Springtime in London

By Jen Selinsky

Springtime in London by Jen Selinsky
Copyright © 2020. All rights reserved.

ALL RIGHTS RESERVED: No part of this book may be reproduced, stored, or transmitted, in any form, without the express and prior permission in writing of Pen It! Publications. This book may not be circulated in any form of binding or cover other than that in which it is currently published.

This book is licensed for your personal enjoyment only. All rights are reserved. Pen It! Publications does not grant you rights to resell or distribute this book without prior written consent of both Pen It! Publications and the copyright owner of this book. This book must not be copied, transferred, sold or distributed in any way.

Disclaimer: Neither Pen It! Publications, or our authors will be responsible for repercussions to anyone who utilizes the subject of this book for illegal, immoral or unethical use.

This is a work of fiction. The views expressed herein do not necessarily reflect that of the publisher.

This book or part thereof may not be reproduced in any form, stored in a retrieval system, or transmitted in any form by any means- electronic, mechanical, photocopy, recording or otherwise-without prior written consent of the publisher, except as provided by United States of America copyright law.

Published by Pen It! Publications, LLC
812-371-4128
www.penitpublications.com

ISBN: 978-1-954004-68-9
Edited by Cassy Cochrun
Cover Design by Donna Cook

Chapter 1

Kate Richards sat in her seat on the plane, hands folded in her lap. She was seated in between two portly men, both of whom, thankfully, had not paid much attention to her during the entire flight. Though this was not her first time on an airplane, she wished that she would have been able to look out the window during takeoff and sporadic times throughout the flight. With both of those fatsos in the way, however, she did not stand a chance. Kate took off her hat and began to fan her face, only three more hours until her plane touched down in England.

After looking around, Kate noticed that many people were reading newspapers or magazines. She packed some books for her trip, but those she had put in the suitcase were not included with the carry-on luggage. Lamenting the fact that she had nothing to read, Kate decided that she would take a nap instead. Hopefully, it would last long enough that she would not have to wake up until the captain announced that the plane had landed safely.

***

Two hours later, Kate awoke, abruptly.

One of the heavy men beside her moved his elbow and accidentally poked her in the ribs.

"Pardon me, ma'am," he said, realizing his mistake.

"It's all right," Kate replied. She then turned away from the man because there was nothing more that she wanted to say to him. She checked the time on her watch. 4:35, only one more hour to go.

Though she wished that she was still asleep, Kate decided it would be pointless not to try and stay awake now. Soon, she would be in London, and she would have some new territory to explore.

Then, maybe, she could forget that her parents had sent her away on this trip.

It was May 12, 1971, and Kate was the daughter of a wealthy dairy farmer from Colcord, Oklahoma. She was twenty-two years old, and less than a year out of college.

Kate was also very beautiful, with long blonde hair and blue eyes. She also had a fair complexion, which was rare for anyone who owned, or worked on, a farm. Kate had a medium build, and she was tall rather than petite. Though she'd never quite lost all her "baby fat," it, along with her baby face, was one of the qualities that made Kate appear younger than her twenty-two years.

While Kate enjoyed her life back home, her father insisted that she get out of the country for a while and go someplace new. Kate had a cousin Gloria who lived in Putney, London. That was why he decided to send her there. Though Kate's father had tried to sugarcoat the situation by saying that she was young and should try something new before she tied the knot, she knew that was not the real reason why she was traveling abroad.

Kate did not know exactly what her parents were up to, but she was a little leery, nonetheless. She did not want to worry about that now, however, because she had every intention of enjoying her vacation. Kate had gladly applied for a passport a while back so she could leave the country and travel for shores unknown.

Kate's parents were very wealthy, but they were also very conservative. Her father was very protective of his only child and did not want her associating with any man whom he'd consider riff raff. He kept insisting that the certain people were "low-life degenerates" and they "would not amount to anything."

After all, the only child of a conservative dairy farmer was meant to marry a gentleman of good breeding. He was to be the type of man who would formally ask permission to date his daughter before so much as trying to ask her out, himself.

Kate's mother also agreed with her father on this issue, but she was not as vocal about it.

Mr. Isaac Richards was a very conservative man. He wanted a pious and reliable son-in-law who could, one day, own and operate the farm.

Of course, Mr. Richards would not even consider the extra farmhands he hired to help run and maintain the farm. In his eyes, none of them were even remotely good enough for his daughter. He also wanted many grandchildren so the farm would thrive and continue to keep the Richards' name in business and continue to have good standing in the community.

This is what Mr. and Mrs. Richards wanted, but Kate definitely had other plans.

London! She could hardly imagine all the kinds of things that were happening across the pond. Kate attended college at NYU, where she got to make friends with some very interesting people. While her roommate was shy and conservative, just as her parents would have liked her to be, Kate went out and made many friends with people whom the older generations considered to be outside the social norm.

None of them had actually been to England, so had her parents even known about all the "drug-induced promiscuity" that went on in London, they would never have let her go in the first place. But that was what Kate liked, the whole idea of freedom. She had never smoked cigarettes, or done drugs, but she thought she would still like to be friends with some of those English folks, anyway. It's not as if she was going to succumb to temptation and live a life full of hedonism and debauchery.

Kate still had high moral values and was a strong believer in God, but she did not like the idea of having her father, and some chauvinistic, smug hick of a husband, controlling her for the rest of her life.

There was this new phenomenon called women's liberation that was taking America by storm. While she did not know anyone who had the "audacity" to support these *strange* new ideals, Kate knew that there were women out there who wanted to change the world. Ever since college, she intended to be one of them.

Kate's father had an older sister, Olivia, who was Kate's aunt. She went to England when she was young and married a "nice English gent," whom the Richards approved of because of his wealth and great, moral standing.

Since Olivia was only twenty when she got married, and her father thirteen, Kate had hardly gotten to know her expatriate aunt. Thinking back on it, she only recalled having met her twice: once when she was five, then again when she was seventeen.

Aunt Olivia and Uncle Stuart also had a daughter, Gloria, who was two years older than Kate. Kate's cousin had been a Londoner all her life. Though Gloria and Kate had written letters to each other for most of their lives, the two of them never got to meet, that is, until today.

Well, Kate thought, *at least I will finally get to meet my cousin after all these years*. A smile then formed on Kate's lips. She was beginning to enjoy her voyage rather than worrying about how her mother and father were doing back home. Though they would miss her, and she them, Kate was sure that they could manage to get by without each other for the next three months. With a sigh, and a smile on her face, Kate closed her eyes.

"Ladies and gentlemen," the voice of the pilot announced. "We will be landing shortly. At this time, I would like to remind you to fasten your seatbelts and make sure that your chairs are in the upright position. Also, please adjust your trays so they are properly locked up on the seat in front of you. Thank you for flying TransAmerica Airlines."

Kate took a moment to refasten her seatbelt and prepare for the landing. She was a little nervous because she thought the plane felt a little shaky during the takeoff, but she could have been overreacting a little.

***

Minutes later, the plane landed, and all the passengers gathered their carry-on luggage and were herded off the plane. Kate was expecting to see lots of rain because she'd heard about England's infamous and gloomy climate. She was pleasantly surprised, however, to see the bright sun streaming through the windows of the boarding area in the terminal. It was like a good omen, come to foreshadow the rest of her trip.

After several seconds of looking around for a familiar face, Kate recognized a woman who could only be her Aunt Olivia, sitting in one of the chairs. Her head was down, and she was reading a magazine. Slowly, Kate started to make her way over to her aunt. Since Olivia had not seen her in such a long time, she wondered how she would react after Kate announced her presence.

"Auntie Olivia?" Kate asked, a little unsure of herself.

Olivia looked up from her copy of *Woman's Weekly*. She stared at the young woman standing before her, not seeming to recognize her at first.

Then, recognition struck Olivia. Kate quickly wondered if her aunt had held any occupation outside the home, but she then remembered one of Gloria's letters describing her mother as a "stay-at-home wife and mum."

Kate smiled.

"Katie!" the warm voice of her aunt responded. Olivia rose from her seat and gathered Katie in a fond embrace. "My, how you've grown! Has it been five years already? How old are you now, twenty-four?"

Kate formed a tiny smile across her face. "I'm twenty-two," she said.

"My, my, then you are two years younger than my Gloria. Oh, she also wanted to come with me to meet you here. She and your Uncle Stuart."

Uncle Stuart? Kate thought as she stiffened. Obviously, she had never met the man her aunt had married, but he must have been really conservative in order for Grandpa to have approved of him. Kate was aware that England and America were virtually the same during the staunch 1950s, so she was a little afraid of meeting this conservative Englishman. She hoped she would not have to present herself in a completely formal manner.

"There they are, Daddy!" a voice cried from a distance.

Kate and Olivia turned to see a young woman and an older man approaching them.

"Your Uncle Stuart and Cousin Gloria," Olivia said. She seemed to have a propensity for stating the obvious.

As they got closer, Kate noticed that Gloria was not dressed conservatively. She wore a loose-fitting shirt with red, yellow and orange floral designs. Gloria also wore blue jeans and black leather boots.

Gloria was twenty-four, but her youthful face and small frame made her look a little younger. Kate could also tell that her cousin had a certain, childlike charm about her. Though, it was not Gloria she was worried about.

Stuart, as she had feared was wearing a grey suit and matching hat. He appeared to be quite a deal older than Olivia, which might not be a good thing.

"Kate!" Gloria shrieked, gripping her cousin and holding her in a strong embrace.

Though Kate did not feel smothered, she wondered if Gloria ever planned on letting go.

"My God, I can't believe I am *finally* getting to meet you! I mean, we used to send letters back and forth all the time, but now you are here in person! I begged Mum and Daddy to bring me here with them; I simply would not take no for an answer."

Just as the embrace was broken, Gloria hugged her cousin again. "This is just making up for all the lost time over the years."

"Easy now, darling, or else you are going to squash the young lady to death," Stuart said.

"Sorry," Gloria replied, speaking to both her father and cousin.

"Don't think her strange, Kate; she is just very excited to meet you, as am I."

Judging from the tone of Stuart's voice, Kate was a little doubtful about that. Though he did not seem particularly cold, Kate was still a bit leery of her uncle. Perhaps he was holding out until he got to know her a little better.

"It is such a pleasure to meet you, my dear. I am your Uncle Stuart, and you are very welcome in our home."

"Thank you," Kate replied, trying her best to sound sincere. It's not that she wasn't grateful; it's just that she was a little shy around strangers at first. Even her cousin Gloria had come off as a little impetuous. She acted a bit like a child, even her voice was a little child-like, but Kate didn't want first impressions to get in the way of bonding with her newfound family. She wanted to like these people, and she was very anxious to start her English journey.

"Hey!" Gloria shrieked, as if she had just stumbled upon some great realization. "What an adorable accent you have, Cousin. Is that how everyone in America talks? How was your flight?"

Kate, feeling slightly embarrassed, did not quite know how to respond to the first question. Since she has lived most of her life in Oklahoma, she never really noticed anything unique or "funny" about the way she spoke.

That was not entirely true, however, because people had teased her about her voice when she started school in New York. Her friends would sometimes call her "Rebel" or "Peggy Sue," but Kate did not mind. To her, these were merely terms of endearment given to her by her friends.

"Well," Kate replied. "This is how most of the people I know talk. Some would call this a southern accent. People in the northeast have different accents." Kate hesitated. "I suppose it's the same over here."

Kate smiled, and Gloria nodded.

I suppose if I try to talk in an English accent right now, you would know it was false, Kate thought, not feeling comfortable enough to say that statement out loud. *You would be able to tell the difference right away.*

No one spoke for the next few seconds; they were all busy thinking different things.

Olivia, having just looked at her wristwatch, then noticed that it was getting late.

"Oh!" Olivia exclaimed. "It's about time we headed home. Let's go over to baggage claim and help Kate with her luggage."

Aside from her small carry-on, Kate had brought along three large suitcases, which an airport official put onto a cart and wheeled them out of the terminal to the cab waiting for them outside.

"My God, girl," Stuart said once the bags were outside and the trunk of the car opened. "What kind of luggage do you have? I don't think we are going to be able to fit this all into the trunk of the car."

Kate bit her lip and dared not to think of a response. She was really worried that her uncle was prepared to give her a hard time even before they got a chance to know each other.

"Oh, don't pay him any mind, dear," Olivia said. "He's only joking. We brought two cabs out here, but the luggage will fit into *one* of them just fine."

Stuart then winked at Kate and laughed.

She began to think that maybe her uncle was not such a bad guy after all.

"You can ride with me, dear, and Gloria will go in the other car with her father."

"That sounds fine to me," Kate replied, a little disappointed. She really hoped that she could ride with Gloria because she wanted to bond with her cousin some more.

Kate soon pushed the thought out of her mind, though, because she felt that there would be plenty of time for that later.

All during the car ride home, Olivia talked about virtually everything. After all, London was such a large city, and there were plenty of things to look at and enjoy.

Kate saw so many businesses and stores on the car ride home, probably more than almost the entire state of Oklahoma. Though she found her aunt to be very garrulous, Kate liked Olivia and could tell that years of living in England hardly left any trace of her Oklahoma accent.

***

Olivia laughed when Kate said she had never seen a car with the steering wheel on the right side. Olivia said that took her some getting used to but not as much as having to learn to drive on the left side of the road.

Kate was very impressed with her aunt. She also seemed well-adjusted to life as an English lady, and Kate noticed that she hardly made any mention of what she was like while she lived in America.

"And this is where I met your uncle," Olivia said proudly as she pointed to a very large and old building. She chuckled. "That was a long, long time ago when your auntie was very young."

Kate heard the story many times, about how Aunt Olivia had won a scholarship to Oxford. She was very excited about her "award," as she thought it was an honor.

While Olivia looked forward to attending school there, her father was not very thrilled about the prospect about sending his only daughter overseas. But, seeing as how important it was to his daughter, David did not want to come in the way of her goals. Of course, David didn't seem to mind when Olivia had met the very upscale, very rich (and considerably older) Stuart Cunningham, who had inherited tons of money from his father's investments.

Long story short, Olivia moved to England, married Stuart, who had generously paid for the entire family to fly over to England for the wedding and got another start on her life. That was one reason why Kate admired her aunt.

Olivia was a good, humble woman, but she was not afraid to pursue her goals. So, in essence, Kate thought of her aunt as a great inspirational figure in that she was a woman who would let nothing get in her way. And, since Kate had done extremely well in high school, she was not afraid to ask her father to let her attend college at NYU. Though not everything she experienced in New York was great, she was certainly glad that she pursued her goals and obtained her degree.

Kate looked out the window and marveled at the size of the building. She had never seen anything like this back in Oklahoma. Sure, there were historical buildings and such, but they were nothing like this. Some of these places looked very majestic and grand, and they appeared to be older than any land on which she ever stood.

It was almost at this exact moment when Kate seemed to lose all her concentration because she was tuning out her garrulous aunt.

She had already become completely enthralled with England and all that it seemed to offer.

She had just realized it now. While Kate was on the flight, her nerves seemed to override her anticipation. She worried about how she would be received by her aunt, uncle, and cousin, and she feared that her parents may try to find some way to monitor her activity through Auntie Olivia.

Kate pondered this for a while then tried to get her mind to think other thoughts, more pleasant thoughts. While she was in college, for instance, her parents did not seem to interfere much with her life or have anyone report back to them from New York, and for that, she was grateful.

Of course, things seemed different now that she was in England. This was a place which was different from that of her conservative hometown.

Kate had often heard that people from Europe seemed to be more "liberal" as one would say, but her father would never let her enter the world of sex, drugs, and rock 'n' roll. As long as her conservative aunt and uncle were there to keep an eye on her, he knew that everything was going to be all right.

***

Just when Kate found herself distracted again, the cab had reached Aunt Olivia and Uncle's Stuart's house. Even though they lived in London, the famous capitol of England, Kate was expecting something provincial, or at least some old house one would get a mental picture of from reading *Wuthering Heights* or something written by Virginia Woolf; perhaps she was thinking of "A Room of One's Own." It was neither.

The house was almost modern and looked very much like one a person would see in the United States. It was white with a red roof and red shutters by the windows. The front door was also red. There were not many gables, but there was a chimneystack poking out of the roof, presumably one from the living room. Flowers and many neatly trimmed bushes lay around in evenly arranged beds of mulch. Kate thought that her Aunt Olivia must be the one who tended to the flowers, since she could not imagine Gloria being interested in such a thing.

Though Kate had worried about the manner of her conservative uncle, she was slightly disappointed that she was not going to be living in an "old country house" for the next three months. This was certainly not a modest farmhouse like one would find in Oklahoma.

As soon as the cab was stopped in the driveway, Olivia and Kate climbed out.

The driver opened the trunk so they could take out Kate's luggage.

Just as Kate retrieved her last trunk, the other cab pulled into the driveway.

Stuart and Gloria got out in time to help carry the luggage inside the house.

Kate then sized up the modern house as she stood in the driveway for the first time.

So, she thought, *this is where I'm going to be living for the next three months.* She noticed that the windows were very large, large enough to see some of the furniture in both the upstairs and downstairs rooms.

Gaping windows were not a new feature to Kate, but they seemed to convey a message to her, nonetheless. It was if they wanted to welcome her into the house, to make her feel like this was her home away from home, so to speak. Kate let her mind wander for a third time before she heard someone talking to her.

"A little different than what you expected, eh, love?" her Uncle Stuart asked. He had obviously noticed her starting intently at the house.

"Yes," Kate replied, who had still not fully come back into reality. She looked from the windows to the front door and formed a smile on her face. Intuition told Kate that she was going to feel very welcome here.

"Well," Olivia said. "Let's not just stand around here talking. Let's take Kate inside and show her to her room. I'm sure she'll want to relax a little before calling her Mum and Dad."

Aunt Olivia was right. Kate felt like she was suffering a little bit from jet lag, and she did feel like she could use a quick nap.

"Yes, let's go inside, Kate!" Gloria exclaimed. "You'll be staying in our guest room, which is right across from mine."

Kate could feel the enthusiasm in Gloria's voice. She reminded her of a best friend, or little sister, who was eager to gossip and share girly things. Of course, since both Kate and Gloria were only children, they were the closest thing to siblings as each other could get.

Once inside the house, Kate noticed that most of the furniture was red to match the roof, shutters, and the front door. Some of the furniture was also many other colors, such as the lime green couch in the living room and the green and yellow floral designs painted on several flower vases.

While Kate did not want to have to use the word "garish" to describe the house, she did find some of the colors and decorations a bit tacky. Again, this was obviously the doing of her eccentric auntie, whom, despite her decorating habits, she was really starting to like.

"Gloria, my dear, won't you show Kate to her room?" Uncle Stuart asked while putting down one of Kate's suitcases. "You girls don't worry yourselves about the luggage. I will carry it up for you in a little while."

"Thank you, Uncle Stuart," Kate replied. "That is very generous of you."

"Please, my dear, call me Uncle Stu if you like." Just as he did earlier outside the airport, he winked at her again.

"Yes," Kate replied, "Uncle Stu it is."

"Charming," Olivia said. "Now, let's give the girl some privacy. She may want to take a quick nap before tea. How does that sound to you, my dear?"

"Sounds great, Auntie. I am a bit tired from my flight. I've never had tea before, so I am looking forward to that." Kate smiled. She hoped that her words were charming enough to be seen as nothing but grateful and polite. There was no doubt in her mind that she wanted to be as little trouble as possible to her newly acquainted family.

Kate knew that while she was here, there was so much she wanted to do, but she felt that it would be wise to focus on one thing at a time. Now that she was here, she just wanted to unpack and take some time to relax before having to phone her parents.

"Shall we go up, then?" Gloria asked. She grabbed Kate by her wrist and led her upstairs.

"This is my room," she said, giving Kate a quick glance into what looked to be a hippie domain with beaded curtains and a lava lamp sitting on one of the desks.

Kate wondered what her Uncle Stu thought of his daughter's strange dwelling.

"And this," Gloria said, leading her cousin into the guest room, "is where you will be staying."

Kate peered into the guestroom. She was both relieved and surprised to that it looked more modest than any of the other rooms in the house. The walls were painted a light pastel blue, and all the furniture matched, although, this was also one of the rooms which had one of those gaping windows. This was one she had not looked into while standing outside on the driveway. Had she still seen it while she was still outside, it may have calmed her nerves a little bit.

"Well, okay, then," Gloria said, aware of the fact that her cousin was admiring her room. "I see that you fancy this room. Mum will be pleased. I actually thought about sharing my room with you, but then I figured it would be too much to handle, what with the decorations and all."

You can say that again, Kate thought. She was literally frightened by the idea of spending the night in Gloria's hippie domain.

Gloria then left her cousin and retreated back to her own room. Gloria could have that room, and all the others, for that matter.

Kate was perfectly content with the guestroom, which would be her safe domain for the duration of her stay.

No sooner had Kate first sat down on her bad had her Uncle Stuart and Aunt Olivia come into the room with her luggage.

"Here we are, my dear," Uncle Stuart said, "luggage all safe and sound, just as promised."

"Thank you."

"Well, let's give her a moment to call her parents. Then she can rest up a little before tea," Olivia said.

"Yes, that sounds good," Kate replied as she stood up. She noticed that there was a telephone in the guest room, which she had never seen before. Her family only owned two phones, one in the living room and one in the kitchen. In certain parts of her town, electricity was still a luxury as recently as ten years ago.

"Well, let's leave her alone so she can arrange all her things." Aunt Olivia led her uncle out of her room. She closed the door behind her.

Kate was now left alone with her thoughts, which gave her a little leeway before she decided to call her parents. Kate looked at her luggage, which was piled on the floor beside her bed. While she had every intention of unpacking her suitcases right away, she wanted to get the chore of talking to her parents over with before she did anything.

Kate sighed and picked up the phone. She looked at the paper that was lying beside the phone with her parents' phone number on it. Kate punched in the numbers she needed to dial and waited two rings before her mother answered.

"Hello," Mrs. Richards said on the other end.

"Hello, Mom," Kate replied. She was relieved to hear that her mother's voice sounded happy.

"Ah, Kate! How was your trip, dear?"

"It was nice. The airplane ride was a little shorter than I thought it would be, though."

"That's nice. Have your aunt and uncle got you settled in yet?"

"Yes, Uncle Stu even helped carry up my luggage for me."

"That was sweet. What do you think of your cousin, Gloria?"

Kate hesitated for a second, her first impression of her cousin was mixed. On one hand, she thought Gloria was a little flighty. On the other hand, she liked her individuality and free spirit. She really hoped that the two of them would become fast friends.

"She's really nice, Mom. You know, I've written her letters for so many years, but you never really get to know someone until you meet them in the flesh. The two of us should get along just fine."

"I'm glad to hear that. Gloria seems like a lovely young lady."

"That she is," Kate replied, smiling at her newly found reassurance. "Is Dad around? It would be nice to talk to him, too."

"You know your father. He's out there milking away. I offered to go out there and help him, but he insisted that I sit here in the kitchen and wait for your call."

"Oh," was Kate's only response. Part of her was actually relieved that her father was not available to talk to her, but another part was a little skeptical.

She loved her father dearly, but she had not been comfortable talking to him for a while, especially since she came back from school. It seemed like only yesterday when she had felt so close to him, though, indeed it has been nearly two years since Kate felt she could tell him anything.

"Don't worry, dear," Kate's mother said, picking up on her disappointment. "Your father will be pleased to know that you had a nice trip and that you arrived safely. As soon as we hang up, I will go outside and tell him that you called."

She hesitated. "You should call us in another day or two once you get settled. I know that you will have such a marvelous time with your uncle, auntie, and cousin. I should get going now to see how your father is doing. Please tell everyone that we said hello. Goodbye, darling."

"Goodbye, Mom," Kate said. She hung up the phone. Kate could tell that her mother sounded a little different, though she wasn't exactly sure why. Perhaps it was because her only child was over 4,000 miles away from them and she was worried. Perhaps it's because she knew she would be lonely with only her father around, and he did not keep good company sometimes.

People who knew Mr. Richards on a personal basis would go out of their way to say what a good husband and father he is, but only his family knew his true, quiet nature. Isaac made it known that he was in charge of his family, but he really hadn't taken the time to talk to his wife and daughter in quite a while. Even though this was the case, no one ever sought to question it because that's just how things were; it was just how things became.

Kate went over to her bed and began unpacking. She started with her carry-on bag, which carried the essentials, toiletries, her toothbrush, a tube of toothpaste, a hairbrush, and other such things. She then moved on to the larger suitcases, which contained all her clothes. Kate neatly hung each dress in the closet and stood back to look at them when she was finished.

Unfortunately, the dresses had gotten wrinkled during their time in the suitcase, but tomorrow she would ask Olivia if she could use her iron to press them. Kate then took out all her shoes and placed them on the closet floor, all lined up according to the dress they matched.

Then, having confirmed her fastidiousness, Kate closed the closet door. She then retrieved all her undergarments and nightclothes and placed them neatly in the drawers on the dresser which was across the room.

Kate knew that the remainder of her third suitcase contained all her books, which she desperately wanted to read. She could have used one of them on the flight. Then, maybe, she would have had an excuse not to look over and talk to the portly man who elbowed her in the ribs. As much as Kate wanted to read her books, however, she declined in favor of sleep. She could get in an hour and possibly forty-five minutes before tea.

Kate went over to the door of her peaceful room and closed it. Then, she carefully removed her dress and neatly hung it up in the closet. Kate still had on her slip and undergarments, but she did not want to fully undress herself because she would have to get up and go to tea in less than two hours.

In a matter of seconds, Kate pulled down the covers and slipped into her comfortable bed. It took even less time for her to fall asleep, the state in which she remained before Aunt Olivia knocked on her door and told her that it was teatime nearly two hours later.

Chapter 2

"Look at you!" Gloria exclaimed. "You look like a regular Pollyanna cowgirl." Gloria studied her cousin from head to toe.

Kate wore a long, conservative dress, similar to the one she had on yesterday. The sleeves were short and puffy, and the hemline was only slightly higher than her ankle.

Gloria also noticed that she wore flats to match her purple dress. She could also imagine that her stockings were made up of the finest nylon.

"We need to get you some trousers," Gloria said.

"Trousers?" Kate asked.

"Yes, pants, as you call them over there. I think a pair of blue jeans will do rather nicely." Gloria hesitated then looked at her cousin again. "Do tell me that you've worn blue jeans before."

"Yes, I have, thank you very much," Kate replied, almost feeling the need to defend herself. "I've worn britches, as my father calls them, when working with him on the farm. That was nearly every day during my childhood but a little less as I started to grow older. When I entered junior high, both he and my mother agreed that since I was becoming a lady, I should start to wear dresses. After all, ladies do not dress like men in social situations."

Kate hesitated, wondering what her father would think of the conversation they were having right now. Would he reprimand her for even getting the idea of wearing pants in a social setting? She would like to think that he would not, but she knew better.

Gloria scrunched up her face, and Kate knew that her cousin could not believe what she was hearing.

Despite her recent upbringing, however, Kate wanted to start wearing pants again, especially since she was not back home in her conservative town of Colcord, Oklahoma.

Gloria was certainly a modern woman, and she knew she would be the one to help transform Kate's wardrobe.

"You will get me a new pair of pants?" Kate asked.

"Yes, we will get you a new pair of *britches*," Gloria said, doing her best imitation of a person with a southern accent.

Kate laughed.

Gloria liked the fact that her cousin has seemed to loosen up since yesterday, but she could still sense that she was hiding something, something about her past that she may not have wanted to mention.

"So," Gloria resumed, "I know that you are a good girl from farmland America, but don't tell me that the only time you ever wore pants was when you were working on the farm with your daddy."

"No," Kate said, almost laughing again. "I used to wear them all the time in college, you know, to classes and everything." Kate hesitated for a brief second. She did not normally like to talk about college because of some of the things that happened during that time.

"I still have a few pair at home stuffed up in a box in my room. My mom rarely looks in my closet and pokes through my personal things, so I guess they are safe there."

"Well, that's a good thing," Gloria said.

Kate smiled. She was starting to feel a more comfortable around her cousin. Maybe being a farmer's daughter "on holiday" in England was not such a bad thing after all.

"Well," Gloria started again, "since you have no plans for tonight, I want to take you to a clothing shop. It's the same place where I get all my things." She paused to study the look on Kate's face, which did not change. Gloria wondered what she was thinking.

"It's called Strawberry Orange Dreams, and it's absolutely delightful! They have so many cute pairs of trousers there; we're bound to find you something."

"You think so?"

"I know so. We also need to buy you some cute tops as well. How much money do you have?"

"All I have are one thousand American dollars," Kate said mournfully. She wished her father would have given her more, but he didn't think she needed that much to begin with. Besides, it was a rather generous sum.

Kate knew that she would have to go to a bank to convert her dollars into British pounds. Kate had not been outside the house since she arrived there yesterday, though she had the feeling that was about to change very soon.

"That's all right, it'll be my treat. You just have to promise me one thing."

"What's that?"

"You have to wear them as soon as I buy them. Strawberry Orange Dreams is the most happening place in town, and we can't have you going around looking like an American hick who's on her way to a Sunday church picnic."

Gloria stopped herself right after that last statement. She was afraid that she'd hurt Kate's feelings with what she had just said.

"Sorry, I didn't mean anything by it. It's just that I don't think you are truly happy wearing these clothes, because they certainly don't look comfortable to me."

Kate smiled again then laughed.

"No, it's all right. Well, now that you mention it, they do seem a little uncomfortable and out of place. But, whatever you buy, I'm going to leave completely up to you. After all, your clothes are so…pretty and unique," Kate replied, looking for the right words to say.

"Right, then; it's settled. After tea, we are going to Strawberry Orange Dreams to give you a whole, new wardrobe! Of course, I've gotta let you keep your bra and knickers. It won't do to have a proper lady parade around town without those."

Kate laughed and thought of herself parading around town like a feminist hippie. How that kind of thing would send her parents spinning into their graves!

As soon as tea was finished, Gloria announced that they were going to the shops.

Olivia seemed delighted at this news and told her daughter what a good idea that was.

Stu told them to have a good time, though he did not have much to say about it after that.

***

"Hello, Judy," Gloria said, as she came bounding into the store. This here is my cousin, Kate; she's a farm girl from America. And as you can judge by the state of her wardrobe, she desperately needs your help!"

Kate had her hands clasped together in front of her, looking like a shy schoolgirl faced by an abrasive teacher. She was wearing a purple dress, matching flats, and a straw hat, with purple trimming, on her head. She felt embarrassed and shy and did not want to say a word.

Kate took a moment to study Judy. She appeared to be a little older, and Kate estimated her age to be around thirty-five.

Judy, however, contained a certain kind of beauty. Just looking around at all the clothes and decorations made Kate think of her cousin's room back at home. She smiled nervously as she felt the eyes of Gloria, Judy, and all the other customers in the shop on her.

"Yes, I can see that," Judy replied. "I'm Judy Spellman," she said, extending her hand.

Kate gave it a gentle shake. "Kate Richards," she replied.

The timid American woman did not say anything else, and Judy could tell by the look on Kate's face that she was a little frightened.

"Don't worry, love," she said to Kate. "I know just what you need."

Judy went to another part of the store and retrieved some clothes from the shelves. She came back and handed them to Kate for her to try on.

"The fitting room is over there," Judy said, pointing to the back of the store. "When you are done putting the clothes on, please come out and show us how they look. Not only do I want my customers to be satisfied with the clothes they try on, but I want them to have my approval as well."

"Um, okay," Kate said, not quite sure how to respond to that comment.

"Don't worry," Judy replied, "very rarely am I dissatisfied with what my customers have tried on. They also almost always seem to like the choices I make as well. It's a mutual thing that we've got going on here."

"Sounds fair to me," Kate said as she walked to the back of the store. She liked Judy. Though the woman had come off as a little strange, Kate could see that she had the intent of truly pleasing her customers. Also, she couldn't be a bad person if she was friends with her cousin.

A few minutes later, Kate emerged from the dressing room. She froze, looking like a store window mannequin, while waiting for Gloria and Judy's approval. Some of the other customers in the store stopped what they were doing just to look at this beautiful stranger don her new clothes. Two or three men even whistled.

"Wow, Cousin, you look delicious!" Gloria exclaimed.

Kate was wearing a pair of tight blue jeans and a tie-dyed T-shirt, which was somehow both loose and formfitting. Kate felt very silly standing there like that, especially since she was still wearing her purple flats which matched her dress.

"Very nice," Judy replied, while studying Kate in her new apparel. "But there's still one thing missing; hold on a moment." Judy then went over to the counter then reached underneath.

She produced the coolest looking boots Kate had ever seen. They were brown suede and looked like they would be a good addition to her new outfit. Judy brought them over to Kate.

"Here," she said, "try these on."

One at a time, Kate kicked off her purple dress flats and tried on the boots. Once both of them were on her feet, Kate walked around in them to make sure that they were comfortable. She then stopped and turned to face the small crowd that had gathered around her.

"I like them," Kate said, referring to the entire ensemble. The people in the small crowd smiled then went about their business.

Gloria and Kate went to the counter to pay for the clothes.

"Let's see," Judy said. "With the tie-dye shirt and the pants, the total comes to £20.80."

Gloria handed Judy the money.

"What about the boots?" Kate asked.

"The boots are on the house," Judy replied. "I would recommend starting off slow while you break them in. They could get uncomfortable in the heels if you wear them too long at one time."

Kate's eyes widened. "Thank you!" she exclaimed, showing grateful sincerity in her voice.

"Just do me one favor," Judy said. "Yes, anything."

"Be sure you tell people where you got these trendy threads. That's Strawberry Orange Dreams on Winchester Avenue."

"I'll be sure to spread the message," Kate replied. "And here, please take this for all that you have done for me. I know this is worthless in your country, and I haven't had time to get to the bank yet, but I want you to have them, anyway."

Kate put down her dress, slip, and purple flats onto the floor. She then took out ten American dollars from her purse and handed them to Judy.

"Thank you," Judy replied, looking up from the counter. "I've never actually seen American money before." Judy was clearly touched by Kate's generosity. "My father is a collector or rare coins and foreign currency. He'll really appreciate this. Next time I go over to visit, I will give these to him."

"You're welcome," Kate said. "I'm glad that I was able to give something to make you happy."

Judy looked at the ten dollar bills which lay in her hand. They were a little crumpled but still in good condition. She knew her father would be happy to receive them.

"Oh! I almost forgot," she said, looking up into Kate's smiling face. "Let me get you a sack to put these...your *old* clothes into." Judy pulled out a brown paper bag and set it onto the counter.

Kate reached down and retrieved her clothes and shoes. She placed the purple flats into the bag first. Kate neatly folded her dress and slip and put them on top.

Gloria smiled as Kate did this. *At last,* she thought. *I am actually helping my cousin get rid of those awful Sunday clothes!*

Gloria and Kate thanked Judy again and walked out of the store.

"Wait!" Gloria exclaimed, as soon as their feet touched the curb right outside the door. She reached inside Kate's bag and pulled out the straw hat.

"You should put this back on."

"Okay," Kate replied, not sure why she knew why Gloria thought that it would look any better on her head while she donned her new clothes. Kate put the hat back on, and she couldn't help but think that it felt a little strange.

"It looks good," Gloria said. "Kind of sends a new message that says something like, 'No matter how much I try to be a hippie, no one will ever take the farm girl out of me!'"

Kate laughed then lightly slapped Gloria's arm.

"Be serious," she said.

"I am being serious. You look really good in that combination." Kate laughed again, which made Gloria very happy. In fact, this was the happiest she had seen her cousin since her arrival.

"I think we should get going. Your mother said that we should be back home in time for dinner."

"Right you are. Let's get on out of here." Gloria held out her arm. "Shall we?" Kate linked her arm with Gloria's, and the two of them headed on down the street.

Chapter 3

Steve and Russell were sitting on the curb, red fire hydrant between them, legs and feet stretched out onto the street. They passed a marijuana joint back and forth to each other and soaking in the atmosphere of the evening.

Corner shops and pubs were beckoning potential customers to come in from off the streets. Tonight, being a Thursday night, sometimes drew people looking for a good time out of their homes and into the center of town. And, tonight, there were also more people out than usual.

Though Russell and Steve had a scheduled gig at one of the pubs, the Banner Alehouse, tomorrow evening, tonight they were just relaxing and picking up energy from those who walked by.

Russell was already a little lit when he started smiling at all the pretty women who passed right in front of his view.

"Would you look at that, Stevie?" Russell said, as he passed the joint over to his friend. "Girls with bare, long legs and miniskirts all the way up to their arses. I wouldn't be surprised if some of these girls aren't wearing knickers." Russell paused a moment to take a hit off the joint that Steve had given him back.

"I mean, life don't get no better than this. All these gorgeous women, man. We could have ourselves a regular shag fest." He paused to look at a tall, leggy brunette pass them by.

Russell tried to tilt his head to the side, hoping to view something naughty, but she moved too quickly for him to see anything.

"It's about time that we find you a new girl, after Sherry…" Russell trailed off after seeing the look on his friend's face.

Though Steve had been smiling only seconds before, there was now a frown which seemed to match the hollow look in his eyes.

"I'm sorry, mate," Russell said, apologizing. "I didn't mean to mention the she-devil's name. 'Course I can't blame you for being upset, the way she tore out your heart did a number on your soul, the bloody witch!" Russell passed the joint back to Steve.

"That's all right," Steve said with more than a hint of sadness in his voice. "I know you meant nothing by it. Now, let's just drop the subject so we can go back to talking about pretty girls."

Though Steve smiled after he said this, Russell could tell that his friend was still hurting.

Sherry, as one could easily guess, was Steve's ex-girlfriend. The two of them were deeply in love and practically inseparable. They had made plans to remain together forever.

***

Steve, Russell, and some of their friends were in a band, The Peppermint Eyes, who were creating quite the local stir. Their music was beginning to take off, and they had hopes of getting their demo tapes out to record executives. More music meant more equipment, and more equipment meant a van and roadies. That was where the trouble began.

It wasn't long after The Peppermint Eyes began giving shows that Sherry had taken an interest in one of the band's roadies Ox. Though he was not very attractive, he had a large build, and something about him must have intrigued Sherry.

She and Ox had been sneaking around behind Steve's back for six months until Steve caught them going at it on the floor behind one of the large speakers.

Though he had every right to be upset, Ox was the one who got riled up because their so-called "lovemaking" was disturbed.

Sherry screamed and struggled to quickly put on her clothes.

Ox had gotten up, naked from the waist down, and tried to charge at Steve, whose poor mind was just beginning to process what was happening.

Though Steve did not consider himself a fighter, a blind rage consumed him, and he charged at Ox full on. Steve sent punch landing into Ox's stomach.

Ox doubled over, but he did not fall to the ground. He went after Steve and tried to grab him, but Steve was quicker.

He grabbed his guitar and whacked Ox right on the shoulder.

Ox uttered a curse before falling on his back. Given any other circumstance, this situation might have been a little comical, but both men were seeing red. They made it an unspoken vow that they would not stop going at it until some blood was spilled.

Within seconds, Ox was back on his feet, and Steve did not run away from him this time.

Steve motioned for him to come over to him, which he did.

Ox grinned a sinister grin and head-butted Steve, sending him to fall back. He remained on the ground, stunned, until he felt a thin stream of warm liquid sliding down his forehead.

Steve placed his fingers to his forehead and gently patted it. When he brought them around to his face, he saw that it was blood. It was bad enough that the son of a bitch had stolen his girl, but he also humiliated him and made his bleed. Steve decided that he was not going to take this lying down.

He uttered some curses of him own before charging at Ox, this time with enough force to knock them both down on the ground.

Before anyone else really knew what was going on, Steve and Ox began rolling on the ground, throwing punches at each other.

Russell and another member of The Peppermint Eyes, John, ran over to try and break up the fight. When they finally managed to separate Steve and Ox, there was still enough tension in the air to make the entire place explode.

Ox was still staring daggers at Steve, who just stood there, brokenhearted. He wasn't sure how the whole ugly affair even got started, nor did he care.

Sherry was his entire world, and Ox had taken her away from him. People were talking and looking at him in the background, but Steve did not move a muscle.

When a tearful Sherry standing by a no longer half-naked Ox, tried to apologize, Steve turned on his heels and left the room. It was weeks before he would even talk to either Ox or Sherry again, and at that point, he only wanted to confront them and tell them what he really thought.

Needless to say, Ox was fired, and Sal, another friend of theirs, took over the job.

The only thing Steve could bring himself to say to Sherry was, "You broke my heart! How could you?" and that was that.

Sherry stopped coming to their performances, and it was rumored that she and Ox ran off together. That was six months ago.

***

Steve exhaled, and the smoke came out of his lips in a thin stream. There were many people out and about tonight. While many of them were pretty girls, they were hanging off the arms of other men. He thought about Sherry and Ox and wondered how long it would be until she broke his heart. For all he knew, they could still be together. Then again, maybe they weren't. Steve took a hit then passed the joint back Russell.

It was then when Steve looked up and saw her. Two young ladies were walking down the street. The slimmer one with the dark, curly hair was kind of cute, but she was not the one who caught his sight. The other woman, the blonde wearing the brown boots, the tie-dyed shirt, and the tight blue jeans was simply stunning.

He also noticed that she wore a straw hat on top of her head, which made her look really cute. Steve thought that she was the most beautiful woman he'd ever seen! She was laughing, smiling, and talking to the dark-haired girl.

She carried in her arms, which were crossed over her chest, a brown paper bag.

Steve wondered what was in the bag. He also wondered who this beautiful creature was as the women approached their direction.

As soon as these two women approached the fire hydrant where they were seated, Steve immediately got up on his feet.

Russell, also liking what he saw, brought it upon himself to let out a wolf whistle, which attracted the attention of neither Gloria nor Kate. After all, there were many other women walking the streets; he could have been whistling at any one of them.

While Steve thought Russell's action was crass, he couldn't help but stare at Kate. He liked her smile and her long, blonde hair. He liked the way she moved. He couldn't help but notice how her tight blue jeans stretched across her ass and legs, revealing their shapeliness. Feeling like a lovesick little boy, Steve knew he wanted to get to know this woman. He felt that this was the part where he was supposed to say something.

"Hello. What's your name?" Steve asked.

At this point, Kate and Gloria had already made their way past them, probably not even having noticed their presence. Steve knew that he had to try again.

"Hey! Beautiful lady carrying the paper bag; please, tell me who you are."

This time, both Kate and Gloria turned around. They looked skeptically at Steve and Russell, who they figured were probably the town letches.

Kate blushed, but Gloria was the one to speak.

"Who are *you*?" she asked.

Steve just looked at her.

Russell was already standing by his side, leering at Gloria with the joint still in his mouth.

"I'm Steve," he replied, "and this is my friend, Russell."

"Hello," Russell said. It was clear that he was smitten with Gloria. He grinned and smoked the rest of the joint as he gave her the once over. Russell couldn't help but smile because he really liked what he saw.

"What's your name?" Russell asked.

"I don't think I want to tell you that," Gloria replied.

"Why not?" Russell asked, sounding almost completely dejected.

"Because," was all that Gloria had said.

Russell couldn't believe this gorgeous girl was talking to him. He was determined not to let this one get away.

"Where are you two going?"

"Home."

"But how will we know where to find you?"

"You won't," Gloria replied, giggling. "You will just have to come out and look for us!"

With that, Gloria and Kate turned and continued to walk down the street.

Steve had not said another word since Russell and Gloria started talking. He did not even want to say another word because the beautiful blonde woman did not even bother talking to him.

Steve then had vision of himself as an old man, alone and unloved. His bitter breakup over six months ago was bad enough, but since this beautiful woman hardly even took the time to turn her head in his direction, he'd considered taking a vow of chastity. Steve figured that it would be easier than having to deal with all the complexities involved with dating women.

He then turned to Russell. "How about the rest of that joint, man?"

"Sorry," he replied. "I just finished it all."

"Thanks a lot," Steve said, sarcastically.

Russell shrugged his shoulders by means of apology. Today was not shaping up to be a good day for Steve. His only moment of happiness was ruined after the beautiful lady refused to acknowledge his presence.

Maybe I'm better off, anyway, Steve thought. *She's probably some prissy snob out to tease and torment men like myself. She probably wouldn't give anyone the time of day.* Steve then sat down by the fire hydrant, no longer happy, but wondering why.

Who was this young lady to him, and why did he care? He did not know her from Eve, and yet he found himself infatuated. Steve then wondered if she might be an evil bitch, like Sherry.

She's probably the kind of girl who would bang a roadie, Steve thought after looking at her departing figure one last time. But, then again, maybe she was not; he felt this way because he'd actually looked at her face. It was full, but not plump. It also seemed to radiate a certain kind of innocence that Steve had not seen in many women before.

Even though this woman had rejected him, he could still see that there was something sweet about her, and not only her appearance. Steve then softened a little, not thinking that he'd been rejected. Maybe he and Russell would track those two down one day, and a conversation would follow. From there, Steve would start a new and get to know the real woman he once saw walking down the street.

After Steve began to fill his head with pleasant thoughts, he seemed to tune out the rest of the world again. Time seemed to stand still around him, as everything else was put on hold.

The world was floating, and nothing else had ever seemed as spectacular before.

Steve did not hear Russell call his name until he came up right in front of him and put his hand in front of his face.

"Hello. Steve, are you in there?"

Steve turned around to see that Russell looked confused. He knew that his friend was always the type to space out when something like this happened, something earth-shattering.

"Yeah," Steve replied. "I'm all right, mate. I just found meself in another world for a second."

Russell was no fool. He knew that Steve had a thing for the mysterious blonde woman who had just walked down the street with her friend.

"How about those two bits of crumpet? They are a bit of all right." Russell couldn't help but smile at the recent memory of the two women passing by. "I know I've seen that cute dark-haired girl around before, and I never forget a pretty face, but I've never seen the blonde one. She must be new to the area."

Or an angel from heaven, Steve thought. He was clearly still smitten. She had a lovely face, and his deepest desire was to one day make that pretty face smile because of something good he'd done.

"She is beautiful," Steve said.

"Yeah," Russell agreed. "She certainly is, but she may be one of those stuck-up types. You noticed how she did not say a word to either one of us. Come to think of it, she did not even talk to her friend."

"She may just be shy," Steve suggested. "I've actually known some women to be like that."

"Yeah, but none of the ones you see around here," Russell replied. "That cute little curly head sure seemed to be a chatterbox. Boy, I would like to see her put those lips to good use on me one day."

Steve laughed. "Always the subtle type you are, Russell. That's what's so appealing about you. I'm sure that both those women would agree with me."

"Maybe, maybe not. She did say that we would have to come out and find them if we wanted to talk again."

"And that is what we are going to do, Russell," Steve replied.

***

Gloria and Kate returned home after their successful shopping venture. Kate loved the way she looked and felt in her new threads. The attire that she had on had given her a certain confidence, a new way which she had thought about herself.

No longer was she the pretty but modest farmer's daughter; she was now the sexy woman who had emerged after trying something new.

While the two of them were gone, Kate did not think about her aunt and uncle and whatever reactions they would have regarding her new apparel. It was not until the two of them were greeted by Olivia, as she came into the living room, did conversation about the clothes start.

"My goodness!" Olivia said, studying her niece. "You look so…so…different."

Kate's only response was a smile, and Olivia could already tell a difference in her niece. She had only seen Kate wear pants, once when she visited the Richards' dairy farm when Kate was a child. There, she was helping her father milk cows.

If Olivia still knew her brother, and she thought she did, despite the distance, she knew that he would not approve. The jeans looked very tight, leaving little to the imagination. Not to mention, the tie-dyed shirt was a little formfitting, even though it appeared to be modest. The boots, however, she thought were a nice touch.

"Isn't it great?" Gloria asked. "I took her to Strawberry Orange Dreams, and Judy hooked her up with these wonderful clothes! Now, she can say goodbye to those awful fifties dresses."

But what if she likes wearing those dresses, darling? Olivia had wanted to ask, but she did not. Instead, she decided to change the subject.

"Oh, Judy. How is she doing?"

"Great, Mum. You should have seen the look on her face when she knew what a good job she did on Kate here. Never in all the years have I seen her had she been more pleased at how a customer looked in her new threads!" Gloria paused to pat her cousin on the back.

Kate smiled a weak smile. It was one thing to wear these clothes outside the house, but her aunt and uncle many not approve of such a thing when she was in their company.

"Kate was a right trooper," Gloria continued, "especially when everyone stared at her after she donned her new clothes."

"I see," Olivia replied. "That must have been an interesting experience for both Judy and Kate. I just hope that you didn't scare your cousin too much with these extravagant trips to all the shops in town."

"We only visited the one," Gloria said. "What we experienced there was all the excitement that I thought she could take in one day."

"Well, that may have been a wise choice. Kate may need more time to adjust to life in England. I know that I certainly did."

Kate smiled at her aunt, who was prompt to return the facial gesture.

To say that Olivia was a bit shocked would have been a great understatement. After all, Kate was this sweet girl from America, who happened to be her brother's only child.

Olivia knew that Isaac had sent Kate here in hopes that she and her husband would be able to "straighten her out" and lead her down the right path. While she knew that Kate's parents had told her nothing about this, she also knew that she must have figured something out by now.

Her niece may have been a good southern girl, but she was not stupid. Olivia then smiled, knowing that Kate had started coming into her own.

Now she knew that she had misjudged her niece. Olivia could see that Kate was a woman who was daring enough to branch out in a new town before rooting herself to this place. It was at that moment when Olivia decided that she would no longer worry about her brother's instructions on how to manage Kate while she was living in their home. It was also the same moment when Uncle Stuart had walked into the living room.

"Darling, have you seen my…" He took a moment to stare at the beautiful woman who was standing in the living room with his wife and daughter. "Is that Kate standing in our living room, or is that a gypsy?" Stuart asked. He squinted then looked at his niece again. "Blimey, is that Kate? And here I thought the circus was in town."

Though Stuart had kept the mood light, he was only half joking. He did not want to think that this strangely dressed, yet sexy woman standing before him was his niece.

"Dad!" Gloria exclaimed.

"Stuart!" Olivia said. "Don't you say anything nasty, now. Come over here and tell your niece how beautiful she looks."

Stuart, still in his disoriented state, went approached Kate and tried his best to compliment her attire.

"Well, my dear, it's certainly…colorful," he said, struggling to find the right words to say. Stuart was not one to take things lightly all the time, especially since he knew that his brother-in-law was counting on him and Olivia.

After Stuart finished his sentence, an awkward silence filled the room.

All three women were now staring at him, and this made him feel like he was put on the spot to say something else.

Stuart decided to change the subject.

"Yes, well, I suppose it's getting late. Would you two girls like to wash up for supper?" He hesitated again to look over at his niece. "Perhaps Kate would like to change into something more comfortable before we dine."

"Actually, I'm quite comfortable in these clothes. But I would like to wash my hands and freshen up before we eat. It's been a lovely day, and we can talk about it more, if you would like, at the table. I will be back down in a few moments." Kate started up the stairs, heading to the bathroom that was located near her guestroom.

Olivia and Gloria looked at each other. They couldn't believe what they were hearing. It was only yesterday when Kate would not be the type of person who would even dream of contradicting something that anyone would ask of her.

Olivia thought that this just goes to show how a change in atmosphere can completely change a person.

***

Moments later, everyone was seated at the table, and well into their dinners.

Though Kate had shown some excitement earlier about her new outfit, she had toned it down a little for the time being. In fact, she had taken Judy's advice and gave her feet a rest from the boots. Kate left them upstairs in her closet, where they must have felt out of place with all her dress shoes. She then padded downstairs in her bare feet, which did not seem to stir up any conversation. After all, she did it at home all the time.

Stuart had just taken another sip of wine. His mutton was delicious, but it was also very filling. He figured since he was nearly done with his supper that now would be a good time to make his announcement.

"I talked with James and Lois earlier today, and they told me that they want to come to tea sometime next week."

Gloria cringed in her seat. She started to make faces, but Olivia saw this and glared at her, telling her to stop.

Kate just sat there, sipping her wine. Even though she was remotely interested in knowing who these people were, she did not go out of the way to ask any questions because she was still evaluating the atmosphere.

Kate turned her head and looked into the living room. The very same furniture that Kate had found very ugly before did not seem to bother her as much today. She still preferred the aesthetic comforts of her guest room, but she was no longer concerned with what she thought were hideous decorations and color schemes anymore.

"James and Lois are Stuart's brother and sister-in-law," Olivia explained in a neutral tone.

Kate picked up on the tension that was now present in the dining room. Despite the warm companionship that everyone had felt only moments before, the atmosphere had suddenly become very chilly. Kate was worried that things would soon get hostile.

"Oh," Kate replied. She did not know what else to say, because, obviously, she did not know the people about whom they were talking.

"Yes," Stuart replied. "My brother James, and his wife, have been frequent guests to our home. I have always done my best to make them feel very welcome here." Stuart then glanced at his wife then his daughter. This, however, was not a kind glance. It was one that indicated resentment and warning.

Kate quickly deduced that her aunt and cousin did not care much for James and Lois, which began to worry her. Just as she was starting to come out of her shell, she did not want to have to deal with who she thought might be prudish people, the kinds of people whom her father would approve.

"The reason why they want to come is to meet Kate," Stuart continued. "I told them that we have a guest in our house and that she is Gloria's cousin from America. When they heard that news, they insisted that I invite them over."

"Really, Stu," Olivia said, clearly showing her disapproval. "Shouldn't we have asked Kate if she was all right with other guests coming over to meet her?"

Both Gloria and Kate could feel the tension growing. If things continued this way, it was not going to be a pretty scene.

Kate realized that her uncle had put her on the spot, and that was not exactly fair, but she knew that she had to say something soon in order to diffuse the situation before it got any worse.

"I don't mind at all," she replied, not completely telling the truth. "I think it would be lovely to meet your brother and sister-in-law, Uncle Stu. I hope that you told them that I would be delighted to see them." This statement seemed to please Stuart, as he shot Olivia and Gloria a triumphant glance.

"Splendid, my dear," he said. "Yes, of course I told James and Lois that you would be delighted to have them come over so you could meet them."

Upon hearing this, Gloria did a mental eye roll. This meant that she would have to listen to all their mundane stories and bragging about their twin sons, Gloria's *other* cousins, whom she did not like very much, Syd and Sebastian. They were twenty-six years old and studying at Oxford. Both of them had started earning their doctorates.

Sebastian was studying psychology, and Syd was into architecture, both very promising fields. They also shared a flat.

Though Stuart and Olivia found this to be very impressive, they did not look down their nose at their only child, who had not attended college.

It's not that Gloria wasn't intelligent. She'd earned many A levels during her secondary school career, some of them for advanced classes, and graduated on time with the rest of her class. Gloria, however, did not really intend to go to college, as she was undecided about what she wanted to do with the rest of her life.

She figured that after a few more years of searching, something would just reveal itself to her naturally. Gloria made another face.

She did not want to upset her father's good mood at Kate having taken the news so well, but she felt the need to say something.

"And are they going to bring up again the fact that I never attended university?"

Stuart almost choked on his wine. He couldn't believe that his daughter was bringing this up again, much less in front of Kate. He put down his glass.

"How many times are we going to have this discussion?"

"Dad, I'm sorry, but you know how I feel about your brother and his family."

Stuart could feel heated blood flowing through his veins. He didn't want to argue about this issue anymore. As far as he was concerned, James and Lois were wonderful people, and he would not hear anyone say otherwise, especially his daughter.

"My brother also happens to be your uncle," Stuart said, and he felt the anger rising within him. "And you will address him as Uncle James. If he and Lois want to talk about Syd and Sebastian, then they will be allowed to do so. There will be no closed topics here! You will dress up and present yourself as a nice young woman." Stuart turned to his niece.

"The same goes for you too, Kate," he said to her, but in a softer tone of voice.

"Yes, sir," Kate said meekly from her seat. In the brief time that she had known her uncle, she never feared that he would lose his temper. Just when Kate had started to grow comfortable in his presence, he had to go on and make the situation tense again.

It was clear that the women of the house felt that the extended family's presence was not welcome, especially Gloria, who seemed more impetuous before. Rather, she was showing the rebellious streak which was currently making its claim on her. During this time, Olivia had remained quit in her seat. Tonight, however, Gloria was clearly testing the limits.

"Now," Stuart resumed. "This subject is closed. Let's not hear anymore nasty remarks about my fine relatives."

An eerie silence loomed over the table for what seemed like an eternity after Stuart had made his last statement. Not only did he stop talking about his brother, but all conversation had ceased on his end.

It was not much longer until he decided to leave the table and retire to his study. This was something that Stuart frequently did when he was upset.

Neither Olivia nor Gloria, however, had seen them do that in a long time. In fact, they didn't remember when the last time was. But Olivia, always the diplomat, decided to quickly apologize and keep the peace.

"I'm sorry you had to witness that, my dear," Olivia said. "But, sometimes, your uncle gets sore when he talks about James and Lois." Olivia then shot an accusing glance at Gloria, which made her want to lower herself in her seat.

"Sorry, Mum. I didn't mean to upset Dad. It's just that you know how I feel about those people, especially Sebastian and Syd and all their braggadocio. It makes me sick. Why can't Uncle James and Aunt Lois be a little more sensitive to me?"

"My dear, you know how your uncle is. Your father was just like him some years back, but I have helped him shed some of his conservative views."

"Thank God!" Gloria replied, shuddering upon remembering how her father used to be while she was growing up in his house.

"Come now, darling, be nice. You know that your father loves you dearly, and he would not let anyone say anything ill about you. Why, I, for one, can say that I am very proud to have you as my daughter."

"I wish that Father felt that way."

"He does," Olivia replied, trying to reassure her daughter.

Gloria started fiddling with her fingernails. She would like to believe what her mother was saying, but it seemed like every time that James or Lois mentioned her cousins, Stuart's face would light up enough to make the rest of the room look dim in comparison.

"Yes, but whenever someone talks about those smug bastards, the whole table seems to erupt with good cheer. Having those two around is *not* a holiday."

"Well," Olivia replied. "Those bastards, as you call them, are your cousins, and they are still very much a part of this family."

"Thank God they aren't my only ones!" Gloria said, glancing fondly at Kate, who was seated next to her.

"Now, no more of that kind of talk; you've upset your father enough as it is."

Gloria glanced at the clock on the mantel in the living room.

"It's getting late. It's best that you two go upstairs. Perhaps after a good night's sleep, you will feel better."

Gloria rose from her seat, still upset about what had just transpired. "I suppose so," she said. "Besides, I want to talk more to Kate. I think we will retire to my room. G'night."

Kate quietly rose from her seat as well.

"Good night, Aunt Olivia. Thank you for supper."

"You are very welcome, my dear. Now, get on upstairs, the both of you. I will see you in the morning."

Kate followed her cousin up to their rooms. Gloria still seemed very upset, and Kate knew that whatever she wanted to talk to her about was not going to be very pleasant. Still, Kate did not know the feeling of sibling or cousin rivalry.

Her only other cousin, Jacob, was only seventeen. He was her mother's brother's child, also born into a family of farmers. Her Uncle David owned a poultry farm, which kept the boy busy on a relatively steady basis.

Jacob, from what Kate could gather, was a bright young lad, and despite his busy schedule, he seemed to do well in school. She was not sure if Jacob had any plans for attending college once he graduated high school next year, but she hoped that he gave it some thought.

Kate didn't want Jacob to make any hasty decisions, which he might later regret. Kate shuddered, thinking back to her college days. Surely, his parents would need him around the farm to help with all the birds. Kate did want to think about her other cousin anymore. Right now, they were headed into Gloria's room to talk about God knows what.

"Have a seat," Gloria said, pointing to her chair by her small desk.

Kate sat down. Even after Kate's wild experience earlier this evening, she still felt a bit unsettled about being in the "hippie room," as she had earlier dubbed it. The decorations throughout the entire room looked very similar to Judy's shop, which made Kate wonder if her decorating was inspired by that of the store's.

"I hope that your dad is not very upset," Kate said, immediately regretting her statement. She then glanced over at Gloria, who, thankfully, did not seem to mind what she had said.

"No, he always seems to get a little tense every time we talk about his family. I know that Mum is not very fond of them, either, but she at least, has enough sense to hold her tongue."

Kate nodded, indicating that she understood.

"I'm sorry. I can appreciate how you must not feel very strongly about your cousins."

"They're buffoons. They may act smart, but they are really stupid gits."

Kate listened with an eager ear. She was curious as to why Gloria thought of her cousins as buffoons, but Gloria did not elaborate any further.

"Do you have any cousins besides meself?"

"Just one," Kate replied, again thinking about young Jacob.

"What's his or her name?"

"Jacob Stone."

"How old is he?"

"Seventeen."

"Do you detest him just as I detest Syd and Sebastian?"

"No, I don't even know Jacob very well. His family lives in Nebraska, which is quite a ways from Oklahoma. His father owns a poultry farm, which keeps Jacob very busy."

"If he's seventeen, then I suppose he's planning on attending university."

"I'm not sure about that. My guess is that his parents would prefer that he stay home, so he can continue to help with farm."

"Just as well," Gloria replied. "After all, he sounds like a nice kid, very much unlike those two pompous arses who are my cousins."

Kate laughed, as did Gloria. She started to feel better, knowing that her words were starting to cheer up Gloria.

For a long while after that, neither one of them said anything.

Gloria was lying down on her belly, facing Kate.

Kate turned around in her chair and looked at the decorations that hung all around the room. She turned again and felt that something lightly touched her head. Kate looked up to see many streams of colored beads hanging directly above her. She reached out and touched some red ones with her thumb and index finger.

"Do you know what the real bitch of it is?" Gloria asked, breaking her cousin's concentration.

"What's that?" Kate asked, still playing with the beads.

"The fact that Dad is going to make us dress up." Gloria made a face. "I mean, I suppose I don't mind, being that I am a lady after all, but I hate the fact that he is making us do it for *them*." Gloria emphasized the last word, like she was spitting out venom.

Now it was clear that Kate did not want to meet her "semi-cousins" because of the tone of voice that Gloria had used to describe them, the general hatred which she portrayed whenever someone had brought up their name.

Kate was an optimist who tried to see the best in everyone, and it seemed that her cousin was the same way. If Sebastian and Syd were the exceptions of Gloria's understanding and love, then Kate certainly did not want to meet them.

A few more seconds of silence had passed, after which Gloria rose from her bed and started to walk out of her room. "Where are you going?" Kate asked, as Gloria had not said anything more for a while.

"Come on," Gloria replied. "We're going into your room."

Without any more hesitation, Kate followed Gloria into the guestroom.

Gloria immediately went over to Kate's closet and started shuffling through the dresses that were neatly placed on their hangers. She hastily looked through them, causing them to get a little wrinkled. Dejected, Gloria let go of the last dress and walked over to the bed. She sat down with her face in her hands.

"Can I help you with something?" Kate asked, not sure how to take her cousin rummaging through her personal possessions.

"Not really," Gloria replied. "I was just looking through your closet to see if there were any dresses that I would allow myself to be seen in."

Kate suddenly started to feel really bad for her cousin. She could tell how this whole thing was just eating her up inside. She went over to Gloria and put her arm around her, determined that she was going to help her through this entire ordeal.

"Is there anything in there that is tolerable?" Kate asked.

Gloria lifted her face from her hands. "No, every single one of your dresses is absolutely horrible."

Kate laughed. "I see. What are you going to do when your aunt and uncle come over next week?"

"I don't know, and I don't care. I suppose I could borrow one of these horrible garments when the day comes. I just hope that it will be earlier in the week."

Kate could tell that Gloria's tone was less acidic. Still, she could not quite understand why Gloria wanted the visit to take place earlier in the week instead of later.

"Why earlier?" Kate asked, full of curiosity.

"Because the longer they wait to come over, the more time I will have to build up my anger. Thinking about them any longer will get me completely enraged, and I don't want to have to go through all of that again."

Kate put her arm around her cousin again. She could certainly understand that. Were she in the same position as Gloria, she would not want the horrible anticipation to drag out any longer than it had to. Gloria started to fiddle with her nails.

"You know, I would get out of the place if I could. I mean, I love my mum and dad dearly, but sometimes I think that I may be a slight disappointment to them. I always dreamed that I would get married someday.

"I thought it would be nice to find the right man, settle down, and start a family. Who knows if that will ever happen? They already think of me as an old maid."

Kate looked over at Gloria. In all their years of corresponding back and forth, Kate had never heard anything about this. But, then again, pen pals did not always disclose their innermost secrets with each other, even if the other person happened to be their cousin.

"I can't see how getting married would be unpleasant," Kate said. Now it was her turn to think other thoughts. Kate had been involved with a man whom, at first, she wouldn't have minded marrying one day, but that was a long time ago. The relationship did not work out, and the breakup very was acrimonious.

In fact, it pained Kate to even have to remember the whole ordeal, especially because the relationship was a mistake. It just took her a while to realize it. As of late, Kate had not thought about marriage, not even when her parents had brought up the prospect. Their idea of marriage was nothing Kate wanted to dwell upon at this time.

***

When Kate was still in high school, her father had constantly observed what he thought to be upstanding young men. Isaac studied each and every man to see if he would be worthy of his only daughter.

There was one time when he actually approached a young man at the local supermarket because he looked rich enough and appeared to come from a good background. He went over and introduced himself to this strange person and went through the trouble of inviting him over for dinner.

Even though the young man was everything Kate's father had hoped for, the dinner turned out to be a disaster. Despite Isaac's best efforts to "promote" him, he could not get his daughter to agree to go on a date with the young man.

In fact, Kate was very upset at what her father did, that she hardly talked to Chester, which was his name, during the entire dinner.

When she did, it felt like forced conversation because her father kept glaring at her from the other end of the table. Though Isaac was very upset at Kate for not showing any interest in the Chester during dinner, a part of him sympathized with his daughter, and he promised that he would never to anything of that sort again. That was over four years ago, and Kate has hardly thought about it since.

***

"I notice that you have some of your books over there," Gloria said, after a few moments of silence. She pointed at a stack of books on Kate's nightstand.

"Yes," Kate replied. "I only unpacked a few last night after supper. I was very tired, and I just wanted to take a shower and hop right into bed."

"You mind if I take a look?" Gloria asked.

"Be my guest," Kate replied.

Gloria got up and walked over to the dresser. She picked up three books from the pile and read the titles. Her eyes saw *Jane Eyre* by Charlotte Brontë, *Daisy Miller* by Henry James, and *The Invisible Man* by H.G. Wells. There were also other titles that Gloria had looked through, all of them older books.

"You must be into the classics," Gloria said, slightly disappointed by the lack of variety in Kate's collection.

"For the most part," Kate replied. "I remember reading a lot of these titles for school assignments. Most of the other students in my class absolutely hated them, but I grew to love them, at least, once I completed all my examinations."

Gloria smiled.

"Is this one any good?" she asked, holding up the copy of *Daisy Miller* by Henry James.

"I like it," Kate said, "but it is a bit tragic at the end."

Gloria made a face and started paging through the book. When she was finished, Kate was a little surprised that she did not set it back down.

"Well, I can handle a little tragedy; it will prepare me for my uncle and aunt's visit next week."

Immediately after that statement, both Gloria and Kate managed a giggle. After all, it was Mrs. Richards who often liked to say that laughter is the best weapon against adversity.

"I suppose I should get myself off to bed. Thank you for letting me borrow your book. Since it is not very long, I should have an easy time getting it read soon. I will see you in the morning. G'nite."

"Good night, Gloria. Sleep well."

Gloria left the room and closed the door behind her.

Though Kate was sure that her cousin was still upset about what happened during supper, she was glad that she was able to lend her some moral support.

Kate allowed herself a few moments to lie back on her bed before she headed to the bathroom to brush her teeth and wash her face.

Kate was ready to retire for the evening. She took off her clothes, starting with her jeans. Kate neatly folded them up and put them in an empty drawer in the dresser.

She began to take off her tie-dyed shirt and hung it up right in between the purple dress she had worn yesterday and a blue one. Kate couldn't help but laugh a little as she noted the contrast between the different types of clothes. It was silly to see such a casual garment stuck between her most formal wear.

After Kate removed her undergarments, she tossed them on the floor for now with the intention of putting them in the clothes hamper tomorrow morning.

While Aunt Olivia made it clear that Kate would not have to do any work around the house, Kate felt that it would be wrong to stay in their home and not contribute anything. Sometime later this week, she would insist on taking care of the laundry. Kate then slipped into her nightgown.

Mere minutes into reading her copy of *Jane Eyre*, Kate felt her eyelids begin to grow heavy. She reached over and turned off the lamp on the nightstand. For some moments, she lay in her bed, trying her best to sleep, but there was something on her mind.

For some reason, she thought of that man who called out to her on the street. The thought seemed to come completely out of nowhere. It was sort of disturbing her how she could bring her mind to think about such a meaningless encounter. Kate did not even know his name, nor did she necessarily want to, but her mind would not let her think of anything else.

Oh, stop being so silly, Kate, she thought. *You will not very likely see that man again, and if you did, you probably won't even remember what he looks like.*

After a few more attempts of trying to reason with herself, Kate finally gave up on logic and tried to let her mind become a complete blank until it finally ceded and allowed her to go to sleep for the night.

Even while deep in slumber, Kate had some strange dreams, all of which she would forget the after she awoke the next day.

Chapter 4

Steve could not get the beautiful blonde he'd seen earlier on the street out of his mind. He tried to talk to Russell about the mysterious woman, but all his friend could offer in return were questions about her companion, the other cute girl.

Steve was starting to feel something entirely different, and for this reason, he wondered if there was something wrong with him. He had only known of this person's existence for a few hours, yet it felt like the mere memory of her consumed him whole.

Steve had never felt something like this upon first seeing a woman, not even for Sherry. He wondered if Russell felt the same way, if he felt as deep, whatever his feelings were for the dark-haired girl.

Still, the last thing Steve thought he needed at this time was another relationship, especially when he had just gotten out of one! There was no logical explanation for his recent infatuation, at least none that he could think of. For all he knew, this woman could mess him up far worse than Sherry had.

Being that as it may, however, Steve knew that there was no way that her milky white skin was going to let his mind escape unscathed. She was going to haunt his dreams.

Russell and Steve shared a flat near the pub which they most frequently held their gigs. Most of the time before their gigs, however, the other three members of the band spent the night there, since it was roomier than their place. This made for very crowded and close quarters much of the time, but everyone seemed to have no trouble finding their way around.

Steve was having difficulty trying to fall asleep. He got up and looked out the window, across the street, to see the banner advertising their performances. The banner was white, and it read in large black letters:

Banner Alehouse Proudly Presents:
The Peppermint Eyes
In Concert 14/5-16/5
8:30-10:00

Steve smiled. He and the rest of the band were really looking forward to their upcoming sets. Things had been a little difficult for a while because of the transitioning of their musical genre, but people had started to pay more attention. Now that The Peppermint Eyes had established a fan base, they could draw in their regular crowd, whom, the band hoped would spread the word about their music.

Steve then smiled because was happy, knowing that tomorrow would come, bearing the hope of new promises.

***

Kate had gotten up early. She awoke earlier than anyone else in the house, so she decided to go into the kitchen and help herself to some fruit. Kate decided not to get dressed since no one else would be joining her, but she wanted to have a quick meal before she was caught being seen in her nightgown. For all that she knew, they could all wake up and come downstairs any minute now.

Though Aunt Olivia made it perfectly clear that Kate was welcome to help herself to anything in the kitchen, she hoped that eating an apple and a banana while everyone else was still asleep was not considered rude.

After moments more of waiting around and hearing no noise from upstairs, Kate decided to go back into the guestroom to read. No sooner had she picked up her recently unpacked copy of *The Man in the Iron Mask* did she hear feet shuffling from across the hall.

Gloria had just woken up and would probably come and knock on her door soon. Kate, however, decided to keep reading until her cousin came to get her. There was no sense in putting down the book right now.

Moments later, Kate heard a knock on the door.

"Hello," Gloria said. "Cousin, are you awake?"

"Yes," Kate replied, "come on in." Before coming to this house, Kate would have been exasperated if someone knocked on her door and asked her if she was awake while reading one of her favorite books. Since becoming more familiar with her surroundings and her cousin, who she could easily now say was her best friend, things had changed. Kate set down her book and wondered what kind of plans Gloria had for them today.

Gloria came into the room, greeted by the sight of Kate, still in her nightgown.

"So," Kate said, "what's the plan for today?"

Gloria shrugged her shoulders. "Nothing, really. Mum said that you wanted to go to the bank to have your dollars converted into pounds. After that, I suppose we could go somewhere and have breakfast."

"That sounds great, except that I already ate. I had an apple and a banana down in the kitchen. I hope you don't mind."

Gloria shrugged again.

"It's all right," Gloria reassured her cousin. "We can go out for lunch instead, but do you mind if I go down to the kitchen and have some breakfast while you get dressed? I'm starved!"

Kate smiled. "Sure, go get yourself something to eat, and don't hurry. I'll just be right here."

"Okay," Gloria said before leaving the room.

Kate went over to her closet and opened the door. She looked at the outfit she had worn yesterday. Too bad she didn't have anything like that to wear again. For a brief second, she thought about asking Gloria if she could loan her something to wear, but she didn't think her clothes would fit because Gloria looked like she was a size or two smaller. Kate sighed and began to look through all the dresses hanging on the rack.

Though it took her a few minutes, she finally settled on the one that looked the least formal. It was white with pink, blue, and purple little flowers. She retrieved the white flats from the closet floor and took time in getting herself dressed.

Kate had her purse in her hand and was about to leave the room, when she realized that something was missing. She went back over to her closet and opened the door again. Kate saw what she wanted on the top shelf. In order to retrieve the item, Kate had to stand on her toes. She grabbed what that she wanted and set her feet back down on the floor. She then smiled as she put on her little straw hat and closed the closet door. Kate turned around and left the room to go downstairs and join her cousin.

"Good Lord!" Gloria exclaimed after her first glance at Kate. "What in God's name are you wearing?"

"Oh, it's just my little floral dress," Kate said.

Gloria glared at her cousin. She, herself, was dressed in blue jeans, a white blouse, and sandals, which was kind of a mismatch, but one had to consider the fact that this was Gloria and her slightly odd taste of clothes.

"What? It's the least formal dress that I own. I used to wear this when I went on family picnics."

Gloria made a face, which seemed to indicate both shock and disgust. She considered herself lucky that she did not have any food in her mouth because, if she did, she would have spit it out on the table.

"What about my clothes?" Gloria suggested.

"I don't think that they would fit," Kate replied, which was the honest truth. Besides, she didn't want to have to impose on her cousin like that.

"Well, farm girl, looks like we are going to have to take another trip to Strawberry Orange Dreams."

Kate smiled. She liked Strawberry Orange Dreams, and she did look forward to getting herself even more "hip" clothes. Today, however, she decided to stick with the dress because she was already wearing it.

"Mum said I could take her car to the bank. It's on the other side of town, a little too far to walk, especially if you're wearing something like that." She gestured to Kate's outfit with her hand.

While Kate wanted to laugh at the fact that Gloria was always so concerned about her wardrobe, she didn't want to upset her. After all, there was all that nasty business that took place last night at supper. Kate decided that it would be best to just agree with Gloria at this point.

After allowing some time for Gloria to digest her food and get dressed, the two of them decided that it was time to take their daily venture.

"Ready whenever you are," Kate said, ready to embark upon today's adventures.

"Right," Gloria replied. "Let me just go get my purse and Mum's keys. I'll be right back."

Seconds later, Gloria returned, and the two of them got in the car to go to the bank.

This must be the conservative end of town, Kate thought, as she observed the building and people surrounding the area.

While Putney, on the whole, seemed a bit like New York City, Kate thought that this part of town was the only part that was not overrun with hippies and young people.

First Savings and Trust was the same bank where the Cunninghams took all their business. Most of the people who worked there knew Stuart and his family very well.

Kate followed Gloria inside the bank. She looked around to see what other people were wearing. Outside of the people who worked there, it seemed that most of the men simply wore fancy suits and dress shirts. Most of the women wore blouses and skirts. Gloria, to Kate's knowledge, seemed to be the only woman who wore pants.

"Hello, Gloria," the enthusiastic voice of the bank teller, Mrs. Ripple, said. "How may I help you today?"

"Good morning, Mrs. Ripple. This is my cousin Kate. She is visiting from America."

"Oh, how nice!" Mrs. Ripple replied. "What state are you from?"

"I'm from Oklahoma," Kate said. "It's very nice to meet you, ma'am."

"And you, too, dear. But my, that is a lovely dress you're wearing! And what an adorable little hat to match."

"Thank you," Kate replied. She did not even have to look over at her cousin, who was just itching to make some kind of sarcastic remark.

Gloria, however, wisely decided to bite her tongue.

"Now," Mrs. Ripple resumed. "What can I do for your ladies this morning?"

"I would like to have my American dollars converted into English pounds, please."

"That should not be a problem. I can take care of that for you right here. How much do you have?"

"Nine hundred and ninety American dollars," Kate said, giving the money over to Mrs. Ripple.

"Let me just take this in the back so I can change out the currency for you. I won't be but a moment."

"Thank you," Kate replied, certain that she was drawing some unwanted attention to herself.

Neither Kate nor Gloria said very much while Mrs. Ripple was in the back exchanging the money.

Gloria did manage to tell Kate that Mrs. Ripple was a very nice woman, despite the fact that she worked with snooty people all day.

Moments later, Mrs. Ripple had returned. She handed Kate a bank envelope and counted out the cash in front of her.

Twenty, forty, sixty…in total, this comes to seven hundred and eighty-seven English pounds."

"Thank you," Kate replied, putting her pound notes into the bank envelope and then into her purse. She did her best to hide her disappointment. Since no one had told her about British advantage when it came to exchange rates, Kate expected to get more money back.

Well, she thought. *At least I have something. As long as I keep a close watch on my finances, I'll be all right.*

"Is there anything else I can do for you young ladies today?" Kate looked over at her cousin.

"No," Gloria replied. "I think this will do us for today."

"Well, thank you both for stopping by to see us." Mrs. Ripple turned her head to the woman in the flowered dress. "Kate, it was lovely meeting you. Please do stop in and say hello to us again. Gloria, please tell your mum and dad hello for me; be sure to give them my best wishes."

"I will do that," Gloria replied. "Thank you for all your help today."

"It was my pleasure," Mrs. Ripple said. "Goodbye, Gloria. Goodbye, Kate."

"Goodbye," the two chorused as they walked out the door.

"She seems very pleasant," Kate said, regarding Mrs. Ripple's polite manner.

"I told you so," Gloria replied. "She's the nicest person working here. Everyone else acts nice on the surface, but you can tell that all they want is your money. Are bankers like that in America?"

"Not really, at least none that I've encountered. People from my hometown are usually very polite and friendly."

Very different than some of those from New York, Kate wanted to say, but she didn't. After all, she couldn't make such a generalization based on one person, even if that one person was someone whom she regretted having anything to do with in the first place.

Gloria glanced at her wristwatch. It was nearly 11:30. "How about we go have that early lunch? I know this nice little restaurant in the middle of the town. Don't worry, it's nothing fancy," Gloria said, noting the worried expression on Kate's face.

"It's just a little diner." She paused. "I know that you are a little bit overdressed, but I can just explain to people that you are a foreigner who is a stranger to our ways."

"Very funny," Kate replied, amused at Gloria's creative remarks.

"Well, I'm just saying…" Gloria said, trailing off.

"Okay, let's just get into the car and go to lunch at this little dinner you wanted me to see."

Gloria and Kate got into the car and went off to the middle of town.

Though the ride was not very far, the two girls were glad that they did not have to walk, especially because it looked like it was going to start raining any second.

Sure enough, their prediction was right. Raindrops fell from the clouds as they climbed out of the car, giggling.

Kate took off her hat and shook it once they got inside the building.

Right away, they noticed that there was a line formed behind the counter. Apparently, everyone else had the same idea about where to get lunch.

"Well, that was close," Gloria noted.

"Yes, the only time it rains here, and I have to get caught in the middle of it."

Gloria raised her eyebrows.

"Consider yourself lucky. You're in England now, surely you've heard about all the fog and rain that we get."

"Yes, I have heard that. Back home, we have lots of sunshine, which can sometimes be a bad thing for farmers, especially if there's ever a drought."

"Well, has there ever been a drought in your neck of the woods?"

"No, thankfully, there has not been. It is a terrible thing for those farmers who grow and harvest plants, but it could be bad for our business as well. Those poor cows would not be able to give us much milk if they weren't properly nourished. Not to mention that they would keel over from dehydration."

"You've got a point there," Gloria replied, although she knew absolutely nothing about life on a farm. They heard the door open then close behind them.

***

"Hey," Russell whispered, as he nudged Steve in the arm. "Look at those two chicks in front of us. One of them looks like she's dressed up in her Sunday best. I didn't know that church had just let out."

Steve looked at the two girls to which Russell had referred. He thought nothing of it, until he noticed that the blonde one was wearing a straw hat. Then, something in his mind had registered as he remembered the beautiful girl he had seen last night. She, too, was wearing a straw hat similar to that one. Could it be the same person?

"Russell," Steve whispered back. "I think these are the two girls we saw on the street last night."

Russell squinted.

"No, it can't be. If I recall correctly, the blonde was not dressed like some schoolmarm from the 1800s."

Steve looked at Kate again, really trying to determine whether or not it was her. It was hard to tell because their encounter had been very brief.

"But she's wearing a straw hat. The cute girl from last night had one on as well."

Russell then focused on the dark-haired girl almost directly in front of him.

"Come to think of it, the one in front of me looks very sexy from where I'm standing. Maybe these *are* the two girls from last night."

Steve rolled his eyes. "That's what I've been trying to tell you," he hissed. "I wonder what they're doing here."

"Who cares? Steve, this is the chance we've been waiting for. Let's talk to these girls and see who they are."

Steve looked hesitant. It's not that he didn't want to talk to those lovely ladies, but what if the two of them were not the same people he saw last night? He didn't want to be wrong and make an absolute fool of himself.

"All right," Steve said. "Let's see who they are. But I want you to talk to them first."

"Figures," Russell mumbled, knowing his that his best friend didn't have the guts to make the first move.

***

"Hello, there," a voice said from behind. Since there were many people in the diner, Kate and Gloria assumed that this person was talking to someone else, so they ignored him.

"Excuse me, lovely ladies," Russell said, addressing them again.

This time, Gloria and Kate turned around. They came face to face with two men who were smiling at them. There were also three others standing behind the two men who had just addressed them. Clearly, they were just as curious to know what was going to transpire.

"Yes," Gloria replied in a plain voice. She studied the men for a few seconds until it registered; she couldn't believe her eyes.

"Oh, my God, Kate; it's those blokes from last night!"

Kate's face turned a crimson shade. Clearly, she was embarrassed at having run into these men again, especially since was dressed so differently today.

So, Steve thought, *the beautiful blonde is named Kate.* He was delighted also to know that this was the same woman with whom he somehow became smitten.

"Looks like we found you," Russell said, a smile set deep in his face.

"That you did," Gloria replied.

"Well, it appears that you did not give us much of a challenge. Keeping that in mind, I believe that you now have to tell us your names."

Gloria smiled. "Gloria Cunningham," she said, extending her hand for Russell to shake. "And this is my cousin, Kate Richards."

Kate merely smiled. She held up her hand and gave a slight wave.

"Hello, Gloria," Russell said. "My name is Russell Stokes, and this is me best mate Steve Maddington." He reintroduced both of them in case the girls had forgotten their names.

"Hello," Steve said right before shaking Gloria's hand.

"And," Russell continued. "These three shy bastards back here are John Thomas, Geoffrey Stevenson, and Henry Atkins."

The three men each leaned over to shake Gloria's hand by means of introductions.

Kate, moderately embarrassed, still had not said a word.

Gloria turned to look at her cousin. "You'll have to forgive my cousin here; I'm afraid she is not very talkative this morning," Gloria said through rueful laughter. "Don't be so shy, Kate!"

Kate blushed again; she still said nothing. In fact, if there was anything in the restaurant behind which she could have hidden, then she would have done it.

"Kate," Gloria hissed through her teeth. "Talk to these people; they're not going to bite you."

"Hello," Kate said, only doing so because Gloria had instructed her to speak.

Gloria rolled her eyes. "Sorry, gents, but Kate is a foreigner in this land and a stranger to our ways. She comes from a dairy farm in Oklahoma."

"Oklahoma," Russell said, clearly intrigued. "So, you're American?"

"Yes," Kate quietly replied. She felt like she could have kicked Gloria for what she was putting her through at the moment, but she decided it would look even worse if she did that in front of all these people.

"Well, it's a pleasure to meet you, love," Russell said, taking her hand in his. He then put his arm around Kate's shoulder. "Don't be a scared of us Englishmen. Despite what you may have heard about our people, we're mostly harmless."

Gloria laughed.

A tiny smile formed around Kate's lips.

Steve felt better knowing that the girl was just shy after all. At least he now had the feeling that she was not snubbing him when she did not speak to him yesterday. He decided that now was the time to make his move.

"Hello, Kate," Steve said. "Are all women in America as beautiful as you, or are you the best-looking one they've got?"

Kate stiffened. She was afraid to speak or even move.

Steve, sensing Kate's nervousness, did not wish their presence to be intimidating. He knew that he had to find a way to make Kate feel at ease.

Steve took her right hand and placed it to his lips. "Well, anyway, it is a pleasure meeting you, Miss Kate."

"Th...thank you?" Kate replied, more as a question than a statement. It's not that Kate didn't find Steve handsome. He was very good-looking, which was the problem. The man she had met in New York was also very handsome, and she knew what kind of trouble she had landed into because of that. Steve Maddington, however, seemed to be a nice guy.

She wasn't sure why or how she knew, but Kate detected something special in him, a certain kindness that had started to make her feel almost immediately comfortable in his presence. She began to feel the shyness inside her melt away as she looked into Steve's eyes and saw his genuine sincerity. She smiled again.

"Oh, look!" Gloria exclaimed, as she looked outside the window of the diner. "The rain has stopped."

So it has, Kate thought, widening her smile.

Despite the fact that the diner was crowded before, it seemed that many people purchased their lunch orders to go. Just as luck, or coincidence, would have it, two large booths recently became open after the new friends ordered their food. John, Geoffrey, and Henry all shared one booth, while the cousins shared one with Russell and Steve.

Though Kate had felt very shy toward Steve only moments ago, she now felt almost completely comfortable in his presence and was delighted to be seated across from him.

The four of them chatted all throughout lunch and came to know each other a little better.

Russell and Gloria seemed to be hitting it off, as there was a mutual attraction moments after they met.

Though Steve and Kate shared something similar, it was more along the lines of establishing a friendship than anything.

Both Steve and Kate talked some about their families and home lives.

Since Steve has lived in London all his life, he was not familiar with farms and farm towns, especially ones overseas.

Kate brought up the fact that she was an only child, but she mentioned that she had another cousin besides Gloria.

Steve found it interesting that Jacob Stone and his family were also into agriculture.

Kate listened as Steve talked about his mom and dad.

He had a younger brother, named Nick, who was twenty. Steve was twenty-four, the same age as Gloria.

As time progressed into late afternoon, Steve and Russell started talking about their band, The Peppermint Eyes, which elicited some strong excitement on Gloria's part.

"I've heard of you guys!" she exclaimed. "Though I've never seen one of your shows, I have a friend who is a big fan of yours. Do you chaps know Judy Spellman, the proprietor of Strawberry Orange Dreams?"

"Know her?" John bellowed from the other booth. "Me girlfriend practically lives in that place. She takes me in there all the time, you know, but they've also got stuff for guys."

"Who's your girlfriend?" Gloria asked out of curiosity.

"Her name is Joan Archer."

"I know her!" Gloria squealed. "Sometimes, I talk to her in the store."

"Huh, small world," John said, returning his attention to Jeff and Henry.

***

The time seemed to fly by as the lunch progressed, and everyone was enjoying their conversations.

Steve took another glance at Kate before checking the time on his watch. Once he saw that it was getting close to 2:30, he frowned.

Their gig was scheduled to start at 8:30 tonight, for which they would have to leave an hour before for the sound check.

"Dammit," Steve said, cursing under his breath. He knew that he and the boys had to get back to their flat to rest up for this evening's gig. Plus, they would have to grab some supper before their sound check started, but Steve knew that they could take care of that at the pub. Steve knew, however, that even a task as menial as eating did take up some time.

"Guys," Steve said, hoping to get his friends' attention.

Russell was still talking and laughing with Gloria, while John, Geoffrey, and Henry were busy carrying on conversations of their own. It took only mere seconds before Steve decided to resort to more drastic measures to get everyone to listen to him. He put his index and middle fingers into his mouth and made a loud whistling sound.

Not only did his friends stop talking, but everyone in the diner stopped what they were doing and looked over at Steve.

"Uh, sorry," he said, slightly embarrassed. "I was trying to get my friends' attention."

Everyone then took one more look at Steve then resumed whatever it was that they were doing.

"What is it?" Russell asked, sounding slightly exasperated. "Can't you see that I'm talking to Gloria?"

Gloria smiled. She could tell by Russell's exasperation at being interrupted that he was really into their conversation. She regarded this as a high compliment, indeed.

"Yes, I can see that," Steve replied. "But if you all notice what time it is, then you know that we should get going."

"Oh, right," Geoffrey said from the other table. "I suppose we need to get some sleep for tonight, then?"

"I don't get it, what's going on tonight?" Kate asked.

"It's Peppermint Eyes' first gig at the Banner Alehouse tonight. We will be playing there for three nights in a row." Steve hesitated, looking over and seeing the disappointed look on Gloria's face.

"Sorry, love," Russell said to Gloria. "Steve's right; we've got to get going for now."

"But today was so much fun! When will I ever get to see you again?" Gloria extended her lower lip, indicating that she was pouting in her mind.

"Come see our band tonight."

"Yes, please, come and see us play," Steve said to Kate. "Banner is just right down a few blocks, on the corner of Chesmond Avenue and Crimson Lane."

"We know where that is. Right, Kate?" Gloria said. "It's only a few blocks down from Strawberry Orange Dreams."

"Right you are," Russell replied.

"I don't know," Kate replied. "It sounds like fun, but what about Uncle Stu and Auntie Olivia?"

"Don't worry about them," Gloria replied. "They will have no problem with us going to a pub. I go to them all the time."

"You see," Russell said to Kate. "Everything will be fine. It's just a little bit of fun and music, that's all."

"Well," Kate said, as Steve waited in anticipation to hear her answer. "I suppose it does sound like fun. I've never been to a bar before, let alone and English pub."

"Great, so it's settled! We will see you lovely ladies tonight around 7:45."

"See you then," Gloria said in a chipper voice as she rose from her seat.

Just as Kate was about to do the same, Steve placed his hand on her shoulder.

"Thank you for agreeing to come hear our music tonight," he said. "It really means the world to me."

"You're welcome," Kate replied, not sure what else she was supposed to say. "It was really nice meeting you all." Kate got up out of her seat and joined her cousin.

The two of them waved as they headed out the door.

No sooner had the door closed behind Gloria and Kate did Russell lean over and lightly punch Steve's arm.

"Oh, man," he said. "Aren't you glad that I made you talk to those girls? Now, they will come see our gig tonight!"

"Yeah," Steve replied. "Kate's beautiful, isn't she?"

"And so's Gloria," Russell said. "Gloooria!" he moaned as he started singing the Van Morrison song. Russell stopped singing, and both men erupted with laughter.

"Well, I suppose it's time that we pay our bill then shove off."

Kate and Gloria had left before the waitress came by with their check, but neither Russell nor Steve minded because they were happy, having just met the women of their dreams.

Though they knew that they all had to leave soon, Steve wished to remain seated at his booth for a moment. He wanted to bask in the glow that Kate had left behind her.

I can't believe that the beautiful woman from last night is the same woman with whom I sat and had lunch today, Steve thought. *She did look cute in that spring dress of hers, although I must admit that what she had on last night looked better.* Steve smiled as he remembered the shape of Kate's body.

Though he wanted to put an end to her shyness, Steve also vowed that he would take things slow. He did not want to pressure Kate or rush into the sack with her, despite what his body was telling him. Besides, that is what he did with Sherry, and he did not want to repeat that mistake twice. No, with Kate, things were going to be different.

This time, Steve had a feeling that things were going to be different. Perhaps, he finally found a love which would last.

"Well, that was interesting," Kate said once they made their way to the sidewalk, still a little nervous from their encounter.

"Come off it, Kate," Gloria said, slightly exasperated with her cousin. "Those men are very nice fellows, but it took a lot of prodding on my part to get you to even talk to them. See, it's that Sunday picnic dress that you're wearing; that's the problem right there. We need to get you a whole new outfit just for tonight," Gloria said. "Something sexy!"

Kate felt her pulse rise. The concept of purchasing yet another sexy outfit excited and frightened her at the same time. Kate knew what this meant, but she had to ask, anyway.

"So, this *does* mean another trip to Strawberry Orange Dreams, right now?"

"You bet your arse it does!" Gloria replied, opening the passenger door for her cousin. "Now, come on; get in. We have to go see Judy, and we have to make it fast!"

The two of them got into the car, and Gloria drove a few blocks to Strawberry Orange Dreams.

As usual, the store was crowded again, most likely with people who wanted to purchase clothes for the upcoming concert tonight. Gloria parked the car, and the two of them got out and made their way over to the store.

Judy was ringing up a customer when she saw Gloria come bounding into the door.

Kate followed close behind her.

Judy smiled when she saw the two of them.

"Back again?" she asked, shortly after finishing her most recent transaction. Judy took one look at Kate's dress then instantly became aware that she had lots more work to do.

"You bet," Gloria replied. "Now, as you can see, my cousin's wardrobe is once again in disrepair."

"Yeah, I can see that," Judy said, taking a closer look at the hokey flower designs on Kate's dress.

"Anyway, Kate here has a date with the guitarist *and* lead singer of The Peppermint Eyes!" Gloria paused. "And you're the only one that we can trust to help us."

Judy smiled. "Really?" she asked as her eyes lit up. "Well, don't you worry. Just leave everything to me," she said as she led Kate back to a vacant dressing room.

Chapter 5

"Hello, girls," Olivia said from the kitchen. "How was your day out?"

Gloria noticed that her father was not about, which meant that he was probably in his study. She had not seen him since last night, so she was a bit worried that he was still upset with her. Perhaps she would try to apologize to him at tea. After all, that would be the adult thing to do.

"It was great," Gloria replied. "I took Kate to the bank to have her currency changed. Mrs. Ripple says hello."

"Oh, how nice," Olivia responded. "I haven't seen her for ages. She is a lovely woman, wouldn't you agree, Kate?"

"Yes," she replied. "Mrs. Ripple is very pleasant. She treated me very courteously when she handled my money."

Even though they went to the bank only a little over four hours ago, it seemed like days had passed since then. Kate was still worried about tonight. Since she had never been to a pub and knew next to nothing about rock 'n' roll music, she obviously didn't know what to expect.

"What else?" Olivia asked, having meant if they did anything else fun today.

"We went to Molly's diner for lunch today, and we met some nice lads."

"Oh?" Olivia asked, this statement having piqued her curiosity.

"Yes, they're in a musical band, and they invited us to see them play at Banner's Alehouse. Their show starts at 8:30 tonight."

"How do you think Kate will feel about that? Do you think she could handle that much excitement?"

"Mum, she'll be fine. It's about time that someone took her out and let her experience some of our culture."

Olivia laughed.

"If you say so, but I still did not hear an answer from Kate."

"Yes, Auntie, I trust Gloria completely to show me a good time." As the words were leaving Kate's lips, however, she couldn't help but think that it was not entirely true. She was worried that Gloria would show her too much of a good time, and she would end up emptying the contents of her stomach before the night was over.

"Well, all right, then. If you are sure that you are up for that kind of thing. Don't mind me, I'll just be in here fixing us some tea. You girls can go upstairs and make more plans for your concert tonight if you'd like."

"May I help you with anything?" Kate asked, feeling that she should help her aunt in the kitchen. "I feel as if I am not doing my share around here."

"Nonsense," Olivia replied. "You are a guest in our home; consider your stay here as a vacation. Lord knows, as an only child and a farmer's daughter, you've done your fair share of work back in Oklahoma."

This was true, Kate did have many responsibilities on the farm. Ever since she was old enough to walk, she had been old enough to work. Thinking about this a little more, she felt less guilty, and she realized that this was the first real fun she's had since college. Though, she'd had some major regrets about her days at NYU.

"Well, since you insist, Aunt Olivia. We will just be upstairs talking about…clothes and things," Kate said, not completely sure how to finish her statement.

"Fine, fine, my dears," Olivia said. "Go upstairs and do your thing; I'll let you know when it's time for tea." Olivia went back to work. She placed some freshly made crumpets into the oven.

"Oh, I almost forgot," she called to Gloria and Kate before they started to make their way upstairs. "Your Aunt Lois called, and she said they will be coming for tea Monday night."

Gloria hesitated, dreading what she was about to say next. "She also said that Syd and Sebastian are on holiday, and they will also be joining us. I just felt I had to tell you now before your father did."

Upon hearing these words, Gloria's face fell. That was the thing she wanted least in this world, especially since Kate was there. Just thinking of that pretentious side of the family made her blood boil, but Gloria was no longer a child. Though she had learned the fine art of diplomacy long ago, she knew that her technique needed improvement.

"I know they are not your favorite people, dear, but you know how much your father is looking forward to this. Please don't disappoint him."

Gloria sighed, she wished that she did not have to hear this news right now, but she knew that she had to say in order to appease her mother. After all, having heard this news from her mother came less of a blow than having her father announce it at the table. At least she would now be prepared more for when he made his announcement.

"Thanks, Mum, I appreciate the heads up. And don't worry, I will not make such an ordeal in front of Father as I did last night."

"I know that he will appreciate that, as will I," Olivia replied. "Now, go on upstairs. Tea should be ready shortly."

Gloria and Kate did as they were told. They had a few things they would like to discuss, anyway, about this evening's concert.

"Don't tell me that you've never been with a man before!" Gloria exclaimed. The two of them were upstairs in Kate's room, sitting on the bed, having a conversation which was close to making Kate blush.

"No," Kate quickly answered. Gloria was unbelieving. She stared at her cousin, open-mouthed.

"What about you?" Kate asked, with the same skepticism that her cousin was currently portraying.

"*Moi?*" she asked. "Why, sure I have. Of course, that was almost a year ago. His name was Glenn, and he was my second boyfriend, though not my first, if you catch my drift."

Kate nodded like she understood. "Well, you don't have to go into detail, especially because I have never been down that road before."

Gloria shot her cousin another skeptical look.

"Are you absolutely sure?" she asked again.

"Yes, I'm sure. I'm surer of that than any other absolute truth in my life."

Gloria nodded, not indicating either way if she believed her cousin.

Kate had lied. In fact, she *had* slept with a man before, back when she was still in college. He was her boyfriend from NYU, Fred Beaumont.

Fred was born and raised in Rochester, New York, and he knew almost next to nothing about rural life, nor did he seem to care. When Fred first noticed the beautiful, but virginal, Kate who hung around his circle of friends, he became intrigued. He'd then found out that she was a farmer's daughter, which highly amused him.

Fred then made it his mission to get to know Kate better, and by know her, he meant in the carnal sense. They soon started dating, and it did not take long for them to fall into bed. Fred also got her started drinking and tried to offer her drugs, which she promptly refused.

Kate figured that a little alcohol would never hurt anybody, but she knew that heavy drugs were a whole different story. Drugs, more than alcohol, were what turned Fred into a monster. And this was only the beginning of the story, as there was so much more, but Kate did not want to think of that right now. She also didn't want to tell Gloria about any of it.

Steve seemed to be a whole different story. In the short time Kate had gotten to know him, he seemed nothing like Fred. It was strange how she could feel so at ease with a man who was practically still a stranger. Kate liked Steve, however, and she thought that if she could forget her bad past, all of it, then the two of them may actually have a shot at starting and sustaining a good friendship.

"You know, it would break his heart if you did not go," Gloria said, looking over at her cousin.

"I beg your pardon," Kate replied.

"Steve. He really likes you. Can't you tell by the way he was trying to flirt with you?"

"I highly doubt that," Kate said, seconds away from bursting out into laughter.

"You can't deny what was happening; I was a witness to all of it!" Gloria insisted. "The man kissed your hand. He was ready to get down on one knee and recite some poetry to you."

"Don't be preposterous! We literally just met hours ago; no one can determine such strong emotions in so short an amount of time."

Despite what she had just said, Kate was not so sure about the validity of her statement. She had fallen in love with Fred only *minutes* after he introduced himself to her. Most of that was due to the fact that he had been so self-assured and smooth.

It took months after she'd left Fred to realize why his false charm had worked on her. Kate lowered her guard; thus, she had put herself in a vulnerable position, allowing him to dupe her. Now that Kate had realized what happened to her as a result of falling in love too soon, she was determined that she would never let it happen to her again.

"Quit trying to kid yourself, Kate. You told me yourself that you thought Steve was a nice guy. It was only moments after we finished having lunch."

Kate, who was no longer in the mood to argue with her cousin, decided to concede defeat because she could not hide the entire truth from her cousin.

"Yes, I said that I like Steve. He seems like he is a very nice person. It's just that I'm afraid because I haven't seen anyone for a long time."

Gloria laughed. "You, afraid? I never would have thought that possible."

"Please, Gloria. This is serious! It's been a while since I've dated anyone. If, *hypothetically*, something does happen between Steve and me, I want to take things slowly. Steve may be a wonderful man, but I feel I need to get to know him better before I go rushing into some whirlwind romance.

"How awkward would it be to say that I love man before I even get a chance to meet his parents, to sit down and actually have dinner, or tea, or whatever with someone in his family?"

Kate shuddered. Just the mere thought of mentioning Steve to her parents made her feel a little queasy. It was not so much her mother's reaction she was worried about; it was her father's. She knew that this would be enough to send him over the deep end.

"So what do you think about Russell?" Gloria asked, slightly changing the subject.

Kate stifled a giggle. She did not have to think long and hard about this one.

"I think that Russell seems like a nice guy. You two do certainly have a lot in common, from what little I can gather, if that is what you want me to say."

Gloria smiled. She was glad that an outside observer thought that she and Russell would go well together. Now, if she could just convince Kate that the same was true of her and Steve.

"You think so? That's good. I hardly know him, but I think I like the bugger. Even though he seems like he is a bit randy, he has a certain kind of charm. I can't quite put my finger on it, though."

"You don't have to worry about such things now," Kate responded. "After all, you just met the guy. Maybe you should take it slow, just as I intend to."

Gloria stuck out her tongue, play mocking her cousin.

"Listen, missy, there are two things that Miss Gloria Cunningham does not do. The first one is to take things slow, and…I forget the second one."

Kate laughed. "Dear Cousin, you are a mess. What are we going to do with you?"

"We are going to leave Gloria alone so she can make her own decisions. And, as for you, I am making you go on a *separate* date with Steve. You know, so you can 'get to know him better.'"

This prompted Kate to start to fake wanting to stay home. She wanted to test her cousin's limits.

"And what if I've changed my mind? What if I refuse to go? I already told you, I hardly know a thing about new rock 'n' roll music. My father only listens to a little bit Elvis Presley."

"Then, I will have to tie you up and throw you over my shoulder," Gloria replied, ignoring her cousin's second comment about music. "I will proceed to carry you to the pub, even if you're kicking and screaming all the way."

Kate snickered then decided to test Gloria's theory.

"You wouldn't dare," she said.

"Watch me," Gloria replied, determined that she was not going to let Kate back out of this one. She considered herself a good judge of character, and in Steve, she saw a winner. Besides, she had some ulterior motives. She was determined to let Kate experience being with a man, even if it was the last thing that she ever did.

Kate does not know this yet, but I am going to fix her up with a good man, Gloria thought. *Besides, years from now, they may even get married, and she will be thanking me for all that I did for her.*

Gloria smiled. Her mind had already begun scheming, and her plans would not stop until she successfully got Kate and Steve together. Gloria did not worry so much about herself since she and Russell had hit it off; she already knew that the two of them would make a great couple.

Chapter 6

"We should get a move on," Gloria replied, looking at her watch. It's nearly 7:15!"

"Wait a moment," Kate said, staring down at her dress. "At least give me a moment to change into my new clothes."

Gloria glared at Kate. There was no way that she was going to let her cousin put on her new clothes while they were still in this house.

"Oh, no, darling," Gloria said. "We can't let you try on your new outfit here. If Mum and Dad saw us going to a pub wearing these clothes, it would send them spinning right to their graves! Besides, I have a little bit of work to do on you which doesn't involve your outfit. You just have to relax and leave everything to me."

Kate smiled nervously. It's not that she didn't trust Gloria, but she knew that "fixing up" did not have anything to do with getting her ready for a quiet evening with Gertrude Stein. Kate knew how much Gloria could accomplish when she got her mind set on something. And tonight, being Kate's first date with an Englishman, was sure to land both Gloria and Kate in infamy.

***

Steve was standing in front of the stage, watching the roadies set up all their equipment. He was pacing back and forth. This was the first night of their three-gig stint, so everyone felt that they were entitled to being nervous. Unlike all the other members of the band, however, Steve was sitting on pins and needles, but not because of the gig. He was afraid that Kate would decide not to show at the very last minute. So many thoughts were racing through his head that it was hard to keep track of them all.

Russell, sensing that Steve's anticipation looked more like anxiety, went over to talk to his friend. "Don't be so nervous, mate. You're making me nervous with all this pacing around. Gloria said that she and Kate would come 'round see us tonight."

Gloria was not who had Steve on edge. He knew that *Gloria* would be there. It was her beautiful cousin about which he was not very sure.

"It's just, you know, Kate is very beautiful. She's practically perfect, and she's American. She might not be very accustomed to being in the company of loud, randy Englishmen."

Russell laughed, but he knew that his friend was serious.

"I mean it, Russell," Steve said. "Today, in the diner, I saw something in Kate. As she was looking into my eyes, I was looking into hers, and I saw something there that I have never seen in any other woman before. I cannot quite describe it, but I'm pretty sure it's something special."

"It's your hormones," Russell replied, with a grin on his face. "You know you want to jump this pretty girl, so you were looking into her eyes to see if the word yes was anywhere in there." Russell began guffawing, which also caused Steve to snicker.

"No, it's not like that. I mean, yes, she's very beautiful, but what I saw was something pertaining to our souls." Steve wanted to go on describing what he was feeling, but he felt he could not accurately portray his thoughts with mere words. Besides, he did not want to wax poetic with Russell standing there beside him.

"Ah, always the romantic," Russell said, placing his arm around Steve. "No worries, mate, I know in my heart of hearts that those girls will show up. Besides, did you see the way Gloria was flirting with me during lunch?" Russell stretched out his arms and exhaled a proud breath. "She couldn't get enough of me. And, in all seriousness, I could not get enough of her. How is it that women, who have always been mysteries to us men, find a way to get to us so easily?"

"I don't know," Steve replied, knowing full well that he had a great mystery of his own to solve. "I don't think that there is a man out there alive who can answer that question."

***

At 7:40, while the band was still backstage getting ready, Gloria and Kate entered the pub. As soon as they walked in the door, they were bombarded with whistles and stares from strange men.

Gloria wore one of her favorite pairs of jeans. They were an older pair, but they were as comfortable as they were tight. On top, Gloria had on a low-cut, purple shirt with long sleeves. She had also borrowed Kate's brown leather boots, which she had gotten from Strawberry Orange Dreams yesterday. Gloria was full of confidence tonight; she knew that these were the kinds of pants that Russell would go for.

Kate, on the other hand, looked completely different than she had this afternoon. Gloria had done her makeup and hair, which was an interesting experience for Kate. The only other time Kate had worn makeup was at her high school prom, and that was only a little lipstick and blush. Gloria certainly had given her the works tonight because Kate was also wearing mascara and eye shadow. Gloria had also spritzed Kate with some of her favorite perfume, Love Potion #9.

Even though Gloria prided herself on her makeup job, that's not what attracted people the most. Kate was wearing skintight, black leather pants, which accentuated her features. Matching her black pants were black leather boots. On top, she wore a white long-sleeved shirt, similar to Gloria's. And, though, they did not have to admit it, neither one of them had worn a bra.

Gloria had talked Kate into that, and Kate, feeling a little reckless, actually agreed to it.

After saying hello to a few people that she knew, Gloria introduced them to her cousin Kate, who had managed to enthrall everyone she met during that brief period of time. Several men tried to ask them out, but Gloria promptly turned them down, stating that they were already taken. Gloria had fun looking at the disappointed faces of men after she told them that they were not available.

Gloria also tried to talk Kate into going backstage, but upon seeing that it was almost 8:00, they decided they would wait to see the boys after the show.

Besides, Gloria thought. *If we wait, it will give them something to look forward to.* She smiled at knowing how Russell and Steve were going to be happy to see them, very happy.

Most of the seats close to the front of the small stage area were already taken, so the two cousins had to seat themselves a little farther back. Though they were seated where they could see the center of the stage, Gloria was not sure how many people would be getting up to dance and cheer, thus blocking their vision. She decided, however, not to let such thoughts enter her mind. Tonight was going to be fun, and that's all that there was to it.

After a few more moments of anticipation, The Peppermint Eyes made their way onto the stage.

Gloria stood up and cheered wildly when she saw Russell come out carrying his bass guitar. She was not sure if he heard her or not, however, because so many people were cheering for the band.

Gloria knew that The Peppermint Eyes needed no introduction, because everyone there was already a fan. That was, everyone except for Kate. She wasn't quite sure what to expect regarding both the music and the crowd.

"Good evening, everyone," Steve said into the microphone. "Thanks for coming out tonight to see us perform!"

This drew a big reaction from the crowd.

"We'd like to start with one of our newest songs, one that we just wrote last week. Here's 'Out There Tonight.' "

There were more cheers and applause.

The band began to play, and Steve sang,

"It's been a while since I've heard
You or seen you
It's been such a long, long time

It's been too long since
I've seen your smile
Don't you think it's time to rise?

And I can sense it, I know it
You're somewhere out there tonight
Don't need to hide it or disguise it
You can meet me out there tonight…"

The first thing Kate noticed about the music was that it certainly did not sound like anything by Elvis. The second thing she noticed was about the band. They did not quite have the same kind of hippie sound than some of the bands she'd heard in New York, as their name seemed to suggest.

Kate was vaguely familiar with the protest songs people had sung, talking about ending the war in Vietnam. She'd heard them when she went from building to building to her various classes. This sound was rougher; it had a certain edge to it. Another thing which fascinated Kate was the instrumentation.

It was different from the things she'd heard on the radio while out with her friends. Kate listened as Steve continued to sing,

"And if I allow myself to give
Up the fight and go home,
Then I would be nothing…"

Steve stopped singing mid-sentence, as he saw something that completely threw him for a loop. Kate and Gloria were there; they had come to see The Peppermint Eyes perform after all. Then, both Steve and Russell had noticed it. They saw that both girls were dressed to the hilt and looking extremely sexy.

Steve's jaw literally dropped when he saw Kate in that white shirt and those tight leather pants.

Russell stared at Gloria with a lecherous smile on his face. It was then when the audience became dead quiet, wondering why the band had stopped playing mid-song.

Kate and Gloria, feeling a little guilty about the spectacle that they created, sank into their seats. They hoped that the band's performance would not suffer because of them.

"Psst, Oi!" John whispered from his drum set. "What do you blokes think this is? We're giving a rock concert here!"

Despite John's words, both Steve and Russell still stood there, completely transfixed by what they had seen.

Henry peered at the two of them from over his keyboard, and Geoffrey stopped playing his rhythm guitar.

"Oh, for God's sake," Geoffrey said to John. "Here, let me do it!" Geoffrey punched Steve in the arm, who, in turn had punched Russell.

The band, realizing their mistake, felt like they had to say something before they resumed the show.

"Um," Steve began. "Sorry for the temporary delay. We were having slight problems with our, um, equipment."

This generated a little laughter from the audience.

Steve let out a little laugh, indicating his embarrassment. "Yes, well, let's get on with the show, then!"

The crowd cheered again, then the band resumed playing. Steve sang,

"…but a coward turned against the wind
If I don't find you out there, I'll remind you
Out there tonight"

And I can sense it, I know it
You're somewhere out here tonight
Don't need to hide it or disguise it
You can meet me out here tonight…"

"Now won't you come a little closer,

Won't you be right by my side?
Only a little bit further until
I can find you, waiting just for me
And I will be right here, waiting, too
Because I know you're out here for me"

When the song was finally over, everyone generously applauded. Steve and Russell nervously laughed at each other and made a mental vow not to let anything distract them during the rest of the show.

***

Once it was made apparent that Steve and Russell were going to give their full attention to their music, Gloria and Kate sat back up in their seats.

"Let this be a lesson to us both," Gloria said to Kate. "The lesson is that we should no longer wear attire like this while attending a Peppermint Eyes gig."

"Says the woman who wanted to dress me up like England's top model," Kate retorted, though she was not angry.

Both women, having thought more about the silly situation, began to laugh. Their laughter did not stop until they heard a voice coming from someone beside them.

"Wow, you two are *literally* showstoppers!" Kate and Gloria turned to face Judy, who was smiling at them. "If this kind of thing keeps up, it will be really good for my business!"

"Hey, Judy," Gloria said. "So you decided to show up, eh?"

"I wouldn't miss it for the world!" Judy replied. "After all, I had to see how the woman who had won Steve's heart was faring."

"Well, I wouldn't quite say that," Kate protested.

"What, are you mad?" Judy questioned. "Did you see the way he was looking at you? I could see him staring right through that shirt at your tits!"

Gloria laughed as Kate crossed her arms against her chest.

"And you," Judy said, "I could see Russell's eyes devour you whole, like you were the main entrée at a fancy restaurant!"

Gloria giggled and smiled. "Really?" she asked, as her eyes lit up.

"Yes," Judy replied. "Both of you look gorgeous. I wouldn't be surprised if I have all the other girls in here come bang down my door in order for me to sell them more of my sexy clothes!"

Both Gloria and Kate laughed. Judy had, indeed, done a bang-up job on them both.

The rest of the show went smoothly, as there were no more mishaps; sexual, electrical, or otherwise.

Some people had started to leave, but Gloria and Kate were still there, talking to a group of young women. They were telling them where they had gotten their outrageously sexy clothes.

"That's Strawberry Orange Dreams, owned by my good friend Judy Spellman, on Winchester Ave..." Gloria trailed off as she saw Russell approaching. Despite the fact that he was now drenched in sweat, he still looked very sexy. She didn't know whether her heart was going to speed up or stop; all she knew was that something was going on with that vital organ underneath her left breast.

"Hello," Russell said, greeting the crowd of young ladies.

They responded by saying how terrific the show was and how they were glad that they got to see their favorite band live.

Flattery, Russell thought, *there's plenty of it to go around.* Just as the girls started becoming flirtatious toward Russell, he knew that he had to make a hasty retreat. While there were many beauties who were present at the concert tonight, Russell did not feel the need to spend much more time with or look at them any longer. He already had his sight set on the one he wanted, the beautiful, dark-haired woman who stood right before him.

"Excuse me, but I have a message from the rest of the band. They humbly request the presence of you two gorgeous ladies," indicating Gloria and Kate. "We want you in the dressing room in back. Shall we?" Russell lifted his eyebrows and held out his arm, which he linked with Gloria's.

The three of them then headed backstage together.

Steve's heart skipped a few beats as the door to the back dressing room had opened. In walked Russell, Gloria, and Kate.

"Hello," Joan said to Kate and Gloria as they entered the room.

"Hey, Joan!" Gloria said, going over to give her friend a hug.

"Joan, I would like you meet my cousin Kate. Kate, this is a dear friend of mine and Judy's, Joan Archer."

"Hello," Kate said, extending her hand to Joan.

"So nice to meet you," Joan replied. "You must be the pretty American girl who's creating all the fuss around here."

Kate blushed. "I wouldn't go so far as to say that," she said, hiding behind her modesty.

"I would," Geoffrey said, as he looked Kate up and down. He had a smile on his face. "Nice to see you again, love."

"Nice to see you again, too, Geoffrey," Kate said.

Steve couldn't blame his friend for fawning over Kate; she did look extremely ravishing, but part of him started to become a little jealous. Steve couldn't quite put his finger on that feeling, but he supposed the reason why was because other men were also attracted to her. This made Steve want Kate all the more.

"Geoffrey, Henry," Russell said. "If I were you two, I would go out there and talk to some of those ladies. They are single, and they want to meet some of the members of the band."

Geoffrey perked up, and Henry smiled.

"Oh, really?" Geoffrey asked. "How many would you say are out there?"

"Tons," Russell replied. "You'd better hurry 'cause they're going fast."

Geoffrey and Henry then looked at each other then made a mad dash for the door.

"Well," Joan said. "I think we'd best get going, too. It's been a long night, and we need to get our beauty rest."

"What are you talking about?" John asked. "I feel great. I feel like I could stay up for...ow!" John winced after Joan elbowed his ribs.

Joan looked over in the direction of Kate, Steve, Gloria, and Russell and looked back at him.

"Oh, right," he said, finally realizing that Joan wanted to give the four of them some privacy. "Come to think of it, I really could use some sleep. Got another two long nights ahead of us and all." John got up from the couch and took Joan by the hand. They left the room, closing the door behind him.

"So," Russell said, addressing both Gloria and Kate. "How were we tonight? We can take any criticism that you have to give, so don't hold back. We want your honest opinion."

"Well," Gloria replied. "I think that the guy who played bass guitar was very sexy." Russell formed a large grin on his face. "But," Gloria continued. "I really couldn't take my eyes off the drummer. He was absolutely fantastic, and good-looking to boot!"

"Hey, now," Russell said, pretending to be offended. "Don't be talking that way about me mate. You're my woman now." Russell put his arm around Gloria's shoulder.

Kate looked at her cousin and smiled. She could tell that Gloria was completely enamored with Russell, and she was happy for them both.

"And you, Miss Kate," Steve began. "How do *you* think we did tonight?"

Kate hesitated. She wanted to say that the band had done well, despite the fact that she made Steve stop singing in mid-sentence, but she felt she did not know enough about this type of music. Kate could easily call herself an expert in picking out a good dairy cow amidst some dried up, old ones, but when it came to topics such as music, she felt she had no authority to judge such a performance.

"I think you did really well, but..." she began to trail off a little.

"But what?" Steve asked, really wanting to know her thoughts.

"But I am no expert in the field of rock 'n' roll. The only modern musician my father has ever let me listen to is Elvis Presley." Kate hesitated. "Now classical music, that is different story.

I can name music from Bach to Mozart, to Beethoven, even to Ives. I have a whole collection of their music back in my room. Of course, I didn't really start appreciating them until I went to high school and took a music appreciation course."

"Really? Then, can you answer me this one? Who was the first ever composer to credit anything to his name?" Russell asked.

"Yes," Kate replied. "That is an easy one; his name was Léonin. Though I will say I've never heard any of his work. Are you familiar with it by any chance?"

Russell started to guffaw.

"Me?" he asked, still laughing. "Why, not at all. I've never heard of the guy, I just wanted to see if *you* knew who he was."

Kate, already having begun to loosen up, began to laugh with the group.

"Okay, that's enough," Steve chided. "Let's leave the poor girl alone. Don't tax her mind on all the vast knowledge that it contains. We'll save that for another time."

"Well, I am proud of Kate for one thing," Gloria said. "She is certainly starting to come out of her shell. Hey, Steve, I'll bet you're thinking that she's not the same, quiet little girl that you met in Molly's Diner earlier today."

Upon hearing the word diner, something suddenly registered with Kate. She remembered that she and Gloria left before their waitress came by with the check. They must have because they certainly did not pay for anything that they'd ordered.

"Oh, my gosh!" Kate exclaimed. "The diner. It completely slipped my mind! I can't believe that we didn't pay for the lunches we had earlier today." Kate reached into her purse and frantically grabbed for her wallet. "How much was my order? I would like to pay you back."

"Absolutely not," Steve said. "It was our treat, and I don't want you to think about it anymore."

"But…" Kate tried to protest.

"Russell," Steve said, ignoring Kate's unfinished claim. "Does Kate owe us anything for lunch?"

"Definitely not," Russell answered, "and neither does Gloria. See, what Kate may not realize, being an American girl, is that when and Englishman offers to pick up a check, he picks up the check, even if nothing is said about it until after the fact."

"How sweet," Gloria said as a happy recipient of their generosity.

"Yes, thank you both," Kate said. "That is very kind."

"You're welcome," Steve said. "Now, let's not hear another word about it."

More time had passed, and the night continued to wane. Gloria knew that she and Kate would be expected back home soon, so she decided that she and Russell should leave Kate alone with Steve.

Surprisingly, when Gloria had mentioned this to her cousin, she did not put up any protest. Since most of the pub was already cleared out, Gloria decided that she and Russell would enjoy each other's company in one of the private booths.

"Just come get me when you are ready," Gloria said. "But don't wait too much longer because Mum and Dad may start to worry."

"Right," Kate said before Russel and Gloria left the dressing room. She was fully aware that she was left alone with Steve, but she was not frightened about it. If it were any other man, even Russell, that might not have been the case. Kate, however, seemed perfectly all right.

"Shall we have a seat?" Steve asked, patting the couch which was next to where he was standing.

"Sure," Kate said, sitting very closely next to him. Though she felt a bit lightheaded, having to deal with her heart beating at an accelerated rate, this was nothing compared to what she was doing to poor Steve.

My God, isn't she gorgeous? he thought, trying to contain himself. Her tight black leather pants clung to her lower body, beautifully outlining her backside and her long legs.

Steve could also tell that Kate was not wearing a bra, which was driving him insane. Every part of him strove to keep the blood from flowing to his male extremity, which, by the way, was no easy task tonight.

"May I say something to you right now?" Steve asked, wanting to tell Kate how he felt.

"Sure," she said with those ruby red lips.

"You look absolutely stunning tonight. I mean, not that you didn't look beautiful before in your dress. Uh, that's not what I meant to say. I just want you to know that you are one fabulous woman."

"Thank you," Kate replied, feeling the heat rise through her spine, like the red line in a thermometer. "You look cute in your jeans and leather jacket, it added tremendously to your, uh, stage persona."

Steve leaned in closer.

"I wasn't even aware that I had one," he said, his lips coming dangerously close to kissing hers.

"Well, maybe it's just the way that you presented yourself. Maybe—" was all Kate had managed to say before Steve planted a kiss on her lips.

Kate opened her eyes in alarm but quickly closed them again. This was a kiss which she was glad to reciprocate. They did not, however, stop after that.

Before they even knew what hit them, Kate and Steve began making out, their hands exploring each other's shoulders and backs.

Steve moved his hands down her back and kept going, touching Kate's buttocks and feeling the material of her leather pants all over her legs. He moved his right hand up and placed it on Kate's neck.

Then, in the intoxicating heat of the moment, he moved his hand down to her breast and began caressing it through her shirt. He felt her nipple becoming hard underneath. His hand went limp then rested there for a few seconds until both of them had realized what they were doing. Steve promptly removed his hand.

"Oh, no! Kate, I'm so sorry. I didn't mean to..."

"No, I'm sorry Steve. Really I am." Then, looking up at the clock, Kate realized that it was quarter to twelve. "I really should be getting going. Aunt Olivia and Uncle Stu are expecting us at home."

"Kate," Steve pleaded. "Please, don't go! I was completely out of line with what I just did. I'm truly sorry, Kate. Please..."

"I have to go. Gloria is waiting for me out there." She hesitated. "I really did have a good time, and the music was great. Thank you for inviting us out here tonight to see you. Goodbye."

Kate left the dressing room, closing the door after her, leaving a completely devastated Steve. So many thoughts raced through his head, and none of them were good.

Here I was, he thought, *with the most beautiful woman I've ever seen. And what did I do? I put my foot to the accelerator; that's what I did! Stupid! I'm such a stupid git, and that's probably the last that I'll ever see of her!*

Steve knew that the pub would be closing soon, but he did not want to move from his chair. He needed some time to think, alone, before having to walk out the door. Then he would have to get in his car and drive home with no one to join him.

Chapter 7

After Gloria and Kate arrived back home, they were relieved to see that Olivia and Stuart had not waited up for them.

Kate hoped that Gloria would not bombard her with a myriad of questions because she certainly did not want to have to answer them now. Instead, she decided to change tactics and ask her she enjoyed her time alone with Russell.

As soon as Kate mentioned his name, Gloria's eyes lit before she broke out into a smile. She mentioned how the two of them talked more before they made out.

Gloria also said that she promised Russell that they would come by and see their show again tomorrow night, providing that it would be all right with their parents.

When Kate heard this, she was none too pleased. She didn't know how she was going to face Steve after having run out on him the way she did. Since Gloria was adamant about seeing Russell again, Kate felt that it would be wrong to try and make her stay home.

Kate, however, needed to come up with some excuse so she could get out of going tomorrow night. She could say something along the lines of that she was not feeling well or that she needed her rest. After all, Kate longed for a bit of quiet time. She especially wanted it now because of what happened at the pub.

I should have known what I was doing! Kate thought. *How could I let that man work his way into my head?* Steve trying to work his way into her head was the last thing Kate wanted. Steve actually getting into her pants was the *last* thing that she needed! She had to stop thinking about the handsome musician and aim her thoughts at something that would serve her better.

***

Minutes after Kate bid her cousin goodnight, she found herself lying in bed, unable to sleep. She tried sleeping on her left side, then her right; neither worked. Kate then decided that it was futile trying to fall asleep without any attempts to clear her head. She got out of bed then went over to her nightstand. She looked through the pile of books, which were neatly stacked in two rows of five. Kate began to read the titles out loud. "*The Adventures of Tom Sawyer*, no. *The House of Seven Gables*, no. *Tropic of Capricorn*, definitely not!"

After she finished reading through all the titles, she decided to give up on the idea of finding something to read. Then, Kate remembered one book in particular. She had forgotten about her copy of H.G. Wells' *The Invisible Man* because she had put it away last night. It was neatly placed in the drawer, along with some of the other titles which she had showed Gloria.

Kate picked up the book and began reading. Though she liked the H.G. Wells' classic work, she couldn't help but wish that she had the one by Ralph Ellison. She'd not read the second book before, but she knew the plot.

Ellison's *Invisible Man* described the life of an African American man who went into hiding. The unnamed, stereotyped protagonist kept himself hidden away from the world because of the negativity associated with his actions and race.

While Kate did not have the same problems as that poor man, she adopted the idea that it would be nice to hide for a while.

Invisible Woman, *that would be a better title*, she thought, as she pictured herself, nameless and hiding in various places around the world. *I could go where no one would try to manipulate me, where no one would try to monitor every move that I make.*

Kate picked up her book and began to read. Then, without consciously knowing it, she found her secret haven. It was in her mind where no one could reach her.

The power and means of escape had been there all along. Now that Kate had found her secret haven, after having dove into the world of Griffin and Dr. Kemp, it did not take long for her to fall asleep.

***

Breakfast was well appreciated by both girls because their stomachs were practically empty. The last food they had were the small sandwiches and crumpets which Olivia had made for tea. Through all the excitement from last night, they had completely forgotten about supper.

Kate was happy to see that Gloria and Uncle Stuart had made amends. Gloria apologized to her father yesterday during tea. Stuart accepted her apology and made one of his own.

The whole turn of events reminded Kate of the scene in *Romeo and Juliet*, in which Juliet comes home from confession and is greeted by her father. Juliet tells Lord Capulet that she had changed her mind and wants to marry Paris. It was at that point when Juliet and her father had reconciled.

Of course, Kate thought. *Juliet had some ulterior motives, as does Gloria, probably.* Soon, the American abolished all the negative thoughts that came into her head. Gloria, although a bit defiant, was no Juliet. She was just a woman who has succumbed to the reality which was about to happen.

Father and daughter spoke amicably to each other regarding his brother's upcoming visit. Kate also helped the conversation along by saying that she was looking forward to meeting Uncle Stuart's family.

Soon after breakfast, Kate decided to give her parents another call. She had not talked to them since she arrived safely at the Cunningham residence, and she wanted to let them know how she was doing. The phone rang twice before Kate's mother answered on the other end.

"Hello," she said.

"Hello, Mom. How are you doing?"

"Hello, sweetheart," Mrs. Richards said. "It's good to your voice again! Are you enjoying your time in England so far?"

"Yes, I'm having a wonderful time. Aunt Olivia and Uncle Stuart are absolutely wonderful, and Gloria and I have gotten extremely close."

"That's wonderful, dear. I hope that you got a chance to explore London; I don't want to hear that you're cooped up inside reading your books all day."

"Oh, I've been to town, all right," Kate replied, trying her best to make it sound innocent. "Gloria's been taking me to some of her favorite places."

"I'm glad to hear it."

Kate knew better than to tell her mother about Strawberry Orange Dreams and the "scandalous" clothes that she had purchased there. There was also no way that she was going to mention Steve or going to see The Peppermint Eyes at some smoky pub. Not only would her mother disapprove, but she may even try to say that Gloria was a bad influence on her.

"But just so you know," Kate continued. "I have been reading some, and I've even loaned Gloria one of my books."

"That's fine, just as you allow yourself some time for fun. Your father would not want you to stay in the house all day, either."

I seriously doubt that, Kate wanted to say. For all she knew, he thought of Uncle Stuart and Aunt Olivia's house as a cloister. Isaac would be content in thinking that Kate had kept to herself and her books. He would happily like to think that Kate was keeping herself chaste behind these walls.

"Don't worry, Mom, I'm managing to have a good time while being the perfect houseguest. Aunt Olivia and Uncle Stuart would give you their word."

"I won't call you a liar if what you are telling me is the truth," Mrs. Richards said.

Both Kate and her mother laughed.

"Your father and I didn't raise any ungrateful children."

"No, you certainly did not. Speaking of my father, is he available?"

"No," Mrs. Richards said. "I'm afraid he's, er, indisposed at the moment."

Kate knew what her mother meant. Since her father was a teetotaler, it had nothing to do with alcohol. "Indisposed" was sort of a family code.

The Richards had changed the term to mean that they simply did not want to talk to someone. Kate liked to think that her mother had meant indisposed in its original intent of saying that someone was not available. She really wanted to believe that her father was simply busy and that he *did not have time* to talk to her instead of her relying on the family's new definition of "indisposed."

"Oh, that's all right," Kate said, trying not to sound dejected.

Mrs. Richards, detecting the disappointment in her daughter's voice, wanted to reassure Kate that Isaac wasn't upset with her.

"Please, don't think that your dad is upset at you. He just isn't feeling really well today. When I say that he's 'indisposed,' I mean just that. I made him some chicken and mashed potatoes for supper last night, and it must not have agreed with him."

"Oh, then I'm sorry that he isn't feeling well," Kate said, knowing that what her mother had said sounded legitimate. She had seen her father sick before, so it was nothing to get alarmed about.

"That's sweet, honey. He will appreciate that you asked about him."

"I just hope that he gets well soon and that I get to talk to him next time that I call."

"Yes. I know that he was sad that he missed your call last Wednesday, and I'm sure he will feel the same about tonight. He knows that your aunt and uncle are talking very good care of you."

And so is Gloria, Kate thought. *She is taking such good care of me that I am the talk and toast of the town.*

"Well, aside from your poor father being sick, nothing is happening around here. Oh, well, I did talk to my brother, and your cousin is doing well, but working hard. You know how diligent Jacob is."

"Yes. Jacob is a very hard worker from what I have heard. If only I could have inherited the same thing." Mrs. Richards laughed.

"Quit teasing, Kate. Both your dad and I know just how much work you've done around the farm! Just because you are off enjoying yourself does not mean that you have to feel guilty."

"Oh, Mom, you know that I was only joking."

"I know, dear. I was just testing to see if you were paying attention."

Kate laughed. "But I don't feel bad. I'm really enjoying myself being 'across the pond,' so to speak. Aunt Olivia and Uncle Stuart are keeping a good eye on me."

Kate paused. Why did she just tell her mother that? She knew such a statement would please her father, once Kate got to actually thinking about it, she wondered whether or not her mother would mind her having such a good time.

She did not want to take any chances, however, because her mother might relay the wrong information to her father. In no way would that be a good thing for any of the parties involved!

"Well, that's nice. Every time dad and I get to missing you too much, we just have to think about what a nice time you are having."

Kate smiled. At least her mother was not going to give her any kind of guilt trip about her recent adventures abroad.

"Oh, there is another thing. Monday afternoon, Uncle Stuart is having his brother and his wife over for tea. Gloria's other two cousins, Syd and Sebastian, will also be there. I told everyone how much I am looking forward to meeting them."

"Well, that sounds lovely! I'm sure that you will impress them all with your intelligence and good manners."

"I hope so."

"You will, and your aunt and uncle will have everyone know just what a wonderful niece they have."

"Thanks. That means a lot to me." Kate hesitated. "It's nice knowing that I am loved."

"And I'll bet that Gloria is looking forward to seeing her other cousins."

"Well, to be completely honest, Gloria does not seem to enjoy their company very much."

"Oh. Is that right? I wonder why that is."

"It might have something to do with the fact that they are both serious students at Oxford," Kate replied, not wanting to get into any detail about how Gloria did not like that side of the family.

"Hmm. That does sound very prestigious." Mrs. Richards hesitated. "Well, I suppose how something like that could be intimidating, but it won't be like that for you. After all, your father and I never went to college."

"Yes, I know that," Kate replied, doing her best not to sound exasperated. She didn't want to think that her mother was condescending Gloria. Kate knew how intelligent her cousin was regarding certain things. Her Mom couldn't say anything either way. She did not know Gloria, after all.

There were a few more seconds of silence until Mrs. Richards said that she needed to get going.

"Katie, I'd best go check on your father. He wasn't feeling very well a few minutes ago. Please give me a call sometime Monday evening or Tuesday morning and tell me how your tea went with Stuart's family."

"I'll be sure to do that," Kate replied, with a little less warmth. "Please tell Daddy that I love him and hope that he will feel better soon."

"Yes, darling, I will tell him as soon as I go to check on him. Send my love to Olivia and Stuart. Tell Gloria that her auntie says hello. Goodbye, my dear."

"Goodbye, Mom, I love you!"

"Love you, too, darling. Take care."

Kate hung up the phone. Though her mother seemed genuinely happy that Kate was having a good time, it seemed like that there was something she was not telling her, something that she was hiding. Though Kate did not want to think there was something more than what her mother had told her, she couldn't help but think that she wasn't getting the complete truth.

Up until now, Kate couldn't quite put her finger on it. She didn't know how she could tell, but there was something different about her mother. She then started to think about both her parents and exactly *why* she was here. Kate wondered if her trip to England was more than what her parents told her it was, a nice vacation. She thought that there may be something more to it than that, but she was very quick to dismiss those thoughts because she had enough on her mind as it was.

Chapter 8

What Kate really didn't know was that a few weeks ago Fred Beaumont had actually come all the way from New York to Oklahoma. It was easy for him to locate the Richards' dairy farm because it was the largest and most prosperous agricultural industry in the state.

He, himself, had just gotten out of a bad relationship. The woman he had been with for the last ten months had gotten him into heavy drugs, including heroin. He had met Cynthia almost the same way he'd met Kate. What Fred liked the most was her sweet, innocent-looking face.

Cynthia had strawberry blonde hair, and she reminded him of Kate. The two of them met at a party hosted by one of their mutual friends. Fred saw Cynthia from across the room, and he became enthralled. She was standing in the corner, talking to another man, a glass of red wine in her hand. Fred was the first one to make a move.

***

Weeks passed, and the two of them were seeing each other exclusively. The more Fred got to know about Cynthia, the less innocent she seemed. It did not take long to find out that she was only sweet on the outside. He dove into the belly of the beast only to find that it consists of the most rotten pile of innards, made up of abuse and lies.

Fred had too much male pride to ever admit to anyone that Cynthia abused him. Once, when a friend has asked him where he got his black eye, Fred told him that he ran into something.

Cynthia is just having a rough time, Fred used to tell himself all throughout their relationship. *She's really nice to me when she's sober.*

Cynthia, indeed, was nice to him when she was completely sober, when she was not taking practically every drug known to man. Fred felt confident that that their love would save them, but the abuse did not stop. Cynthia would cuss and hit him every time he mentioned Kate. Other times, she would wail on him for even looking at another woman.

Their relationship came to an end after Cynthia nearly beat him to death in a fit of rage.

The two of them were at a party, and they had parted ways for a while.

Fred was over in a corner, innocently talking to another girl, when Cynthia turned her head from wherever she was standing.

She immediately saw red. When Fred saw her approaching, his heart lurched. His mind began to instantly panic. She went right up to the girl and grabbed her by the hair.

The woman let out a yelp as Cynthia tried to hit her with a beer bottle but missed.

The enraged Cynthia then grabbed the poor girl by the hair again and effortlessly flung her on the floor. She lay there for a few seconds before getting up on her feet and hastily leaving the room.

Without another word, Cynthia picked up another beer bottle and smashed it against Fred's head.

He immediately felt a warm pool of blood forming on his forehead. Seconds later, blood streamed down his face.

Cynthia kneed Fred in the groin, causing him to double over and fall onto the ground. As he lay on the ground with his hands on his crotch, Cynthia began to kick him in the ribs.

Fred did not try to fight back; he just lay there, moaning in pain. He thought about hitting Cynthia twice as hard, but this time he was actually afraid. Fred thought that his best defense in this situation was to simply "play dead."

When someone finally realized what was going on, two men rushed over to Cynthia. It took both of those men to restrain her.

Fred's best friend Ray came over to help him.

Fred's hands were still holding his ribs on his left side.

Ray told him to remove his hands so he could feel if he had any broken bones.

"Does this hurt?" he asked him.

Yes, it did hurt, very much. Fred indicated with a nod.

Ray then asked Fred if he thought he could stand up, to which he responded "No." It seemed like it was a struggle for Fred to even move at all.

All the while, Cynthia was still thrashing around in the arms of the two men who were restraining her, demanding that they let her go.

"You may have some broken ribs," Ray told Fred. "Just stay right there. Don't try to get up, and don't try to move much. We are going to call an ambulance."

Upon hearing this, Fred's eyes widened. He did not want to go to any hospital, broken ribs or not.

"Somebody call an ambulance!" Ray shouted.

At that moment, it seemed like everyone at the party stopped what they were doing.

"Hold the noise down!" someone said before racing to the nearest phone to dial 9-1-1.

Fred could feel himself drift in and out of consciousness. By the time the paramedics arrived, he barely had enough strength to keep his eyes open.

The pained man could feel the paramedics gently place him on the stretcher then transport him to the ambulance. An eerie silence hung about the room as the whole thing took place.

By this time, Cynthia had stopped thrashing.

The men finally released her after her breathing had become more slow and tranquil.

Anyone who looked at her face at the moment would have seen that it expressed thoughts of panic and regret.

Cynthia's heartbeat had already rapidly slowed, and for the first time during the course of their relationship, she knew that she had gone too far.

***

Fred woke up to find himself in a hospital bed. His left side was bandaged. He reached his hands up to his forehead where Cynthia had hit him with the bottle and found that they had stitched up the area. Fred then looked over and noticed that Ray was sitting in a chair beside his bed.

"Hey," Ray said. "How you feeling?"

"Not sure," Fred responded. "It feels like I broke something."

"You did. Doctor said you had a small fracture on one of your left ribs. He also had to give you stitches on your forehead."

"I sure feel it," Fred said as he looked around the room. "Where's Cynthia?"

"She went home. After you left with the ambulance, Rick told her to go home. He said that she disturbed the good mood of his party and assaulted one of his close friends," Ray paused. "He also told her that she was never allowed over to his house again."

Fred smiled. "That's a good thing,"

"Yeah," Ray said, half smiling. "So, I guess it's over between you two."

"Damn straight it is!" Fred replied, regaining his confidence and masculinity. That was the straw that broke the camel's back.

As Fred lay in his hospital bed, he knew that he should have broken it off with Cynthia long before tonight. The first thing he intended to do was to go over to her apartment and tell her that it was over, for good. If she tried to protest, he would simply walk out the door. If she tried to get physical, which would most likely be the situation, then he would simply have to land a strong punch in her face, blackening her eye and knocking her to the floor. That would be it.

"If you ever see her about," Fred resumed, "and she says she wants to come here to visit me, you tell that bitch that I don't ever want to see her again!" Fred paused, feeling a twinge of pain on his left side. "She can get alcohol poisoning and die for all I care!"

Ray just sat in his chair and said nothing. He felt he did not have to respond to his friend's comment because Fred knew that he would carry out his wish. Ray glanced at the clock on the wall.

"I've got to get going now; visiting hours are almost over."

Fred nodded; he didn't feel like talking anymore.

Ray got the message. He got up out of his chair and left the room, leaving Fred alone with his thoughts.

Shortly after, Cynthia barged into his hospital room with tears in her eyes. She walked over to his bed. When she saw him lying there and the part of Fred's hair shaved where the doctors had made the stitches, she began to cry even harder. Cynthia tried her best to create a convincing performance, but Fred was unmoved. He just lay there, staring daggers at his soon to be ex-girlfriend.

"Baby, I'm *so* sorry," she said before dabbing her eyes with a tissue.

Fred did not respond. For the longest time, he just stared at her with cold eyes, hardly moving in his hospital bed.

After several attempts at apology, Cynthia leaned over and lightly touched his forearm. She leaned in to try to give him a kiss.

Fred quickly moved his head. "Don't touch me!" he exclaimed, nearly growling in anger. "In fact, don't ever come near me again, you fucking bitch!"

Cynthia recoiled, as if stung. The expression on her face clearly indicated that she was hurt.

"Get out," Fred whispered, before raising his voice again. "Get out of this room right now. Go outside, turn the corner, and never come back here again. I don't ever want to see you, and I don't ever want to hear you." He paused, taking a sip of water for his parched throat. "I don't even want to hear *about* you ever again for the rest of my life!"

Cynthia looked as if his harsh words had stung her. She couldn't believe that he was talking to her this way; she was his woman. Cynthia started to cry again.

"I don't want to hear any more of that shit," Fred continued. "That's not going to work on me anymore. Just do as I say and get the hell out of here." He hesitated again. "And if I ever see you again, I will personally kill you with my own bare hands!" Fred said his piece then stopped talking.

Cynthia, having changed her mood from sadness to anger, turned around and stormed out of the room. He could hear her heavy breathing all the way until she turned the corner two doors down. Fred then smiled, satisfied in knowing that was the last time that vile woman would ever darken his doorstep. Cynthia was out of his life forever, and not a moment too soon!

As he was left alone again with his thoughts, Fred began to think about Kate again. She had been so good to him, and treated her like garbage most of the time. Now that he'd endured the same kind of physical abuse from Cynthia, he knew how Kate had felt when he did it to her.

Though Fred had felt somewhat sorry for what he had put Kate through, he felt more like he had just rightfully earned his redemption. He realized now that his entire relationship with Cynthia was the penance he had to pay. Now that it was over, Fred knew that he had received atonement for all his sins.

***

Fred was released from the hospital. He went home and continued on with his life like nothing had ever happened. Though he'd done his best to push Cynthia out of his mind, he could not forget her entirely. Fred knew that a part of her would always haunt his memory, and he was all right with that, as long as she was nothing but that, a distant memory.

***

Fred was walking down the dusty road. The person who had driven him to Colcord let him off two miles before he reached the Richards' dairy farm. He had hitchhiked all the way from New York in the hope of finding Kate and trying to win her back. Ever since he was released from the hospital, he felt like a changed man.

Fred did change, however, but it was only on the surface. Once he won Kate back, he knew that he was going to resort back to his old habits. After all, he would be the one who was in charge of the relationship, and he felt it was a woman's place to obey and satisfy her man. Fred was ashamed that he suffered the amount of abuse that Cynthia inflicted upon him; this made him want to dominate a woman even more, and Kate was an easy target because he'd been down that road with her before.

Though the spring air was already warm, he didn't feel the need to complain. Every once in a while, a cool breeze would blow against his back, stirring up the dust behind him. Some months had passed, and he did not hear from Cynthia again since she stormed out of his hospital room that day. Fred didn't even know whether she was happy or sad, dead or alive, nor did he care.

The farm was just up over the hill, in plain view of people driving on the highway. The letters on the red barn read:

Richards' Dairy Farm
Since 1885

Fred couldn't help but snicker. He had already encountered the kinds of hicks who lived in this town, one of them had graciously given him a lift. As he made his way over to the farmhouse, he wondered what kind of people Mr. and Mrs. Richards were. While they were dating, Kate seldom mentioned her parents. This made Fred wonder about them even more.

The farmhouse was only a few steps away, but Fred was not even afraid to meet with these "stern folks" who were not afraid to put a chastity belt on their only daughter.

Fred rapped on the door with his knuckle. He looked down at his feet and shuffled them until he heard the door open seconds later.

"Can I help you?" a man dressed in a white T-shirt and blue overalls asked.

This must be Kate's father, Fred thought, as he estimated his age to be around fifty-five.

The farmer had a distrusting look on his face, glancing at Fred with his loud shirt, his ripped jeans, and his long hair. He did not seem at all amused by this young man showing up at his door.

"Yes," Fred replied. "I would like to talk to Kate. Is she around?"

Isaac Richards frowned upon hearing this degenerate speak his daughter's name. He could feel the blood rush to his face. Luckily, Kate was not home. She was out with one of her friends from high school. They had gone to see a movie.

"Who wants to know?" Isaac asked, feeling like he was only one step away from strangling all the life out of the long-haired, no-good hippie.

"My name is Fred Beaumont," the young man said, extending his hand. Isaac made no motion to shake it. Fred smiled. "I went to college with your daughter."

"Oh, right, that damned school in New York," Isaac growled. "I should never have let her go to that school, but she *absolutely* insisted. I told her that she did not need a fancy degree in journalism to run a farm, but she had her heart set on getting it." Isaac stopped talking, but Fred swore that he heard him grumble under his breath, though he could not make out any words except for *no-good* and *hippie*.

Fred moved his body over from the front of Isaac. He peered in the doorway to get an idea of what the house looks like.

"What do you want?" Isaac asked, wishing that this young man would just leave him alone.

"I would like to come inside so we can talk." Fred said, still not afraid of the older man.

Isaac's eyes widened. "Now, listen here, you son of a bitch! I don't know who you think you are or what you are doing here, but you had better clear off and leave my daughter alone. Just turn around and leave my property right now, or so help me God I will…" Isaac trailed off upon seeing his wife come over to where he was standing.

"Isaac, who is this young man you are talking to?" she asked, wondering why her husband was threatening him.

"This *man*," Isaac replied, still highly agitated, "claims that he went to college with Kate."

Mrs. Richards moved her eyes from her husband to Fred. He certainly did look different from the people who lived around here.

While she had never been to New York herself, she expected that he was what most men from that state looked like.

"Well, aren't you going to invite him in?" she asked, hoping to ease the tension a little.

Isaac gave her a look, which indicated his shock in wanting to invite this stranger, this misfit, into their home.

"We were just getting to that, dear," Isaac said, his voice much calmer.

"Thank you, Mrs. Richards," Fred replied. He stepped around Isaac and made his way into the hallway.

"Please, call me Susan," she said. "I was just in the kitchen warming up some milk on the stove. I also have some cookies and brownies that I set out for dessert. I'm afraid that you just missed dinner."

Normally, Isaac was proud to have a wife as hospitable as Susan, yet he did not like the kindness that she was showing this stranger. For all they knew, he could be a murderer or a madman who escaped from the asylum.

"Thank you, Susan. Your hospitality is very much appreciated," said Fred, as he glared at Isaac. "I won't be staying too long, I just wanted to come by and talk about Kate."

After hearing this, Susan's face fell. She became concerned and thought he was going to tell her that something was wrong with her daughter. Isaac could feel his blood boiling again.

"What about Kate?" he bellowed. "You had better have kept your filthy hands off my daughter!"

"Isaac!" Susan exclaimed. "Why are you standing here accusing this man of something like that?" She turned to Fred. "Don't mind him; he's not having a very good day. His arthritis is acting up again."

Isaac was incredulous. There was his wife, standing here and telling a complete stranger his business. Still, he did not say anything. If anyone was a good judge of character, it was Susan. Though he knew it was going to be hard for him, Isaac made a vow not to judge this young man until it appeared that he was guilty.

"Won't you come and have a seat in the kitchen?" Susan asked.

"Yes, that sounds very nice. Thank you again for the offer." The three of them then headed into the kitchen, waiting to see how the situation unfolded.

"Please, have a cookie," Susan said, giving on to Fred then one to Isaac.

"Thank you," Fred replied.

"Now," Isaac said, looking at Fred with narrow eyes. "Let's get down to business. What brings you here from New York?"

"Well," Fred began. "As I said when you answered the door, I came here to see Kate. We haven't spoken since before she graduated last year." Fred hesitated. Now was the time he was going to tell Mr. and Mrs. Richards all about their relationship.

"Kate and I used to date, but that was a long time ago—"

Isaac cut Fred off in mid-sentence. "You say that *you* used to date Kate?"

"Yes, it was quite some time ago. To be honest, I was hoping she would be home tonight so we could talk things over."

"That's odd," Susan said, "she never mentioned having any kind of boyfriend while she was up there?"

"Really?" Fred replied. The grin on his face began to widen. He could detect the distress that both parents were starting to feel, and he liked it. Fred was confident. No matter how much he shocked or disturbed them, he knew that he was not going to give up until he got Kate back.

"No," Isaac said, his suspicion coming back faster than a bullet through a shotgun barrel.

"I can't see why Kate did not mention me. After all, we dated for almost an entire year. Of course, I wasn't the best boyfriend she could have had."

Now Isaac was feeling the full fury flood back in his head; blood was rushing through his veins.

"You're damn right, mister! If Kate had told me about you, I would have removed her from that college just to keep her away from people like you!" Isaac had dancing visions in his head, of hurting the man who had molested his daughter.

Fred let out a little smirk.

Oh, if these two really knew what went on between Kate and me, Fred thought, *it would be enough to do all three of us in!* Fred smiled again, but it was not the same smile he had shown Kate back at when they were dating. No, this smile seemed sincere, and it could have fooled even the most unbelieving person. Fred, however, knew that it was too late at this point.

"What is all this about, why did you *really* come here?" Susan asked, hoping she would not have to throw him out of the house.

"I came here to apologize to Kate. I won't lie in saying that I was always good to her. I got her drinking and involved with my circle of friends. Rest assured, I did not get her into drugs though."

"Thank God for small favors!" Isaac said sarcastically, feeling the venom rise up through his throat and into his mouth. What bothered Isaac the most was the fact that Fred just announced his latest claim with the greatest of ease, as if he were talking to one of his close relatives.

Mrs. Richards noticed this as well. At this point, Susan was starting to get enraged as well. She did not even interrupt Isaac to keep his temper in check.

"I know that you have touched my daughter," Isaac continued. "I knew this without you having to tell me because I can see it in your eyes, and I can see it in your oily smile. Now, since I am a man of God, I'm going to nicely ask you to leave. Just go outside now and leave our home for good. You are no longer welcome here!"

Susan scowled across the table at Fred, who was still unwavering. Any outside observer would have been able to feel cold the stares of determination from all three people.

Mr. and Mrs. Richards were determined to make sure that Fred would never see their daughter again, and Fred was determined that he was going to find his way back to her.

There were a few more seconds of silence before Mrs. Richards lost every ounce of patience that was still in her body.

"I think you'd better do as he says; just leave," Susan said. All the kindness in her voice was now gone. She wanted to both cry and slap Fred in the face, but she wasn't sure which one she wanted to do more. At moments like this, Susan found it hard to keep her composure. She just hoped that this horrible man would leave before she could do either one!

"All right," Fred replied, getting up from the table, "but don't think this is the last that you'll see of me. I'll be back, and I'll keep coming back until you let me see Kate. Mark my word."

Isaac also rose from his chair. He went into the hallway to open the front door for Fred.

"Now, mark *my* words, you miserable little pissant! If you ever come back to this house again, you'll be sorry!"

Fred merely smiled before crossing the threshold and between the house and the front porch.

Isaac slammed and locked the door behind him.

***

When Kate returned home that night, neither of her parents had really spoken to her. They simply told her that she should go to her room because they wished to be left alone. Isaac and Susan had gotten into a fight over Fred's visit.

Mr. Richards blamed his wife for even encouraging their child go to NYU in the first place, and Mrs. Richards blamed her husband for being too strict, too protective of her. What she had really meant to say was "smothering" but she couldn't let that actual word escape her mouth. She felt that would have angered him even more.

After their argument had ceased, Isaac and Susan went up to their room and got ready for bed, without first saying goodnight to Kate. They decided that they would deal with this situation later. Though the fight was officially over, Mr. and Mrs. Richards did not speak as they turned out to light and went to sleep with their backs turned to each other.

***

Three days later, things seemed like they were back to normal. Neither of Kate's parents had confronted her, so she did not know that anything was wrong. Sure enough, however, Fred remained true to his word and returned to the Richards' dairy farm.

Kate and her mother were busy milking the cows in the barn, much to Isaac's pleasure.

Still anticipating Fred's second arrival, Isaac answered the front door, wielding a shotgun.

"Now, what did I tell you last time, boy?" Isaac asked through gritted teeth. "I done told you to stay away from this place, but did you listen, no?" He hesitated, giving himself a second to wipe the sweat from his brow. "I told you to stop poking around or you would be sorry. Now, you leave me no choice but to shoot you!"

"Yeah, right," Fred scoffed. "You don't have the balls!"

"I'll ask you to watch your mouth around me, you disrespectful long hair!" Isaac exclaimed as he shot his rifle.

The bullet came very close to Fred; it whizzed right by his head and landed somewhere out in the yard. Fred's expression changed from a confident grin to a look of complete horror. He held his left ear, which already felt like it was under water from all the throbbing.

"The next time, don't consider yourself so lucky," Isaac continued. "Because the next time, I am going to shoot you in the head!"

Fred's eyes widened. He looked as if he had just seen a ghost, a ghost which had come back with vengeance. Fred knew that he had to get out of there! He stumbled and nearly lost his footing as he backed away from the door.

Isaac was still standing on the threshold, solid and unmoving.

Fred took his opportunity and started running away as fast as his feet could carry him.

"And don't come back!" Isaac screamed at Fred, who was almost out of his range of vision.

Once Fred was far away from the farm, he still did not stop running. His ears were still ringing from the shotgun blast. He carried on until his felt like they could carry his weight no more. Fred collapsed in the grass by one of the back roads and began panting.

When Susan and Kate returned from milking the cows, they asked about the noise.

Isaac said it was nothing.

Surprisingly, that answer did not lead to any more questions. The three of them took a moment to relax before both mother and daughter went into the kitchen to prepare dinner. Tonight, they decided to have chicken from Stone Poultry Farms in Nebraska. They all knew it was the best chicken farmed in this part of the country.

After dessert, Susan sent Kate into the kitchen to wash the dishes. She knew that Isaac wanted to have a word with her, alone, judging by the way he glanced at her all throughout dinner.

They talked low enough so that Kate would not hear them.

Susan formed a look of shock on her face after her husband told her that Fred had showed up again today.

Shortly after she began to cry, Isaac reassured her that he got rid of that horrible degenerate once and for all.

Susan ceased crying, but she still was not completely reassured.

The two of them talked a great deal more regarding what to do about their daughter. They could not risk her going anywhere in town, for fear that Fred might still be hanging around, waiting to corrupt their child all over again. Neither one of them felt like they could find a good solution until Isaac remembered his sister.

A light bulb went off inside his head. His sister and conservative brother-in-law would be able to help Kate get on the right path. They knew that their daughter had grown close to her cousin, Gloria, by corresponding through letters for all these years.

Kate wouldn't object a trip to England, after all, because she had mentioned wanting to go there one day.

Isaac and Susan kept talking and scheming, trying to formulate a plan that would work. All the while, they had to remember to keep their voices low, even though the water was running in the kitchen sink.

They did not want their daughter to hear that they were going to send her to live in England with her aunt and uncle for a while.

Perhaps, while she was there, Stuart would introduce her to a nice, well-off man who was suitable marriage material.

Chapter 9

Before tea, Kate decided to go outside. She wanted to sit on the patio while immersing herself further in her book. Now more than ever, Kate wanted to be invisible. She wanted the world to forget about her existence for the time being.

Half of this had to do with the phone conversation she'd had with her mother, and another half had to do with avoiding Gloria for the time being. Kate still had not told her cousin that she did not want to go back to the pub tonight. She felt awkward enough as it was, having spurned Steve last night. Kate, however, did not feel like she'd acted wrongly because it was a matter of self-defense.

While she gathered that Steve seemed like a very nice man, she did not want to get involved again and follow the same, dark trail which had led her to Fred Beaumont. He had done enough damage to make her want to take back the last two years. Kate also figured that Steve could be nothing but trouble since he'd been the one who approached her, and she did not need anyone else telling her something different.

The only solution Kate thought of would be to avoid Steve's presence forever, but that was not logical because Gloria and Russell seemed to enjoy each other's company too much. It was inevitable that they would eventually become a couple. She even pictured them getting married. How awkward it would be having to be the maid of honor at Gloria's wedding while Steve would be the best man.

But Kate was getting very far ahead of herself. She knew that Gloria would not do such a rash thing in the near future, as impetuous as she may be. At least, Kate hoped that her cousin would not rush into something like marriage so quickly without any serious thought or consideration.

Kate rose from her seat and started to walk around the backyard. She read her book as she moved aimlessly around the entire yard.

It's a good thing that they have this privacy fence, Kate thought. *Otherwise, the neighbors would start to think that a raving lunatic was walking around the backyard of the Cunninghams.*

Kate dismissed the thought, hoping she had not achieved that feat. Despite all that was going on inside her head, she felt completely normal. She just had to think of a way to get out of going to the pub tonight before Gloria approached her about it.

"There you are!" a voice from behind said, completely interrupting her thoughts. Gloria waved at Kate from right outside the glass door leading to the patio. "What are you doing out here? I thought you were reading up in your room. I asked Mum and Dad if they knew where you were, and they told me to check outside."

"Well, here I am. You found me," Kate replied. Gloria shot her cousin a strange look, one similar to that a concerned parent would give her child.

"Are you feeling all right? Maybe you should come into the shade and sit down for a while."

"I'm fine. I'm just out here, getting some fresh air while reading." Kate paused. "You know, this is the first time that I've gone out to your back yard. It's very nice."

"Okay," Gloria replied, not sure how to respond. "Speaking of going out, what do you say we go to see The Peppermint Eyes again tonight? It would really mean a lot to them if we gave them an encore."

Shit! Kate thought, upset at being caught completely off-guard. *Now what the hell am I going to tell her? How will I get out of this one?*

Kate then reconsidered playing the part of a lunatic, hoping that it would get her out of any future commitments having to do with tight clothing, pubs, and sexy musicians.

"You go on ahead, Gloria. I plan to just stay home and keep to myself tonight. Tell everyone I said hello, though, and I hope that their concert goes well."

Hmm," Gloria replied. "Perhaps if you are out here getting some fresh air, you are not feeling to well after all. Maybe it's best that you stay home and rest."

Kate couldn't believe what she was hearing; had her cousin actually believed what she was telling her? Success! Maybe she could go on without any more worries about having to see Steve, at least, for now.

"Then, I'd best get inside and go back upstairs. Come to think of it, I don't even know how I came out here in the first place. I'm going back up to my room now; please tell your folks that I may not be able to make it for tea."

"Sure thing, Kate, I'll be sure to do that."

"Thank you." Kate headed back over the patio. She was about to go inside when Gloria blocked the entrance.

"May I go inside, please?"

Gloria nodded her head. She made no motion to move.

"Nice try, dear cousin, but I know you, and I can already tell when you are full of shit. There is nothing wrong with you. You just don't want to go the pub again tonight."

Kate crossed her arms. She could feel herself getting exasperated with Gloria, and she did not feel that she had time for these silly games.

"And that is a problem because?" Kate asked.

"Because I know that you need to come out with me again tonight. You can sit around at home and read any old time. I'm asking you to do this with me, as a favor for a dear friend."

"You don't need my permission to go out and see Russell again tonight. We already saw the band last night. Besides, wouldn't your mom and dad object you going out two nights in a row?"

"No, Mum and Dad are completely fine with it, just as long as long as we're home by midnight."

"And what do you suppose I'm going to wear?" Kate asked. She could feel herself getting slightly angry. "As you can recall, I have nothing in my closet but all those dresses that you think are so ugly!"

Gloria winced. She was taken aback by her cousin's hostile tone.

"I'm sorry, Kate," Gloria apologized. "I didn't mean anything by it. I—"

"You know what, fine, forget it! Let's just go back to Strawberry Orange Dreams so I can waste another twenty to thirty pounds on some more revealing clothes. Then, maybe I can have all those horny British men wag their tongues at me again like they did last night!"

Gloria was now feeling defensive. How dare Kate be so ungrateful, especially after all that she had done for her!

"Hey, I took you to Judy's because I know that she has the cutest clothes in town. I knew that you were uncomfortable wearing those dresses, and I wanted you to have other options. And, as you may recall, I bought your first outfit for you!"

"Oh, pardon me!" Kate exclaimed. "Talk about doing great favors for someone. Like having cute clothes is the epitome of happiness. You should write a book on the subject, *Gloria Cunningham's Guide to Complete Happiness*. It would sell in all the finest bookstores!"

The blood began to rise in Gloria's cheeks. If Kate wanted to act like a bitch, then so be it! Besides, Gloria had better things to do then to stay around and watch Kate become even more miserable.

"I was doing you a favor, you bitch! Your so-called 'wardrobe' was in desperate need of repair, and I knew someone who could help, that's all. So, don't pin any of your negativity on me; it doesn't fuel my fire. *I* can live without it!"

"Oh right, as if your bossiness has enriched my life anymore! I was completely fine before I came here. I was successful and might have been able to make something of my life." Kate paused for a moment to catch her breath. "Maybe coming here was a mistake."

"Yes, maybe it was," Gloria replied. She was seething, because this was the remark that had finally sent her over the edge. "So, go on back to Oklahoma and rejoin all the other hicks! See if I care! Put on your little farm girl dresses and go back to your hoe-downs and shin-digs."

Gloria paused again. "Or, better yet, why don't you join those wankers Syd and Sebastian at Oxford? I'm sure they would love to have you, as you would provide them with good company! I would have expected this kind of pompous behavior from them, but not from you. Now I find that the three of you are so alike that I might as well not have any cousins at all!"

That remark angered Kate so much that she did not say anything in response. She merely walked by Gloria, who had now moved out of the way, and stomped all the way upstairs to her room. Kate went inside and slammed the door.

"Miserable bitch, indeed!" she said to herself. "She's the one who's miserable because she's so selfish!" All Kate had wanted to do was stay at home because she did not want to go back to the pub. She did not want to face Steve, or anyone else for that matter, because she decided that she's had enough of this place.

"I'm going to call Mom back, right now," she said, pacing back and forth, letting out bottled anger. "Dad might be feeling a little better, and he would be the one to listen to reason."

Kate did not need these walls to protect her anymore. She wanted to be back on the family farm, where she would be safe and chaste. Kate felt that she did not have to find a man in order to be happy and confident. She was a strong woman, and she could run the family business by herself. Besides, Kate was born and raised on that farm, and no one else could do any job there better than she.

Once Kate had calmed down enough, she decided not to call her parents, especially since the just talked to her mother earlier. Kate decided that she would try to read as much as she possibly could without a single interruption. She smiled as she opened the book and returned to the page where she'd left off. It was only a matter of minutes before she felt all the anger inside her drift away.

An hour or two later, Kate stiffened when she heard a quiet knock on her door. She thought that she may have fallen asleep, but she wasn't entirely sure. Either way, it didn't matter, because she knew where she was, right here.

"Come in," she said, thinking that it was Aunt Olivia bringing up food for her tea.

The door opened, and Gloria emerged, head down to the floor.

"What do you want?" Kate asked in an indifferent tone.

"I've come to apologize," Gloria replied.

Kate softened. The anger she'd felt merely hours before disappeared with all the anger. "I had no right saying to some of the things that I said to you," she continued.

"I'm sorry, too," Kate replied, beginning to feel remorse over the way she'd acted. "You are not some empty-headed girl whose main goal in life is to transform me."

"And you are not a simple farm girl, nor are you a pompous intellectual. Come to think of it, simple and pompous are oxymorons."

Kate smiled. "I didn't mean to blow this entire thing out of proportion, but I meant it when I said that I did not want to go to the pub tonight."

Gloria looked at her cousin sympathetically. She knew what was going on; she did not even have to ask Kate why she wanted to stay home because she could sum it all up in one word.

"Steve," she said.

Kate shed a tear and nodded.

"But why?" Gloria asked, showing some genuine concern.

"It's complicated."

"Try me." Gloria sat down on the bed and put her arm around her cousin.

Kate let a few more tears fall from her eyes. She knew that it was time to reveal to Gloria everything ugly about her past. It was time to tell her about Fred Beaumont and all that he had done to her and put her through. Kate thought that this would make Gloria understand all about why she was afraid to take things any further with Steve.

"We have to talk," Kate said, after mentally preparing herself to hold the following discussion. "But close the door first. I don't want anyone else to hear what I am about to say."

Gloria got up from the bed and closed the guest room door. She rejoined Kate, who began to tell Gloria the entire story.

***

Gloria and Kate decided to skip tea and grab an early supper at Molly's. They were both very jovial. Anyone who observed them in the café found that they seemed carefree. No one would have expected that the two of them had fought merely hours ago.

Gloria and Kate had a long talk, and Gloria explained to Kate that she did not have to think anything serious about Steve. She merely suggested that the two of them could talk and be acquaintances, bordering on a new friendship.

That made Kate blush. If Gloria knew about how Steve touched her last night, she would think that Kate and Steve were far beyond that stage.

"Thank you for letting me borrow your jeans and top. It's really surprising that they fit."

Gloria laughed. Again, her scheming mind was at work. In actuality, the two of them were closer in size than they thought. Gloria had deliberately given her clothes which were a bit tight, proving that she was back to her same old tricks.

"You know me, always ready to assist," Gloria replied with a smile on her face.

"No, really, thank you for all that you have done." Kate, of course, had meant listening to her tell her story and how it related to Steve. Anyone who's had a bad relationship could identify with Kate and loan her their sympathy.

This did not mean that Kate was off the hook, however, as it was still Gloria's intention to hook her up with Steve. If it was anyone else, Gloria wouldn't have cared, but she knew that every time she even mentioned his name to Kate, it invoked something deep.

Her eyes may not move, and her face may still remain the same, but Gloria could still tell that she liked him.

Perhaps it was because the two of them had grown extremely close during the last few days. Perhaps it was because Kate's emotions were easier read than an open book, but it was something, nonetheless.

Chapter 10

After dinner, Gloria drove the two of them to Banner Alehouse. Though many people hung around outside before the show started, Kate and Gloria decided to go inside and find themselves a seat. There was already a large crowd around the front, so they had to find themselves a place to sit farther back.

Both Kate and Gloria smiled, recounting the events of last night. Perhaps it was better that they did not sit as close as they had wanted to. This way, the band would have no more mishaps, and nothing would hinder their performance. Moments later, The Peppermint Eyes were on the stage, ready to perform their first number.

The show was already in full swing when Kate and Gloria took an opportunity to look around at the audience. They noticed that many of the people who were there last night had shown up again tonight. Gloria looked around to see if she could spot Judy and Joan, but they must have been consumed by the audience.

Kate was definitely more into the music tonight, as she already began to memorize some of the song lyrics. Before anyone had time to notice, the show was already over.

Gloria and Kate sat patiently, waiting to see if Russell or Steve would come over and invite them backstage. A few more minutes passed, and they still had not received any word from either one of them. Gloria looked around at the remaining people in the crowd, but she did not see any members of the band.

"Kate, would you be all right if I asked you to go with me backstage? I know you have your reservations regarding Steve and all, but I think it would be good if you sat down and tried to talk to him."

"Yes," Kate replied. "I'll go back with you, especially since I do owe Steve some kind of explanation for the way I acted last night." Kate was ready. This time, she knew she had to go back there and face her fear. Kate encouraged herself mentally as she followed Gloria to the dressing room.

"Come in," Russell said, seconds after they knocked on the door. Steve assumed that Gloria had come back to see Russell. He did not think that Kate had actually joined her until he saw her walk into the room.

"Kate," he said, with a surprised look on his face. "I didn't think that you would come."

Kate just smiled as she acknowledged his presence. She had so many things that she wanted to say to him, but she felt it would be better if the two of them were alone.

"Hello, lovely ladies," Russell greeted Kate and Gloria.

The rest of the band members were also there. They acknowledged the ladies and said their brief hellos before getting up out of their chairs.

"I think I will go find Joan," John said. "What about the rest of you lads?"

Geoffrey and Henry followed their friend out the door, in the hope of finding more pretty women with whom to spend the night.

***

Russell and Gloria followed suit and got up to leave the room as well. They headed out to The Peppermint Eyes' touring bus, which was really an old lorry, but it sufficed enough to carry and transport the band's equipment. Gloria and Russell were already kissing before he opened the door.

"Wow," Gloria said as she climbed inside the truck. "This is actually very spacious."

"Yeah," Russell replied, looking around at all the messy debris. "It's not the prettiest thing in the world, but it serves its purpose."

Russell closed the door behind them. He made his way over to Gloria, who was looked around at all the different equipment.

"Gloria, I would like to talk to you about something," Russell said, moving her over to a blanket lying on the floor. The two of them sat down, and Russell put his arm around her.

"I'm going to be completely honest with you. Ever since I've started this gig with The Peppermint Eyes, I've had me a few women."

Gloria looked over at Russell and smiled. She was no stranger to lovemaking. She'd had two men before, but neither of the relationships lasted very long, nor did they mean very much.

Russell caught Gloria's chin in his hands. "And I will admit that I was having a lot of fun with them while partying, boozing, and you know..." Russell trailed off as he looked into her eyes. Gloria could see something in his as well.

"But tonight is different. Tonight, I am in the company of someone I would like to call my own. I know that we only just met, but ever since the time I first saw you on the street, I've been meaning to tell you one thing." Russell paused to take in some breath.

"I love you, Gloria."

Delighted at what she'd just heard, Gloria reached over and kissed Russell on the lips.

"I love you, too, Russell," she said before the two of them starting kissing again.

After a few more minutes of kissing and exploring each other with their hands, Russell and Gloria lay down on the blanket, where they proceeded to express their newfound love for each other.

***

Steve and Kate sat alone on the couch in the dressing room.

Kate told Steve that she had something to tell him, but he said that he had something that the wanted to say first.

"Listen, I'm glad you came to see me again, and I'm terribly sorry about last night!"

"You are not the one who should be apologizing, Steve, I am. I shouldn't—"

"Shh," he said, completely cutting her off. Steve then turned around to face Kate. He took both her hands in his and looked deeply into her eyes.

"Kate, please, let me finish. I know that Gloria convinced you into buying new clothes; I know that she dolled you up with all that makeup. But the fact of the matter is I was turned on by you, plain and simple. I saw you from the stage, and when you and Gloria came back here, Russell and I just went crazy. My other mates all knew that they had to leave the room because the sexual tension in here was palpable.

"I saw you in that revealing outfit last night, and I just lost my mind. As you already know, I stopped in mid-song because of it. You looked so beautiful and tantalizing that my baser instincts completely took over my actions. I should have kept my hands to myself, but I didn't." Steve paused. He sighed as he looked over at Kate, who listened with understanding.

"Kate, you are a *very* attractive woman, and I can't help but stare at you every time that you come into my range of vision. It was like that since I first laid eyes on you."

Kate looked over at Steve and smiled. She was relieved that he was not only interested in one thing, and she could tell that his words were sincere.

"Steve, please don't think that I was upset at you for *that*," Kate said. "It's just that in the past I've—"

"Kate, I am not finished," Steve said, patiently, as he reached for her right hand. He took it and placed it in his.

"You are an incredible woman, and I hope someday that we become something. But I don't want to rush into a relationship which should take some time. I would like to take things slow and get to know you better. I am very confident that we could make things work, but I will not do or say anything that makes you uncomfortable. Having said all that, I hope that you'll forgive me."

Kate nodded, and tears streamed down her eyes.

Steve reached over and gave her a long hug, one which was more comforting than any she'd had in a while.

"Steve, there is something that I have to tell you," Kate said in a serious tone of voice. She drew in some breath and exhaled. "About last night, I am sorry how I ended things so abruptly and ran out on you. I enjoyed the kissing, and, you know. It's just that I've had some trouble with a man in the past."

Steve, beginning to feel reassured that Kate didn't hate him, wanted to take this opportunity to make things better. He had so many things that he wanted to say, but he felt it was important to listen to her.

"I've not told many people about this," Kate resumed. "I just told Gloria earlier today, and I certainly could not ever mention this to either one of my parents." Kate sighed. She wasn't quite sure how to tell all this to Steve, but she knew that it needed to be done.

"Back when I was in college, I dated a man for about seven months. His name was Fred Beaumont, and we met through one of my mutual friends. Anyway, he approached me at a party, and after the first few minutes of talking to him, I started to fall in love.

"Shortly after Fred and I became a couple, we started doing things together. One night, he got me so drunk that I was sick almost all the next day. That was one of the few times in my life that I tried alcohol. After I refused to drink any more, he tried to get me into drugs. Since I come from a conservative background, I refused those, too."

Kate hesitated to draw another breath. She hated to tell Steve about what came next, but, unfortunately, it was an integral part of the story.

"Then, a few weeks into our relationship, I'd given Fred my body. This was the first time that I was with a man, so I didn't know what to expect. And after that, things started to go downhill fast. Since I'd already slept with Fred, he started to lose respect for me. When I refused to give him sex, whether I was in a bad mood or just tired, he would hit me. Then, his drug problem became worse. He would sometimes lash out at me then as well.

"One time, after he'd shot up, he grabbed me by my hair and kicked me for no reason other than he was messed up on drugs." Kate's eyes began to water, and tears started sliding down her cheek. "He did not stop lashing out until one of his friends came into the room. At that point, I was really frightened about what else he would do to me."

Kate then went into more vivid detail about her abusive relationship with Fred. She talked about the one night where she got the courage to finally stand up to him. Kate told Fred that she could take no more. Despite his attempt to threaten her, she did not back down. With the help of her friend Ashley, and even some of Fred's friends, she was able to get him to leave her alone.

That lasted for two days, until Fred had come back and tried to apologize. He told Kate that she was the only thing good in his life and that he would kill himself if she would not take him back. Since Kate was smart and did not want to repeat her mistake, she told him to leave her alone once and for all. The miraculous thing was that Fred did leave, and she has not heard from him ever since.

After hearing Kate's story, Steve understood a lot more about her. He understood why she abruptly left him last night, and he knew that was why she was so reticent to come back again tonight. Because of this, there was so much that Steve now wanted to do. He wanted to reach over and stroke Kate's hair, place his hands on her pretty face so that he could dry her tears. He also wanted to get a hold of this Fred Beaumont character and rip out his fucking throat!

That son of a bitch never deserved her! Steve thought, blood rising in his veins. *It's a damn good thing that he's in America, or I would have to pound his arse into the pavement!* Steve looked over at Kate again, who was trembling and trying to force back tears.

"I'm sorry, Steve" Kate said, breaking his train of thought. "You must know after me telling you about all this that this is why I ran. I should have given you an explanation last night, but I didn't think you'd be interested in someone like me. Someone, you know, who is damaged goods."

Kate stood up; she tried to head for the door, but Steve stopped her. He took Kate by the arm and turned her to face him. There was no way that he was going to let her leave him again, and he sure as hell wasn't going to let any more harm befall her.

"Kate," he said softly. "There is no way that I am going to let you leave this room, not after what you've just told me, and I will not let you go home before I tell you this: I love you."

Kate looked at Steve, not believing what she'd just heard.

"I have loved you ever since the moment that I saw you walking down the street with Gloria." He paused. "Don't feel that you need to explain it because I don't know how it happened, either. It just did, and I'm not willing to question it."

"Steve..." Kate said. She looked deep into his eyes and discovered that he was serious. Though he promised that he would be good to her, Kate still wasn't convinced that she could learn to love again, at least, not until she resolved all the issues that were still in her head.

"I know what you're feeling right now; I know that you're afraid," Steve said, gathering her into an embrace. He held her tightly and whispered into her ear.

"But please give me a chance. We can take things as slowly as you like, but I feel that we should at least give it a try." Steve let her go and looked into her eyes. In there, he was able to find hope.

Kate didn't know what to say; she felt like she had been backed into a corner. While she liked Steve very much and found him really attractive, she still wasn't quite sure how to respond to his pleas. Kate did not want to falsely lead him on for fear that the relationship would not work, but she did not want to leave him without any hope.

During the few moments that Kate had to think, she decided to throw away any reservations that she had and give it a shot. Steve himself said that they could take things as slow as they wanted, so Kate felt like she had nothing to lose.

"Steve, let's give it a try," she said. "Your kind words and understanding have touched my heart. I know that my past experience with Fred was bad, but coming to England has given me many chances to try something new. I say that we should go ahead and take the risk."

Kate leaned over and kissed Steve, trying her best to prove to herself that she was ready to start again.

Chapter 11

Both girls had returned home that night at precisely 12:00.

Kate told Gloria how she had opened up to Steve and how the two of them decided to take a chance on a relationship.

Gloria hugged Kate when she heard the news, as she was overwhelmingly happy for them both.

Kate also mentioned that Steve had declared his love for her, which did not surprise Gloria. She knew that it was bound to happen sooner or later. Gloria then told Kate about how Russell declared his love for her, thankfully, leaving out all the gory details.

***

Sunday was an uneventful day. Everyone just kept to themselves and enjoyed the peaceful tranquility that was present all around the household. Kate sat on her bed, looking out the window at the streets below. There was little activity outside today, which made everything seem all the more peaceful. She sighed contentedly, knowing that peace had finally crossed the threshold of her mind. Her conversation with Steve had allowed Kate to open up her eyes and realize that dwelling on the past was detrimental to the planning of one's future.

Kate was very close to the end of *The Invisible Man*, but she decided not to finish it at the moment. Today, Kate was feeling great, and for the first time in a long time, she did not want to be invisible.

Since all this positive energy placed itself in her head, however, Kate felt that she had to go out and do something. It was a beautiful day outside, as Kate knew from looking out the window upstairs. Since there was little activity on the streets, Kate decided that she would go out and take a walk. Since she did not want to leave Gloria out, she decided to go to her room and ask her if she would like to join her. Gloria's door was open; Kate looked in to see that she was reading her copy of *Daisy Miller*. Kate lightly rapped on her door.

"Hello, Kate," Gloria said, looking up from her book.

"Hello, yourself. How are you enjoying *Daisy Miller*?"

"Just started into it, nothing out of the ordinary, for a classic book, that is."

"Oh, I see. Would you like to take a walk with me outside?"

"That sounds lovely, but I think I'll have to pass. Russell is going to give me a call later."

Kate could tell that her cousin was already going through separation anxiety.

Aunt Olivia and Uncle Stuart told them that they should stay home because they had already been to the pub two nights in a row. While they did not actually forbid them from going, Gloria saw it as the same thing.

No one had actually come out and said it, but Kate knew it was because the other Cunninghams were coming to tea tomorrow. Surely, Olivia and Stuart wanted both girls to be well-rested and presentable. Kate wondered if Gloria was actually going to mention Russell tomorrow afternoon, but she hoped that she would not. After all, it would be more appropriate to mention him at another time.

Kate went outside and began to walk the streets of the neighborhood. Though they were a little less deserted than they were before, that did not make the experience any less enjoyable. Walks were often good for clearing one's head. Even though Kate had already begun to clear hers, she felt that this activity could only benefit her even more. Kate could feel all the burden fly off her shoulders as she walked down the streets with which had only become familiar in the last few days.

***

Monday afternoon, Kate was in her room getting ready for tea. She had offered to loan Gloria one of her dresses, but she refused, stating that she had one in her closet for just such an occasion. Kate knew it was because Gloria had found every frock in the guestroom closet to be completely abominable.

Kate did her best not to think about Steve too much, but it was all to no avail. Kate wished that she and Gloria could have gone to the pub last night to see the band's final performance. Though Steve now had the phone number to the house, thanks to Gloria giving it to Russell. She didn't know when she would hear from him again. She hoped it would be sooner rather than later. Just as she was contemplating whether or not to put the straw hat on her head, there was a knock on the door.

"Are you almost ready, darling?" Olivia called from the outside. "Stuart's family will be here soon."

"I'm almost ready; I'll be down soon," Kate replied through the door. She went over to the mirror and studied herself. After looking at herself in her pink dress, Kate decided that she looked very presentable. She thought of Steve again and decided not to wear the straw hat. It remained on the top right hand post of her bed.

After Kate made her way downstairs, she saw Uncle Stuart and Gloria sitting at the table. Gloria had on a purple dress which was a little similar to the one she had hanging upstairs. Though she was trying her best to put on a brave face, Kate could tell that she did not want to be there. She hoped, for her cousin's sake, that tea would be quick and painless.

"You look beautiful, my dear," Olivia said, as she fawned over Kate's dress. "Stuart, doesn't she look nice?"

Stuart looked over at his niece.

"Yes, Kate, you look very nice. That dress was a good choice."

"Thank you," Kate replied, feeling a little awkward. She wondered what Stuart's family would think of her, if they were the type of people who could see through a person's dress and manner. For the sake of everyone concerned, she hoped that they were not.

All Kate had to do wait out the last few moments in anticipation. She took a seat right next to Gloria, hoping to help calm her cousin's nerves.

Earlier, the two of them had talked upstairs, mostly about how much Gloria missed Russell. She mentioned that he asked why they couldn't come see The Peppermint Eyes perform their last show at Banner Alehouse, and Gloria said that she blamed it on her "stupid bastard cousins" coming over for tea.

Gloria also told Russell that she would have to invite him for tea sometime so that he could meet her parents. It wouldn't be within the next few days, but Gloria hoped that it would be soon. Since she still had not told her parents about Russell, she figured she would need time to break the news delicately, when she was ready.

The next thing that the four of them knew, the doorbell rang. Kate could swear that she could hear Gloria stop breathing, or was it her? Given the tension of the atmosphere, she wasn't sure either which way.

Uncle Stuart went to answer the door. He was greeted by the face of his brother.

"Stuart, ol' boy! Long time, no see. How are you?"

The two brothers embraced.

"Oh, James, you know it's only been two months." Laughter filled the room.

James then went over to Aunt Olivia, who was waiting to receive his greeting.

"Hello, Olivia, you look really lovely today." James hugged Olivia then kissed her on both cheeks.

Lois followed her husband into the house.

"Stuart, Olivia, marvelous to see you again!" Lois greeted each of them with a hug and kisses.

Stuart then noticed his nephews standing on the porch.

"Lads!" Stuart exclaimed. "How nice to see you both again! Come on inside."

Syd and Sebastian followed their parents. Both of them were tall and lanky, both with their mother's youthful face, light brown hair and blue eyes. They each smiled and greeted their aunt and uncle in the same fashion.

"Olivia," Lois said. "Where are Gloria and Kate? I'm just dying to meet your American niece!" Lois said this forgetting again that Olivia was once an American herself. Though it was many years ago that she married Stuart and became a legal citizen of England, Olivia never forgot her home country. It was futile, however, to keep having to remind her sister-in-law of that.

"They're right there in the dining room," Olivia said. "Shall we all go inside and greet them?" Gloria and Kate stood up when they heard everyone come in from the foyer. They both looked like beautiful, proper young ladies, which is exactly what Gloria's parents had hoped for.

The two cousins, however, knew that this was a complete façade, which they hoped they could keep up for the time being. Everyone walked into the dining room, and Kate was greeted with four new faces.

"Hello, darling!" Lois said as she looked over at Gloria, looking very lovely in her dress. "James, let's go say hello to our niece."

James and Lois went over to greet Gloria, which she took very well. She acted like she was in the company of her best friends.

Kate was even amazed to see Gloria greet her cousins with the same warmth, embracing them with authenticity.

Though Gloria was smiling at Syd and Sebastian, she couldn't help but think how pretentious they looked wearing their blue Oxford jackets, especially because they were currently on holiday. This was something that she barely found tolerable.

"So nice to see you both," Gloria said, wishing that Russell were there to knock them down a peg or two.

"Likewise, Cousin," Syd said, flashing her one of his fake Ivy League smiles. While Gloria was busy having to be nice to her cousins, poor Kate had to deal with James and Lois.

"Oh, and you *must* be the lovely Kate," Lois said with an air of fascination. "My, you certainly are beautiful. You know, Stuart and Olivia did not do you any justice at all in their description."

"Thank you," Kate replied, feeling somewhat awkward. "It's a pleasure to meet you, Lois."

James turned to Gloria's cousin.

Kate couldn't believe how much he looked like Stuart. The two of them could have been twins had her Uncle Stuart not been five years younger.

"It's such a pleasure to meet you, my dear," he said. "Stuart and Olivia have been talking about you to me for the longest time; just last month, Stuart said 'you must come meet my niece sometime.'"

Have they? Kate thought, wondering how long they'd known about her, especially since Kate's parents had only told her about this trip two weeks ago. Stuart cleared his throat.

"Boys, won't you come say hello to Kate?" Syd and Sebastian walked over to Kate, who by now was feeling incredibly awkward and a little shy.

"Kate, it's a pleasure," Sebastian said, taking her hand in his.

"The pleasure is all mine," Syd said.

Kate smiled. "Thank you. How lovely it is to meet you both." It only took Kate a few seconds to realize that Gloria was right; these men *did* seem a little pretentious, but Kate did not want to judge them too quickly. She decided to be nice so that everyone would make it through tea.

Once everyone was settled into their chairs, Olivia filled everyone's cup and brought over the scones and finger sandwiches. She also provided jam and butter to go with the scones.

The food was delicious, and everyone seemed to enjoy plentiful conversation. James and Lois simply adored Kate, who to them seemed like the perfect lady.

"So, Kate, correct me if I am wrong, but I hear that your father is in agriculture."

"Actually, my father owns a dairy farm in the state of Oklahoma.

Upon hearing the word "Oklahoma," Syd and Sebastian stifled a giggle.

Gloria saw this and shot a warning glance at her cousins. She did not like the idea of them making fun of Kate.

"It's simply called Richards' Dairy Farm, and it's the largest in the state. Since I am an only child, I have spent much of my life helping around the farm. My mother and father are relieved to have someone such as me on hand."

Kate hesitated for a second; she was worried that talking about her father's farm might seem a little lowbrow in this mixed company. Kate, however, was very proud of her father and the family business, so she soon decided that there was no shame in talking about his occupation.

"Then, this is your first time out of Oklahoma?" Lois asked, her smile cutting right through her.

"Not entirely, I did study at New York State University, NYU. I received a bachelor's degree in journalism, though I have not had much experience writing outside of class." Kate felt herself getting a little nervous talking about NYU, because she was dangerously close to thinking about Fred and what he had put her through. Kate smiled, hoping that someone would change the subject soon.

"Oh, how nice," Lois responded, sounding like she was praising a small child for an accomplishment. "Both my boys are attending Oxford; Syd for architecture and Sebastian for psychology." She then looked over at Gloria, who was not smiling, but she was doing her best to keep her composure. After all, she promised her parents that she would be on her best behavior.

"Even though they are on holiday," Lois continued. "They never cease to show their school pride. I told them that they did not have to wear their Oxford jackets, but they absolutely insisted."

"How nice," Olivia said, starting to notice how pretentious they all were acting.

"Good lads, eh, Stuart?" James asked.

Stuart nodded over his plate. He was helping himself to another scone.

"Yes," James continued. "Lois and I are certainly proud of these ones."

"As are we of Gloria," Olivia said, doing her best not to let Lois and James get to her.

"Thank you, Mum," Gloria said. She was glad that Olivia was sticking up for her in front of father's relatives.

Stuart, however, seemed immune to the fact that James and his family were trying to brag about themselves. It seemed like this was the case every time they were invited over for tea.

Gloria was the one it affected the most because she felt like her cousins were laughing at her behind her back.

"Of course," Lois replied. "We should all be proud. Gloria is a fine young lady." Lois smiled at her niece again.

Kate looked over at her cousin, not exactly sure what she was thinking, though she could venture a guess.

Polite conversation followed through the rest of tea. Olivia was busy clearing the dishes off from the table and putting them into the sink. Lois had actually offered to help, but Olivia insisted that she enjoy herself because she was their guest.

"James, would you like to go outside and look at the rosebushes that Olivia planted in the back? She put the seeds in last year, but they were slow to bloom. They are just starting to come up now for the spring."

"They sound lovely," he said, not knowing full well that Lois would definitely be interested in seeing their delicate pedals of red.

"Rosebushes?" Lois asked, in almost a singsong voice. "Why, I'd be delighted to see them!"

She turned to her brother-in-law's wife. "Olivia, don't fuss with those dishes right now. Let's go outside and see your lovely roses!"

Olivia turned off the water and led the four of them outside.

Syd and Sebastian, of course, had no interest in looking at flowers. Instead, they remained behind in the kitchen.

Gloria and Kate remained in the dining room. They both felt like congratulating themselves, and each other, for how well they behaved themselves all during tea.

"I must say," Kate said. "You are doing well. One wouldn't even know that you don't very much care for this side of your family."

"Tell me about it," Gloria replied. "Do you see why I call Syd and Sebastian pretentious? To think, they actually came here wearing their stupid Oxford jackets, and while they are on holiday, no less! Who do they think they are trying to impress?"

Kate laughed. She could definitely see Gloria's point.

"Now I can see why you aren't too fond of them. I must admit that they do seem a little full of themselves."

"I told you so," Gloria replied, relieved that their time together would be over very soon.

"Would you be all right with those two in the kitchen while I go to use the restroom?" Kate asked.

"I think I can manage," Gloria replied, knowing full well that her cousins would be talking about stupid things in Kate's absence.

"All right, I'll be back shortly. Try not to break any bones while I am gone."

Gloria laughed.

"We'll see," Gloria said. She was about to head back to the dining room when she heard some laughter coming from the kitchen. Her cousins were in there talking, so she decided that she would eavesdrop. Gloria quietly went to a nearby spot where she could remain unseen.

"So about this little girl from America, it seems like she is a regular fish out of water. What do you think?" Sebastian asked.

"I know," Syd replied. "I almost lost it when she said 'Oklahoma' and started talking about her daddy's farm. She must be one of those American hicks, simple as one can be."

Both boys laughed again.

"She's cute, though," Sebastian said.

"Yeah, she's a nice bit of crumpet, all right, big tits from what I could see. Must be from all that milk she drinks on her daddy's dairy farm."

Both Syd and Sebastian erupted with laughter. Sebastian looked around and started shushing his brother.

"Quiet, man, do you want them to hear us?"

The twins stopped laughing and resumed filling their glasses with the wine that Stuart and Olivia bought for the company.

"I do envy her one thing, though," Syd said.

"What's that?"

"She's been to New York."

"So what, you've heard about New York. It's full of nothing but degenerates, prostitutes, and dirty movie theaters," Sebastian hesitated. "Who knows, with that body of hers, she might fit in with that crowd, too."

The two of them laughed.

Gloria had heard enough; she felt the blood boil in her veins. No one talked about Kate that way, especially not some self-important, pretentious bastards, who did not know their heads from their asses.

"I heard what you just said, and it isn't very nice."

Syd and Sebastian turned to see Gloria cross-armed and staring at them coldly. When they returned her angry gaze, she narrowed her eyes even more.

"How long have you been standing there?" Sebastian asked, angry with his cousin for eavesdropping.

"Long enough!" Gloria replied, who had to fight back every urge to rip off both their heads.

"What are you going to do," Sebastian taunted, "tell Kate what you heard us say about her?"

"I wasn't planning it on it, but perhaps Mum and Dad would like to hear it."

Syd and Sebastian erupted with laughter again.

"As if your parents are going to take your word over *ours*." Sebastian said.

"I certainly think they would, you self-important bastard!" Gloria exclaimed. "I am their daughter, and while you may be their nephews, you're not as revered around here as you think you are."

Syd and Sebastian looked at their cousin skeptically.

"That's right, you're not in Oxford with your closest of peers sucking up to you all the time; you're amongst family. I'm standing here talking with two condescending pricks whom, by the way, I am ashamed to call my cousins."

Syd and Sebastian just looked over at Gloria. Though they did not laugh at her, which is what she expected, they didn't seem to take what she was saying seriously.

"Ashamed of us?" Sebastian asked, still not sure what to think of Gloria's sudden declaration. "Maybe *you* are, but I know that your mum and dad absolutely adore us.

"Yeah," Syd replied. "As if we really care what *you* think of us." Syd hesitated. "What are you going to do, tell Kate and our parents what we said?"

"No," Gloria replied, coolly staring down her cousins. "I won't, but just think about this. Mum and Dad may *seem* to hold both of you in high regard, but I know the truth of the matter." Gloria paused as she heard the bathroom door open.

"Now, if I were you, I would keep your mouths shut. Kate just came out of the bathroom. I will not tell her any of the lewd and demeaning things you've said about her, but if she hears them from the likes of you, then I can't promise that your favorite aunt and uncle will adore you much longer."

Gloria turned to leave the kitchen, and the twins remained quiet. In fact, they did not say anything else until their parents came in with their aunt and uncle. Gloria and Kate just sat in the living room. They talked of polite things until it was time for her father's family to leave.

Moments later, everyone said a long goodbye.

Gloria was relieved because it couldn't have been a moment too soon. Though both she and Kate hugged Syd and Sebastian on their way out the door, they were practicing the fine art of diplomacy.

James told Stuart that he and Lois would have to return to visit them soon. Thankfully, he also seemed to indicate that the boys might not join them next time.

Stuart smiled and said that they looked forward to seeing James and Lois again for another visit.

Gloria and Kate decided to go upstairs to while away the time until supper.

Kate could tell that her cousin missed Russell like mad and was probably awaiting his next call (before she decided to call him).

"So I see you survived the time that I left you alone with your cousins," Kate said. The two of them were talking in the guestroom, each wanting to get the other's perspective on the day's events. Kate said that she did not mind the company, but she felt a little off put by both Syd and Sebastian.

Gloria made a face, indicating that this did not come as a surprise to her.

"Well, Syd and Sebastian are pretentious bastards, all right. Did you see how ridiculous they looked wearing their Oxford school jackets?"

"Yes," Kate replied. "I can see now why you don't like them very much."

"Well," Gloria said. "I don't actually *hate* them, I suppose. It's just that they can both be so exasperating. Their pretentiousness just seems to leak out sometimes." Gloria paused. She was contemplating whether or not to tell Kate about the demeaning things both men were saying about her.

"They did not say very much to me, but I'm afraid it was because they thought I was a simple American woman."

Then, Gloria began to feel some of the anger coming back to her. She finally had the guts to stand up to Syd and Sebastian a little, but she felt that she shouldn't hide their cruel words from Kate. Gloria sighed. Telling Kate was not going to be easy.

"Kate," Gloria said in a serious tone. "About Syd and Sebastian, there's something I should tell you."

"I'm listening," Kate replied. She knew that Gloria had something she needed to get off her chest, and though she did not know what she wanted to say for sure, Kate figured it was something that the Oxford twins had said.

"Well, I was standing in the dining room while you were in the bathroom. I was just there waiting for you to come out when I heard some laughter from the kitchen. When I went over to eavesdrop, I heard them saying some nasty things about you."

Kate's face fell, as part of her felt a little hurt. While she didn't expect Syd and Sebastian to instantly like her, Kate didn't think those two would be that mean.

"What did they say?" Kate asked.

Gloria bit her lip.

"Some of it was just plain nasty. It was mostly sexual; let's just leave it at that."

"Oh," was all Kate had to say in response. She was disturbed that her uncle's sons would say such things about her. Though they were not related by blood, it was disturbing enough to make Kate feel uncomfortable. Gloria was right, she did not want to hear more.

"I'll be right back," Gloria said, getting up from the bed. She went into her room to retrieve something; then she came right back. "I finished this," Gloria said, holding Kate's copy of *Daisy Miller* in her hand.

"What did you think of it?" Kate asked.

"Depressing, like you said," Gloria replied. "I would read more of the books you've brought along, but I think I might find them to be too depressing."

"What kinds of books do *you* have?"

Gloria shrugged. "Nothing much right now. I've been meaning to go to some of the shops in town. I guess we could swing by the bookstore to see what they've got some time."

"And I suppose you want to change my reading habits like you did my wardrobe," Kate teased.

"Hey, let's not start on that again. You looked red hot in those clothes." She smiled. "I know that Steve liked them. It's surprising that he didn't try to attack you."

He almost did, Kate thought, as she remembered Friday night, when they started kissing, and he put his hands all over her. While

Kate *did* enjoy it, and she was attracted to Steve, she was relieved that he'd promised to take things slow.

"He's too much of a gentleman to do that," Kate said. Then, she began to think about how much she missed him. They had not spoken for nearly two days, but those two days were longer than she anticipated, given the fact at how quickly they formed their relationship.

The same was true with Gloria and Russell. The two of them had already made love, and they had known each other only just as long as Kate knew Steve.

In this country, things seemed to be moving much too fast, much faster than things had moved in America. Or, at least, Kate thought.

Kate also realized that the only thing in her life that moved this fast was her relationship with Fred. Though she already knew that Steve was an entirely different person, she could not help but hold on to some of her fears. Kate, however, remembered that she agreed to try a relationship with Steve.

"What can I lose?" she asked herself, while thinking about how much her life had already changed. Kate was beginning to come into her own, and she knew that she would have to make some adjustments in order to keep up with the changes in her life.

Chapter 12

Two weeks had passed, and things were going along smoothly. Kate and Gloria frequented not only Strawberry Orange Dreams but some other stores in the area as well.

Kate particularly liked the bookstore, London Block, which had a diverse range of books for sale.

Gloria suggested some titles which she thought Kate might find interesting. Among them were *The Doors of Perception* by Aldous Huxley, *Howl*, by Allen Ginsberg, and some books by Hunter S. Thompson.

While Kate considered herself to be a cultured person, she had not heard of Hunter S. Thompson or Aldous Huxley.

Gloria assured her cousin that she would enjoy those books.

Both Kate and Gloria enjoyed all the time they'd spent with Russell and Steve.

***

As time went by, Kate felt that she had less to fear from her relationship with Steve. He was keeping his word by behaving like a perfect gentleman.

Kate was now more comfortable with the two of them exploring each other, but they had yet to actually consummate their relationship.

They both figured that they would reach that point when the time was right.

Gloria and Russell, on the other hand, were getting hot and heavy. The more time that they'd spent together, the harder it was for them to part. It had gotten to the point where Russell had invited

Gloria to meet his parents and sister. She was absolutely in love with the idea, but she felt that Russell should meet her family first.

Gloria told her new lover that her father was a little old-fashioned, which was not entirely true, as he'd lightened up a little over the years, but she would feel better if Russell got to know her parents first. When she asked for Kate's advice, however, Kate told her that it wouldn't hurt to meet his parents whenever she would like.

"Think of it this way," Kate said. "If you meet his parents, and you find that you are not very fond of them, you can always call the whole relationship off."

"Kate!" Gloria exclaimed, not believing what her cousin had just said.

"I'm only joking," Kate said, trying not to laugh. She was surprised that Gloria had taken her so seriously sometimes. "No, but you are probably right. I would definitely see how your folks take to him first. This way, you'll feel better. You could always meet his family any time after you bring him home for tea."

Gloria thought about this for a second, and she was glad that her cousin agreed with her on this issue. She thanked Kate then hugged her before the two of them parted ways for the evening and went to bed.

When Gloria told Olivia and Stuart about Russell, they did not seem to have much of a reaction. Gloria knew that her father was not thrilled when she told him that Russell was a musician, but at least he did not resort to talking Syd and Sebastian into bringing some of their Oxford friends over to meet her.

He had actually done that once, and Gloria was none too pleased, especially since Simon seemed to be every bit as pompous as her cousins.

Gloria was talking to her parents, trying to convince him to allow Russell over for tea. While Olivia liked the idea that Gloria wanted to formally introduce her "new beau" to her parents, Stuart was not very convinced.

"I don't know, my dear," Stuart said in his concerned voice. "This young man you speak of is a musician, and I'm just a little concerned."

"About what?" Gloria asked, trying her best to sound like she was not accusing her father of being unfair.

"Well, it's just that, you told me he is a musician." Stuart paused, knowing that what he was about to tell his daughter was not what she wanted to hear. Still, he feels it needs to be said.

"That does not sound like a very stable job, and with that in mind, I don't know how he's going to support you."

Gloria felt herself get a little angry. She did not care about the fact that Russell was a musician without a record contract because she loved him, nonetheless. She felt that her father should at least give him a chance.

"Please, Dad," Gloria said. "Russell is really a terrific man, and I so want you and Mum to meet him. Please, at least just give me that."

Stuart sighed. He looked into Gloria's eyes and realized just how serious she was about this person. He then turned to look at Olivia, who was smiling, as if giving him encouragement to indulge his daughter.

"Well," he said. "I suppose there would be no harm in bringing the young man by sometime. Shall we say, next Monday for tea?"

"Thank you!" Gloria exclaimed, hugging her father. "Daddy, you are not going to regret this. Russell is a terrific man, and you will think so, too, once you and Mum get to meet him."

Stuart just smiled. He was not against the idea of meeting Russell. After all, he would be able to determine whether or not he was worthy of his daughter almost right away. Stuart liked to think that he was a good judge of character. His daughter, however, was a little different.

Though Gloria was already twenty-four, he knew how childlike and innocent she still was. He was just afraid that her impetuous behavior would encourage Russell to take advantage of her. Just the thought alone made Stuart's blood boil, but he did not want to make any kind of scene in the living room.

He decided that he would save all that for later if he did not find Russell to his favor. Stuart had yet to meet the man, so he did want to be fair in inviting him over for tea.

Gloria, meanwhile, was still beaming over her father's extended invitation to her new beau.

"I'll call Russell right away and tell him the wonderful news. He'll be absolutely delighted." Stuart smiled again then chuckled.

"Well, my dear. You don't have to go rushing to the telephone right away. Give it some time."

Gloria decided to respect her father's wishes, but the last thing she wanted to do was give it more time. She had been doing nothing but that until this very moment, but she knew that her parents would not have wanted to delve into a meeting with Russell.

Gloria saw it fit that she should try to explain some "ground rules" to him before he met her parents. For instance, he would have to watch his mouth and not use vulgar phrases to describe people or events. He would have to be polite and eat everything that her mother served for tea, even if he decided to spit it out into a napkin later. And last, but not least, he should not and could not mention his affair with her.

Though their lovemaking was passionate, and Gloria was no virgin, she could not let her parents know that they were having sex. And, if they already knew, Russell should not be the one to remind them! How she envied Kate and Steve, whom she knew had yet to consummate their relationship.

Gloria decided that the best time to use the phone would be when Kate was through talking with her parents. She could not wait to extend the invite to Russell to join their family for tea, but it would have to wait for a few minutes.

If she knew, Kate would have gladly given her cousin more time to talk to Russell, especially since she was afraid to talk to both her mother *and* her father, being that she was now dating an

Englishman, and a rock musician at that! Kate could already see her father's reaction, which would be far from happy, to say the least.

If anything more serious came of this new relationship, Kate knew that she would not be able to hide it from them forever. Still, she did not have to tackle the issue tonight, so she decided that it was time to call her parents. Kate took a couple of deep breaths and dialed her parents' number. Someone picked up on the second ring.

"Hello," Isaac said from the other end.

Kate could feel her pulse quicken. Then, she felt all the blood drain from her hands and face. This was the first time her father answered the phone in all the two weeks that she had been there, and this was one of the few times that she had actually gotten to speak to him.

"Hello, Dad," Kate replied.

"Sweetheart," Isaac's said voice kindly. "It's good to hear from you. How are things over the pond? Is your Aunt Olivia treating you well?"

"Yes, Father. I'm having a splendid time. How's Mom?" Kate hesitated a moment after her question. She hoped that by changing the subject Isaac would not try to pry into her personal matters.

"Your mother's fine. She's getting ready to come inside and fix me supper. She said that she misses having you here to help her in the kitchen."

Kate laughed. She couldn't help but think that her father was in a good mood today, especially because he was making jokes. Perhaps, this conversation was not going to be a bad one after all.

"I've been doing a lot with Gloria," Kate said. "Oh, she's lovely, Dad. I hope someday that you get to meet her."

"Someday," Isaac replied, though his voice seemed to lack the same emotion as it did seconds ago. "So," he resumed after a few seconds, "has anything else interesting happened there?"

Oh, if you only knew, Kate thought. Ever since she has arrived in England, there have been *a lot* of interesting things going on. It seemed as if Kate's whole life had already been turned upside down.

"Well," Kate said, trying to think of something to say. "I met Syd and Sebastian. They are James and Lois's sons, Gloria's cousins."

"Oh, yes," Isaac said, "the Oxford twins. Your Aunt Olivia has told me an awful lot about those boys. It seems like they are regular chips off the old block."

Kate frowned. Her father had inadvertently hit a nerve. If Olivia had really mentioned those boys to him, it would have been news to her. Kate just hoped that neither her aunt nor her uncle would try to hook her up with one of those boys, especially since she wanted nothing to do with the likes of them.

Besides, they were practically family, though they were not related to Kate by blood. Just thinking about the whole thing made her completely nauseous. Kate now felt sick, and she knew that she had to end this conversation soon.

"Well, Dad. It's nearing 4:00, which is teatime around here. I need to get going for now."

"Well, okay, sweetheart. It's a shame that we can't talk any more right now. Your mother just came in, and she's going to start fixing my supper."

"Well, tell her that I love her and not to worry too much about me. I'll be fine."

"Will do, Katie. You have a nice tea. Talk to you soon."

"Okay. I love you, Dad."

"Love you too, sweetheart."

"Goodbye, Dad."

"Goodbye."

Kate hung up the phone. Just when she thought the conversation was going well, her father had to toot the horns of Syd and Sebastian. She was none too happy when Gloria told her that they were saying mean and lewd things behind her back.

It was only when she started thinking about Steve did she calm down a little. Now, there was a gentleman. Steve would never say or do anything to hurt her, and he was very honest in expressing his feelings. Kate smiled, happy in her thoughts about him.

The only problem was that The Peppermint Eyes had been away touring other cities in London for a while, which meant they would be out of town this weekend.

Kate felt that there was no way Aunt Olivia and Uncle Stuart would allow then to go so far out of their way to see the band. Besides, Russell would be here this weekend to meet Gloria's parents. Kate hoped and prayed that everything would go well, but she was not entirely sure because of how protective Uncle Stuart was toward her cousin.

Kate then decided that she would clear her mind of any thoughts that would only upset her even more. She knew that within a few minutes Aunt Olivia would announce that tea was ready. She also knew that Gloria would want some time to talk to Russell. Kate got up off her bed and went over across the hallway to knock on Gloria's door; she told her that it was time that she call Russell.

Chapter 13

Monday was finally here. Though the time in between when Gloria had invited Russell to tea on Thursday and Monday afternoon went agonizingly slow for her, it seemed like the opposite for everyone else. Olivia seemed a little perplexed because it seemed to go in the blink of an eye for her and Stuart.

Gloria, insisting that she help her flustered mother in the kitchen, ensured that tea would be ready on time.

Kate offered to help as well, but both women told her to leave the kitchen, insisting that she let them take care of everything themselves. Just as Kate expected, the tea was formal dress. She hoped that Russell remembered to wear a suit.

Gloria had worn her most formal dress, the same one she had on when her father's family had come to visit.

Kate had on the same purple dress that she'd worn the day she first entered Strawberry Orange Dreams, how many recent memories that it had already brought back.

Minutes before Russell's arrival, Kate felt like getting up and pacing the hallway. Why was *she* the one who felt extremely nervous on Gloria's big day? Perhaps she was just as worried that Aunt Olivia and Uncle Stuart would not like him. Perhaps she thought about how she would feel when her time would come, how she would find the courage to introduce Steve to her parents.

Kate felt that there would not be enough time in the world for her to prepare for that day whenever it did come. First, however, Gloria and Russell would have to get through this day. Though each person living in the house each exhibited a fair amount of tension, Kate knew that it would not last forever.

Besides, Kate thought. *If Aunt Olivia and Uncle Stuart like Russell, then they should have no problem accepting Steve.* The mere thought of that alone was enough to make Kate feel better for the moment.

No sooner had Gloria and her mother set up the table did the doorbell ring.

Gloria, whose nervousness instantly turned to excitement, rushed over to answer it. There he stood, on their threshold, wearing a nice, blue suit. Upon further inspection of the suit, Gloria could tell that it was little wrinkled, but she did not think her parents would notice, unless they got a very close look at him. His hair was still long, but it was slicked back on his head. He'd also shaved his sideburns.

"Russell!" Gloria exclaimed, right before he stepped inside. She then looked at the dozen red roses which he had brought with him.

"These are for you," Russell said, handing them over to Gloria.

"Thank you," Gloria replied, taking the bouquet into her arms. "Please, come into the dining room. My parents are very eager to meet you."

We'll see about that, Russell thought, as he nervously surveyed his surroundings. He noticed that the house, while very well-maintained, did not have the same appearance of some dreary English castle, where people who liked to compare themselves to monarchies, usually lived. Russell followed Gloria into the dining room.

As soon as Kate saw Russell make his entrance, she stood up from her chair. She did not have to wait long until he came over to greet her.

"Hello, Kate," he said, hugging her and giving her a kiss on the cheek.

"Hello, Russell," she replied. "It's nice to see you again." And while Kate was glad to see Russell again, she couldn't help but feel a little sad because she did not get to share this meal with Steve. Kate sat back down and wondered what he was doing at this very moment. She wondered if he was thinking of her.

"Father, Mother," Gloria said, bringing Kate out of her trance. "I would like to introduce to you Mr. Russell Stokes."

Olivia smiled, while James seemed to remain neutral. One could easily tell that he was keeping a close watch of Russell, paying attention to every little detail that he could.

"Hello," Olivia said, acting as jolly when she had met Kate at the airport. "How do you do, Russell? I'm Gloria's mother, Mrs. Cunningham."

"Hello, mum," Russell replied, as he leaned in closer to receive a kiss on the cheek from Olivia. "Now I know where Gloria gets her charm and beauty."

Olivia giggled.

Clearly, though such a display of flattery, he had already won over Gloria's mother. One down, and one to go. Russell then looked at Stuart, whose face still showed no expression while standing stiff as a board.

"Hello, sir, it's a great pleasure to meet you," Russell said, extending his hand to Stuart.

"Hello, Russell, likewise," Stuart replied after shaking his hand. "Gloria tells me that we are in for a real treat tonight."

For a brief moment, everyone else in the room seemed shocked. No one quite knew what Stuart meant by his comment, but it did not sound as reassuring as Gloria and Russell would have hoped for.

Still, the couple was not willing to give up quite so easily.

In her heart of hearts, Gloria still knew that Russell would somehow win over her father. Olivia must have hinted at the tension present in the air, so she figured she would try to bring up a positive subject.

"My, aren't those roses lovely?" she said, admiring the flowers that were still in Gloria's arms. "Gloria, have you thanked Russell for these?"

"Yes, Mum," Gloria said, rolling her eyes. She couldn't help but be embarrassed because her parents still treated her like a little child sometimes.

"Let's get these into a vase, shall we?" Olivia said as she went into the kitchen and retrieved an empty vase which stood on the counter.

"We can put them right in the center of the table while we eat," Olivia said excitedly. She was still in the kitchen, cutting off the ends of the stems so they would fit into the vase. Once she was all finished, she brought out the finished result and put it on the dining room table.

"There, now doesn't that look nice?"

Everyone verbally expressed their agreement. The flowers really looked nice, but there was still that tension between Stuart and Russell.

"So," Olivia said, trying to break the tension, "I hope that everyone likes the food. Gloria and I were working in the kitchen all afternoon."

Russell looked down at the table and noticed that there were finger sandwiches, filled with various meats, a large salad bowl, scones and rolls of all shapes and kinds and a bottle of Chardonnay. There were also butter dishes and containers full of strawberry and grape jam.

While the food looked very delicious, Russell doubted that it took very long to prepare. Though, he was certainly in no position to share his opinion on that. Russell took a scone and buttered it. He took his first bite and let everyone know just how good it tasted.

"Yes, Mrs. Cunningham," Russell said, "the food is delicious."

Olivia smiled. "You can call me Olivia, Russell. Thank you for the compliment."

"No, thank you, Olivia. This is the best scone that I've eaten in a long time."

Gloria was pleased that her mother and Russell were getting along, but she was concerned about the fact that her father had hardly said two words to him. And as if on cue, Stuart had finally spoken up again.

"So, Russell, Gloria tells me that you are in the *music business*." Stuart had emphasized the words *music business* to make it sound like it was not much of a business at all.

Both Russell and Gloria could feel themselves get a little nervous. Though Stuart had simply stated a fact, Gloria did not like his neutral tone. He sounded a little too cold, a little too distant.

"Yes, sir," Russell replied. "Me and a few of my best mates, I mean friends, have started a musical band."

Stuart sniffed.

"What kind of music do you play?" he asked in a bemused tone of voice.

Gloria, sensing her lover's embarrassment, simply wanted her father to stop.

"Dad," she said.

"Gloria, let the young man answer my question," Stuart replied, eyes now locked on Russell.

"Well, we are rock musicians, sir. We have played some local pubs in the town. While we have only just started out, we have generated some interest in the area, and a few local record producers have shown interest in our work."

Stuart raised his eyebrows.

"Really?" he said, picking up a scone and smearing it with grape jam. "And do you think that you could continue doing this work for the rest of your life?"

"Well, sir, if it is quite possible." Russell paused for a moment and scratched his neck. "What I mean to say is that I think it will be able to work." Stuart, now in the middle of eating his scone, never let his eyes stray from Russell.

"Well, what I would like to know is if you ever, say, end up marrying my daughter, could you support her with that kind of lifestyle?"

"Dad!" Gloria exclaimed, trying to interject again.

"My dear," Stuart replied. "Please, let the young man speak. Surely, you do not have to answer for him every time."

Russell began to rub his neck, which was now starting to sweat.

"Well, yes, sir," Russell replied.

Olivia noticed that he had hardly touched his food.

"I think that I would definitely be able to support Gloria if the subject ever came to marriage." Russell paused. "Of course, I would never dream of proposing to your daughter without your consent."

"That's good," Stuart replied, reaching for another scone. This time, he spread strawberry jam on the piece of bread. "That's the kind of answer that I like to hear."

Stuart did not smile, but this was enough to make both Russell and Gloria feel relieved for the moment.

Olivia looked over at her husband and gave him a disapproving look. His face, in turn, did not show any response.

"In fact, our lead singer, Steve Maddington, is responsible for most of our songs and lyrics," Russell said, trying to change the subject a little. "He also plays a very good guitar. He is a very talented musician."

Just hearing Russell speak Steve's name was enough to make Kate want to be in his arms. And, though they had not seen each other for only a week, this was the loneliest Kate has been in a while.

"Yeah, Dad, we should bring over Steve so you could meet him sometime," Gloria said. "I think you would really like him."

Kate could feel herself begin to panic. While she certainly was falling in love with Steve, she wasn't quite sure that her aunt and uncle were ready to meet him yet. Besides, Kate wanted to see how they got along with Russell first.

"Well, that sounds like a nice idea," Olivia said, hoping to encourage Stuart to contribute more to the conversation.

"Let's just get through this dinner first," Stuart said, as though he still didn't know what to make of everything that was going on around the dining room table.

Kate could feel herself starting to get nervous. While she did want Steve to meet her family, it would all have to be done in good time. After all, Kate still had mixed feelings about the relationship and how it was going to work long-term.

"I don't think that's such a good idea," Kate said, hoping that Gloria would drop the subject. "Let's just enjoy the rest of our tea and talk about other things later."

Gloria formed a look on her face, just like she was holding back laughter.

"Don't be silly, Kate; surely Mum and Dad would be interested in meeting the man that you're currently dating."

Upon hearing this, Stuart and Olivia focused their eyes on Kate, who was just about to take a bite of her salad.

"Gloria!" Kate hissed, clearly embarrassed by her cousin's faux pas.

"Sorry," Gloria mumbled, barely audible.

She felt a little embarrassed for Kate as well because she hung her head, as if looking down.

Russell even began to look at Kate, curious to see what else she would say.

Kate's face completely drained itself of all its color. She felt her heart beating inside her chest. Why had Gloria chosen this time to mention Steve in front of the family? She wanted to kick her cousin underneath the table, but she thought that would only make things worse. Kate, however, had to find a delicate way to approach the subject.

"Yes, Gloria. Thank you *so much* for mentioning Steve." Kate hesitated for a second. "Steve and I have been dating for a while."

"Really, is that so?" Stuart asked, raising his eyebrows and looking right over in Russell's direction.

"Yes, sir," Russell replied. "And he's a good man, if I may say so." Kate could feel herself getting really uncomfortable. She hated the fact that the attention was now focused on her.

"Yes, Steve is a wonderful person," Kate said. "But I don't want to talk too much about us right now. This is Gloria and Russell's night."

An uncomfortable silence filled the room for a few seconds, which allowed Kate enough time to reflect on her faux pas.

Us? Kate thought. *I referred to Steve and myself as us?* Kate then thought of the two of them engaging in some kind of secret and illicit affair. She pictured them making love, over and over again, in the most inappropriate places. Just the picture alone was enough to make Kate's face turn a shade of crimson red.

"Quite so," Stuart said. "We will have to meet this young chap sometime soon."

Though Stuart did not seem as stiff as he did moments ago, one could easily tell that he still didn't know what to make of Russell. Gloria, for one, would feel much better if her father would just smile at him.

"Yes," Olivia crooned. "Kate, you will simply have to bring Steven by soon. We are dying to meet him already."

Both Kate and Gloria could tell that Olivia was acting a little strange.

Gloria thought that her mother was still infatuated with the idea of having a young man to tea. Gloria was both relieved and concerned about the way that her mother looked at Russell. It would seem that it was Olivia who was dating him, not Gloria. Still, it helped that at least one of her parents took a liking to him.

The rest of the tea seemed to go very well, as Russell felt himself getting closer to Gloria through her parents. By the time tea was over and Russell got up to say "goodbye," everyone in the room seemed a little more comfortable.

Olivia told Russell that he simply must come to tea again soon, and Stuart had made more effort to talk to him. He'd even smiled at him a few times as they talked more about their families and stories about growing up.

This was a rare thing because Gloria had not brought many men home to meet her parents. The two whom she had brought home before neither of her parents really liked. The fact that they got along with Russell was a promising sign.

Gloria smiled. She knew that all Russell had to do now was win over her father, and he would be in. She didn't care how long it would take. As long as it was bound to happen, love would find a way. Gloria remained optimistic about because she loved Russell Stokes with all her heart.

Gloria couldn't take it anymore. She had to know exactly what her parents' thoughts were upon their first meeting of Russell. While she knew that her mother seemed to like him, she wanted to hear what her father would say. Gloria flat out asked Stuart what he thought of Russell.

"He seems like a nice, young lad," was Stuart's singular response. No doubt, he was still evaluating Russell with careful interest.

Though Gloria was not quite satisfied with her father's answer, she decided to leave the subject alone. She felt that if she "pressured" her father any further tonight, that he would be inclined to change his mind.

After some more general chatter and nice remarks from Olivia, everyone decided to call it an evening and retire to their rooms.

Kate couldn't stop thinking about Steve. She seemed to miss everything about him; his smile, his laugh, his touch, and his overall presence. Stuart and Olivia arranged for a meeting with Steve in two weeks' time.

Next Monday, Mr. and Mrs. Cunningham were going to be preoccupied. They were going out to dinner with Mr. and Mrs. Ripple.

Kate remembered meeting Mrs. Ripple at the bank, when she was kind enough to convert her dollars into pounds. Kate thought she seemed pleasant enough. For some reason, the Cunninghams wanted to designate Monday night to meeting the other young gentleman.

Kate was just about to start into a new book when she heard a knock on her door.

That'll be Gloria, coming to assess the evening with me, Kate thought. She sighed and put down her book.

"Come in," Kate said, grateful that she had time to change out of her dress.

"Hello," Gloria said, with a smile on her face. "Thought you might like to talk about tonight's events." Gloria was wearing her nightgown, which was nothing out of the ordinary because she had seen her in it so many times.

"Sure," Kate replied, "come on in."

Gloria made her way over to Kate and sat down on the foot of her bed.

"So," Gloria said, "I thought that went well, much better than it could have."

"Yeah," Kate replied, feeling slight resentment. Although she seemed genuinely happy that her aunt and uncle seemed to like Russell, Kate couldn't help but think about how her own parents would react to Steve.

Father would probably have him tarred and feathered, Kate thought, knowing full well that that was the *least* Isaac would do. Her mother, as sweet she was, would only accept Steve secretly, as not to upset her overbearing husband. Either way, Kate knew that she couldn't win.

"Are you all right?" Gloria asked, sensing that something was wrong.

"I'm fine. It's just…" Kate trailed off. As dearly as she loved Gloria, she did not want to discuss this with her right now.

"You're worried about me folks meeting Steve," Gloria added, pretty sure that she knew what was ailing her cousin.

"Something like that," Kate replied.

"Don't worry. *You* are not the one who should be worried. Did you see the way Dad looked at Russell all during tea?"

"Yes, I noticed, but you said he reacted better with him than any other man that you'd brought home."

Gloria put index finger to her lips, indicating that she was giving this some real thought.

"You're right, but we still have a long way to go. I mean, what if Russell asks me to marry him? What will happen then?"

Kate's eyes widened. She couldn't even believe that Gloria was thinking about such a thing right now."

"Gloria, don't you think you're getting a little ahead of yourself? I mean, you and Russell just met."

Gloria shot her cousin a look, indicating that her remark had stung her a little.

"But I *love* him, Kate. How can you even question that? Don't you tell me that you don't feel the same way about Steve."

"I do, but—"

Gloria cut her off. "You know, Kate, you don't have to put up any kind of façade with me. I know how it really is between you and Steve."

"But marriage, Gloria. It's not something one should rush into."

"And how would you know?" Gloria asked, beginning to get a little defensive.

"Know? I don't have to know, Gloria," Kate said, rising to defend her claim. "Listen, your mom and dad are lovely people, and I'm not just saying that. The two of them are really good together, and they deserve each other." Kate sighed. "My parents are a different story."

Gloria looked over at Kate, whose eyes started to fill with tears. She knew she had to find a way to comfort her; she wanted to tell her that everything was going to be all right.

"Kate," Gloria said in a sympathetic tone. She moved closer to Kate and put her arm around her. Though Gloria had never met her American aunt and uncle, she knew enough about how conservative they are.

"I'm sorry. I didn't mean to sound a little defensive there. It's just that, you know how much I love Russell."

Kate looked up through her tears and nodded.

"And you know that I would marry him at the drop of a hat," Gloria continued. "But it's not like we're going to get married right *now*. After all, he has yet to even ask me."

Kate nodded again. Though words had not eluded her, a part of her still felt too angry to say anything more. Talking about her parents and how they would react to Steve was not going to make anything better.

"And I know that you are worried about you and Steve," Gloria continued, her arm still around her cousin. "But you're in London, love, which happens to me my home turf! If I could just melt Dad's heart a little and get him to like Russell, I mean really like Russell, then things would work out well for me."

Kate was getting a little exasperated. She thought that Gloria was doing nothing here but rambling.

Just get to the point! Kate wanted to shout. After all, this was not just about Gloria and Russell. It was also about Kate and her future with Steve. It was about wondering, no, knowing that her parents would never accept him as their son-in-law.

"I mean, I know it sounds like I am not making sense here, but what I'm trying to say is that as long as you are on my stomping grounds, nothing can get to you." Gloria looked at her cousin and saw that she was starting to smile.

"And you know you've got Mum and Dad as your allies. I'm sure that they will have no problem accepting Steve."

Kate looked up, drying her tears as Gloria looked reassuringly into her eyes.

"Do you really think so?" Kate asked, her eyes full of hope.

"Absolutely," Gloria replied. "Steve is a nice chap, almost as good as my Russell. I know that you love him, Kate. Nothing should ever take that away from you." She paused. "And if your parents are not willing to come to accept him, then too bad."

Kate looked over at Gloria, a bit surprised at having heard her said those words.

"You heard me," Gloria continued. "Your mum and dad are lucky to have you, and if they don't want to accept Steve as a major part of your life when you introduce him, then they will just have to just learn to come to grips with it."

Kate let out a little laugh. "That'll be the day," she said, though she really appreciated Gloria's efforts to make her feel better.

"Well, let's not worry about that now. We should just take things as they come." Gloria paused. "I should be following this advice, too."

Kate laughed again. Gloria's words had started to sink in, as Kate started to have positive thoughts. Perhaps Gloria was right; perhaps her parents would see reason the day Kate chose to introduce Steve to them.

"Thanks, Gloria," Kate said, giving her cousin a grateful look. "You always seem to know what to say to make me feel better."

"Of course I do." Gloria proudly replied. "Isn't that what cousins and best friends for?"

"Indeed," Kate said, feeling completely at ease with herself. She knew just as long as she took things slowly with Steve that everything would eventually work itself out.

Chapter 14

Monday night was not usually a night when The Peppermint Eyes performed their gigs. But both Russell and Steve wanted to take the girls out for the evening. The four of them decided to dine at the café where they had all met, which was nice because they could all reminisce about old times.

The dinner and conversation had gone well, and Gloria smiled behind her eyes. Tonight, she had an ulterior motive. Since both her parents were busy having dinner with the Ripples, the house would be empty.

Gloria would be going with Russell to their flat, and Kate would have no choice but to offer Steve an invitation to come back to their house. It was sheer genius, and Gloria didn't mind thinking so herself.

***

Shortly after dinner, Russell announced that he and Gloria were going to go back to the flat together. Of course, Gloria had talked to Steve earlier about her plan, and he seemed to like it. The only thing that made him feel uncomfortable was the fact that Kate might not think too highly of it.

"It sounds like a good plan to me, but this is coming from a man who is okay with this. What if Kate gets mad? She could hate me forever after pulling a stunt like this."

"Are you kidding?" Gloria replied. "Kate loves you. She has been aching for you for weeks. And since she is too afraid to admit this to anyone, especially to herself, she may act differently."

Steve smiled. So Kate was deeply in love with him. That was enough to make him leap mountains and fly through the air. If what Gloria was saying is true, then he was the happiest man alive.

"She really loves me that much?" Steve asked, still incredulous.

"Yes," Gloria replied. "Every time someone even mentions your name, her entire face lights up!"

"But I don't feel quite right," Steve said, head facing the ground. "Kate and I have a wonderful thing going, so why would I want to jeopardize that?"

"You wouldn't be jeopardizing anything. I love Kate dearly, as do you, but that woman desperately needs to get laid." Gloria paused for a moment, taking in Steve's expression, which was one of shock.

He did, however, form a tiny smile on his face.

"She's been under so much stress lately, and this would be the perfect opportunity to relieve her of some of that."

Steve looked up. He smiled again then laughed. Though the plan seemed a little half-baked, he did like the idea of making love with Kate, especially since he knew how she felt about him.

"All right," Steve relented. "But if this plan backfires, and Kate absolutely hates the idea, then I am going to hold *you* responsible."

"Fair enough," Gloria replied.

The two of them stopped and stared at each other in awkward silence before shaking hands, making it official.

After dinner, Russell and Gloria made the announcement that they were headed back to his flat. John, Geoffrey, and Henry had their own plans and would be all gone for the evening. Russell and Gloria said their quick goodbyes, leaving Kate and Steve alone to do their own thing.

Kate was conflicted. She wanted to spend more time with Steve, but she didn't know what they would do or where they would go. She knew that her aunt and uncle would be gone for most of the rest of the evening, but she did not think Steve would really want to accept an invitation to their house. Still, she supposed there wouldn't be any harm in asking.

"Steve, I know this may sound a little sudden, but would you like to come back to my aunt and uncle's house with me for a while?" Just as soon as the words came out of Kate's mouth, she immediately regretted it. She wanted to kick herself for sounding so stupid.

"That sounds fine to me," Steve said, being careful not to seem to overanxious.

Once the two of them were alone in the house together, he would have to find a way to make his move. Kate and Steve went outside. Steve frowned as he looked in the direction of the parking lot.

"Oh, bloody hell!"

"What's wrong?" Kate asked.

"Russell, the little bastard; he took the car."

Kate couldn't help but laugh. It was a nice evening out, and a little exercise could never hurt anybody.

"It's all right; we can walk."

Steve smiled. He loved the fact that Kate seemed so easygoing most of the time.

"Well, it's a good thing that you are with me. This way, if someone tries to come up to you, I can protect you." Steve put his arm around Kate, and she leaned in for a hug.

"And this is one of the reasons why I love you very much, Steve Maddington!"

"And I love you, too, Kate Richards. I love you more than words can describe." This much was true. Ever since he had first lay eyes upon her, Steve Maddington was a smitten man.

The wind picked up lightly as the two of them made their way to the Cunningham residence.

The lovers walked toward the house with their arms around each other.

Though Kate was hesitant before, she was glad that she extended this invitation to Steve, the invitation to finally be alone together. Kate had a good feeling. Tonight was the night. Somehow, she just knew. Tonight, she would finally be comfortable enough to fully express her love for Steve in every sense of the word. She smiled, knowing that they only had a few more blocks until they reached the house.

"Good thing Gloria gave me an extra key," Kate said, as she inserted it into the lock.

Steve was right behind her, both nervous and excited about what he thought was going to take place. He did not want to have to blame Gloria if things did not work out.

Once inside, Kate closed and locked the front door behind her. She placed her key down on the kitchen counter.

"Now, I'm going to turn on the lights, Steve, but don't be afraid."

"Afraid? Why would I need to be afraid?" Steve asked, feeling a little nervous. He hoped that Mr. Cunningham was not hiding somewhere, waiting to pounce on him for his sudden intrusion.

"Because," Kate replied, "some of the decorations in these rooms are a little bit…unusual."

Steve let out a sign of relief then laughed. "Oh. Is that all?"

"Don't say that until you've looked around a bit," Kate teased. "Okay, I'm going to flip the switch." Kate turned on the light, and Steve was suddenly exposed to all the red, green, and mismatched decorations in the living room.

"Good Lord," Steve said, looking around, "you weren't kidding."

"Nope," Kate replied. "I love Auntie Olivia dearly, but she is definitely notorious for her bad taste for garish decorations."

Steve nodded. He didn't know anything else he could say that wouldn't offend Kate.

"I see. Is there any part of the house that isn't quite as, uh, unusual as this?"

"Well, there's Uncle's Stu's study, or there's Gloria's room."

Steve recoiled. He was definitely sure that he did *not* want to see Gloria's room, judging by her eccentric taste in clothing and overall mannerisms. Steve leaned in close, his lips inches away from hers.

"How about your room?" he asked.

Kate blushed. She could tell that Steve was getting amorous, but she was feeling the same way.

"Um, would you like me to show you my room?" Kate asked, still a little nervous. "That is, the room where I stay? I mean, I could show you my book collection."

Kate decided to stop speaking right there. She felt like her rambling would only make her feel stupid and foolish.

Steve, however, knew what Kate was trying to say. He remembered back to his conversation with Gloria earlier, and he hoped that she was right. He leaned over and kissed Kate on the lips.

Kate felt the heat rising in her stomach. This time, she knew she would not stop herself if things got any more passionate.

"You can show me *anything* that you want in your room," Steve said, feeling aroused.

"Right," Kate said, still feeling the effects of his kiss. "Just follow me upstairs. My room is right across from Gloria's."

Kate navigated the stairs, Steve following close behind. Just as he had done the first night he had seen her, he stared at her bottom, liking the way it moved as she climbed the stairs. Steve was ready to explode. He felt that he could not even wait the few more seconds it would take to reach Kate's room.

"This is my room," Kate said, standing outside the open door. "Shall we go inside?" she asked, hoping that Steve had not changed his mind.

Steve smiled at her choice of words. He made a sweeping motion with his arm, indicating that Kate should go in ahead of him.

"After you," he said, finding it hard to disguise the desire in his voice.

Kate went into the room first, and Steve followed her inside. There they stood for a few seconds, taking in the atmosphere.

Steve closed the door behind them. His lips curled into a mischievous smile.

It was a good thing that Mr. and Mrs. Cunningham were out for the evening. They were probably in the middle of enjoying their dinner with Mr. and Mrs. Ripple.

Gloria was otherwise occupied with Russell back at their flat.

Steve, however, wanted to take all precautions necessary. He decided to lock the door.

Once safely inside the locked room, Steve went over to Kate. He looked her square in the eyes and saw himself reflected in there his face. The light from the streets outside spilled into the room, which provided enough atmosphere to further enhance the mood.

Steve leaned in closer and began kissing her, his hungry lips overpowering hers. It wasn't long before their hands were around each other's backs.

Kate closed her eyes and imagined herself in an entirely different place. She could have been in Buckingham Palace for all she cared because she was with Steve; the passion was already coming to own her.

The two of them sat down on the bed, still kissing with mad fervor.

Steve then removed his lips from hers and began kissing her neck, which caused her to begin to melt.

Kate left out soft moans of pleasure as Steve caressed her breasts and explored the other parts of her body; she became putty in his hands. She had never felt anything like this all during the time she'd been with Fred. Steve was masculine, yet gentle. He also seemed to know what he was doing, which Kate liked very much.

"You don't happen to have that sexy outfit that you wore to our first show, do you?" he asked.

Kate smiled. She knew that Steve was referring to the white, long-sleeved shirt and the tight, black leather pants.

"Let me just go into the closet and get it," she said. Kate was relieved; she was no longer uncomfortable at the prospect of making love to this man.

In a matter of moments, Kate had put the outfit on, and she lay back down on the bed.

Steve came over and lay down on top of Kate, and the two of them began kissing again. Steve ran his hands up and down Kate's legs; he loved the feel of the leather against his fingers. Then, slowly, as to make sure Kate anticipated his next move, Steve ran his hands up her body again, tugging at her white shirt.

Kate knew what he wanted, so she sat up, allowing him to remove the shirt, leaving her completely topless. Steve hungrily placed his lips on each breast and nipple before moving down to take off her pants, making her want it all the more.

After Kate felt like she could take it no more, she returned the favor and relieved Steve of his clothes.

Mere seconds later, Kate and Steve were completely undressed.

Though he was just as nervous as she, one would never know it because of the way in which he presented himself. Steve's male swagger was enough to turn Kate on, without making her feel intimidated. His lips touched every part of her body, making her moan with passion which she had never felt before.

Her sordid past was all but forgotten, as Kate realized that she had found her true love. Steve was the very reason why God had delivered her to England. The two of them proceeded to lie down and make love for the first time, doing what came to them most naturally.

The two lovers lay peacefully in each other's arms. After their first lovemaking, Kate and Steve wanted to savor the moment and spend as much time in each other's company as possible. Though all the lights upstairs were off, the room was illuminated by moonlight which spilled in through the windows in streams.

Kate and Steve gazed at each other and liked how they looked with the pale white against the black. It was truly symbolic. This was clearly one of the best moments of Kate's life, and she knew that Steve felt the same way, too.

Kate was on the verge of sleep; she was struggling to keep her eyes open.

Steve turned over and placed his arm around her side. "My love," he said, "you were absolutely wonderful."

Kate smiled and stretched her limbs, trying to get herself to stay awake.

"You were quite good yourself," she said, knowing that it was a complete understatement. Steve was absolutely the best. She'd never felt this way with anyone before, and she was glad to be in the company of the love of her life.

"No," Kate said, correcting herself. "You were not simply 'good,' you are *everything* that I look for in a man. And even though it took me a little time to realize it, I am very happy that I am with you."

Steve smiled. Clearly, Kate's speech touched him, as he could tell that her words were sincere.

"Come here, you," Steve said, embracing Kate through the sheets.

He then rolled over and turned on the lamp. Steve looked at the time on the alarm clock.

"It's not even midnight yet," he said. "Russell won't be back with Gloria for another hour…"

Kate did not even have to second-guess what Steve had on his mind. She smiled, blushing.

"I would love to," she said. "That is, if my body can handle all that again." Kate untangled herself from the sheets.

Steve kissed her, and the two of them fully expressed their love for each other a second time.

Chapter 15

"Are you sure that your parents want to have me over *tonight?*" Gloria asked, a little apprehensive. Tonight was the night when Russell and his parents arranged to have Gloria over for tea, and she couldn't be more nervous. Just as Russell was last week, roughly nine days ago, Gloria could feel herself quiver with both fear and anticipation.

"Yes," Russell said, sounding absolutely insistent. "Tonight has to be the night; me mum and sis are in the kitchen right now getting everything ready."

Gloria felt herself getting more nervous by the minute. It took every ounce of self-control in her body not to pace around the room.

"Gloria?" Russell asked, after having heard her say nothing for a few seconds.

"I'm here," Gloria said, still not waiting to leave the house tonight. She told Russell that she wanted him to come by and pick her up because she felt like she was too nervous to drive.

"All right," Russell finally said. "I'll do it on one condition."

"What's that?" Gloria asked with a hint of anticipation in her voice.

"That you don't act this nervous around my family. I've told them all about you, and they like you already. You don't have to worry about a thing."

Gloria smiled. She liked the way that Russell always seemed to have a way to make her feel at ease. She made a mental vow to promise to do just that.

"Okay. I won't be nervous."

"Good," Russell said, "I will be by in a few minutes."

The two of them said their goodbyes, and Gloria hung up the phone. She was relieved at the fact that she did not have to dress up, but she wanted to anyway. She felt like it would make a good impression on his family.

Plus, her parents may object to her going over to meet Russell's family while wearing her "casual attire." Gloria decided to go with a purple dress, which was more casual and comfortable. She figured that would be better than wearing her jeans and an elaborately colored T-shirt.

Gloria had just come downstairs; she was waiting for Russell to come by and pick her up. Stuart and Olivia, who were in the middle of their tea, stopped eating and looked over at their daughter.

"You look lovely, darling," Olivia said, admiring Gloria's choice of clothing.

"Thank you."

"Yes, my dear," Stuart said, nodding his head. "If Russell's family does not think you are absolutely charming and stunning, then it is their loss."

Gloria stopped smiling. How could her father say something like that after Russell reassured her that everything would be all right? Gloria started to feel herself get nervous again, but that stopped as soon as she heard the doorbell ring. She promised Russell that she would not worry about meeting his family for the first time.

Gloria opened the door and let Russell inside. He smiled at Gloria, who looked at little perplexed. Unlike her, he had not dressed up in at all. He was wearing a pair of jeans and a T-shirt.

"Hello, love. You look absolutely beautiful," he said, loud enough for Mr. and Mrs. Cunningham to hear. Russell then leaned in close and whispered in Gloria's ear.

"You do look very nice, but you know you did not have to dress up tonight."

"I know," Gloria whispered back. "I just wanted to make a good first impression."

Russell smiled again.

"You know," he said. "If your parents weren't sitting right in the dining room, I would go upstairs and ask you to change. But we are running a little late as it is."

"But won't you come in and say hello to my folks?"

"For a brief moment," Russell said, trying not to appear at all exasperated, "then we've got to go."

"All right," Gloria said, leading him into the dining room.

"Hello, Olivia," Russell said to Gloria's mother.

"Hello, dear," Olivia said. "I think it's so nice that you are going to take Gloria home to meet your family tonight."

"Well," Russell replied, "they are certainly glad to have her." Russell then looked over in the direction of Stuart, who looked neither amused nor bemused.

He simply sat there, looking at Russell's attire.

"Hello, Stuart," Russell said, doing his best to found formal and polite. "It's a pleasure to see you again, sir."

"Hello, Russell," Stuart replied. "I trust that you will have Gloria home after tea tonight."

"You can count on it, sir," Russell said, "and she will have a lovely time with my family."

"One can only hope," Stuart replied in a neutral tone, no one really knowing exactly what he'd meant by his comment.

After Gloria and Russell bid Mr. and Mrs. Cunningham goodbye, they got into the car and drove to Russell's parents' house. And while Gloria did feel nervous during the car ride, she did her best not to let it show. Russell did not even seem to notice.

As soon as they arrived at the house, Mrs. Stokes opened the door. She must have been waiting for them in the foyer.

Russell took Gloria by the hand and led her to the threshold.

"Hello, Mum!" Russell said as soon as he had crossed the threshold.

"Hello, Son!" she said, kissing his cheek. "It's so great to see you. It's been such a long time."

Both Russell and his mother laughed at the joke. Both of them knew it had only been a little over a week.

"And this must be Gloria," Mrs. Stokes said, looking at Gloria in her purple dress. "My, isn't she lovely?" She then gave Gloria a hug and a kiss on the cheek.

Mrs. Stokes was a tall woman with dark, brown hair and a pale complexion, which was further emphasized by her dark, red lipstick. She wore a flowered dress with black high heels. Gloria found her to be a glamorous woman.

"I'm Julia, Russell's mother. You don't know what a pleasure it is to *finally* meet you. I've kept telling Russell that he needed to bring you by sometime."

Russell looked at his mother and rolled her eyes.

"Mum," he said, "you know that I've been busy with the band. We've had a lot of shows lately."

"Well," Julia said, "what matters now is the fact that we finally get to meet this lovely young lady."

Russell and Gloria were lead into the kitchen, where Mr. Stokes and Russell's sister were already seated at the table.

Upon their arrival, Mr. Stokes got up out of his chair.

"Well, hello, Son," he said, going over to embrace Russell. "And who do we have here? Is this Gloria?" he asked, acknowledging Gloria's presence.

"Hello, sir," Gloria said, greeting him with her best manners.

"Hello, love. You can call me Roger," he said. "No need to be so formal, eh?" Roger winked at his son.

Roger was an older gentleman, a bit portly in the middle. His hair was balding, but he had a very handsome face. Gloria could now see where Russell got his looks. He seemed like the easygoing type, which made Gloria relax even more.

"That's what I've been trying to tell her," Russell said, putting his arm around Gloria's waist.

"Hello," Russell's sister said as she rose from her chair, "I'm Cynthia. It's nice to meet you."

Cynthia had blonde hair, which was similar to Kate's. Like her mother, she was pale, though not quite as tall. Both women were a contrast to Roger and his tan skin.

"Likewise," Gloria replied.

Russell then drew her close and placed a reassuring kiss on her forehead, as if to say to her, *See, there was nothing you had to fear in the first place.*

The family sat down to a nice tea, consisting of chicken finger sandwiches, salad, soup, Earl Gray tea, and buttered scones.

Gloria made sure to compliment Mrs. Stokes about the food that she had prepared. She also contributed to the conversation and laughed at any jokes that anyone told.

Everyone was enjoying their food and talking about most any subject that was raised.

Gloria had mentioned that Kate was dating Steve, which seemed to generate some interest around the table, especially when Gloria told them that Kate was American.

Mr. and Mrs. Stokes thought that Russell and Steve should bring her over to meet them sometime.

Gloria said that she would have to arrange that.

The entire evening was going exceedingly well, except that Gloria had noticed something. Russell's little sister remained quiet throughout most of the meal.

Cynthia was twenty years old, and she still lived with Mr. and Mrs. Stokes. Russell would later explain on the car ride back to the Cunninghams' that Cynthia has always been shy and that she should not take it personally.

Once the actual meal was complete, Julia brought out a lemon meringue pie which she had made earlier.

Once everyone had a slice with another cup of tea, the evening's festivities started to die down.

Before anyone knew it, it was time for Gloria and Russell to say goodbye. Though Russell would have liked to take Gloria out after tea, he was a man of his word, so he delivered Gloria straight home.

***

After greeting her parents and briefly telling them about her evening, she went upstairs to talk to Kate. When Gloria knocked on

Kate's door, she put down her copy of *Alice in Wonderland*, which she hadn't read since she was a child.

Kate invited her cousin into her room and informed her that she took the opportunity to call her parents while she was gone. Kate talked to her father longer this time, but the majority of the conversation was shared between she and her mother.

Gloria was very anxious and excited to tell Kate about her evening, which she did in great detail.

The two of them had talked for hours that night about Russell's family.

Gloria was perfectly content, since she got on very well with the Stokes. She now felt that their relationship was cemented and that nothing could keep them apart.

After the long and detailed conversation was finished, Gloria and Kate bid each other goodnight and went to bed.

Chapter 16

The following Friday night, the boys were playing another show in a rougher part of town. Both girls were eager to see their men perform on stage again, as it had been a little while between shows.

The Peppermint Eyes were happy because this was a higher paying gig. The band would be offered £450, which was a lot for only one show.

Since Steve was the one who was primarily in charge of managing the band's finances, he hoped that the boys would be reasonable with their purchases. So far that he knew, Russell had been doing well by not spending much of his share lately.

Kate and Gloria stood outside the pub, talking to some local girls who were acquaintances of Gloria. They were all fascinated with Kate and seemed to adore her accent.

Once Russell made the announcement that the band was getting ready to perform, Gloria and her friends headed inside, thus leaving Kate alone to soak up the atmosphere. She was just standing there, observing all kinds of people who went into and came out of the pub. As usual, Kate became lost in her own, little world until something brought her back into reality.

" 'Ello, miss," a gruff voice said from behind her.

Kate turned and looked into the face of a heavyset man. He looked a little disheveled, as he had not shaved, and his clothes were dirty. He also looked like he could use a bath.

"Hello," Kate said apprehensively. She felt a little leery of this man, and she would rather he go away and leave her alone.

"My, aren't you a bit of all right?" he said, eyeing her legs and cleavage. He licked his lips. "Where are you from?"

Kate, feeling suddenly very uneasy, decided not to talk to this man anymore.

"Excuse me," she said, deliberately avoiding his question.

The man's face formed a frown as Kate tried to turn and walk away from him.

"Where do you think you're going, my lovely?" he said, gripping her arm.

"I'm going back inside," Kate said, clearly indicating she was disgusted by his manner.

"I don't think so," he said licking his lips again. He took his hand and placed it firmly on her rump, giving it a squeeze.

"Hmm, I like the way that feels."

"Well, I don't!" Kate shouted, trying to free herself from his grip. As Kate struggled, another man nearby approached the two of them.

"Excuse me, mate," he addressed the man, "but is there any problem here?"

The man sneered and let go of Kate's arm. He then looked around and determined that there were far too many people outside to create any kind of scene.

"No problem at all," he said, straightening his collar and walking away.

"Thank you," Kate said to the kind stranger before heading inside the pub. She decided that she would not even leave the building without Steve.

This area was much too different from the pubs back home. Kate was relieved that the show would start soon and that she and Gloria could sit close to the stage.

The show was spectacular, and the band gave their best performance yet. The two girls were in their usual place, right in the front row, cheering them on as they played.

Kate looked intently at Steve, and she was really happy knowing that he was hers. She'd proudly told people that she'd slept with the guitarist and lead singer of the band, and she hoped she would get the opportunity to many more times. It was worth it to see the amused looks on their faces.

She and Steve had not seen each other since Monday night when Russell had brought Gloria back home, so tonight, she was prepared to spend every minute possible she could with him both before and after the show.

As soon as the show had ended, the band had gone backstage and allowed themselves a few minutes of rest and relaxation before rejoining the public.

Everyone was having a good time drinking and talking until Kate saw a familiar face.

"Oh, my God!" she exclaimed, not believing what she was seeing. "Steve, we have to get out of here!"

Steve could see the amount of panic in Kate's eyes, and he knew that whatever she was looking at was enough to cause her a great amount of distress.

She started to make a run for the door, but Steve caught her in his strong arms.

"What's wrong, babe?"

"It's him!" she exclaimed in a frightened voice.

"Who?" Steve asked with a great sense of urgency in his voice.

"That crazy man who tried to accost me outside," Kate said, barely above a whisper. Kate had told this to Steve and Gloria briefly before the show, but the only reason she did so was because they had both asked her why she stayed outside for so long.

Steve looked over at the disheveled man, who was heading over in their direction.

Kate saw that the man was coming closer, and she tried to move behind Steve in order to hide herself.

Steve stopped Kate simply by putting his arm around her. She did not have to hide behind Steve in order for him to protect her. There was no way that Steve would let this man get to her again.

The man stopped a mere few inches away from Steve's face. It was Ox! There was no mistake about it. Even though his appearance seemed to have gotten worse over the last seven months, Steve still recognized him right away. He had gained some weight, which Steve hardly thought possible, given that he was so large before. Also, his hair was a little bit longer and more unkempt.

Ox approached Steve and was only inches away from his face. He did not say anything at first.

Steve could tell that he was inebriated, not only because he saw him wobble on his feet, but also because he could smell it on his breath.

Ox didn't even seem to recognize Steve. He then turned his attention to Kate, who stood quivering into Steve's chest, clearly afraid of what he would try to do to her.

" 'Ello, mate," he said to Steve.

Steve acknowledged Ox in no other way buy by looking him square in the eyes, anger brimming from right behind them.

"Could I trouble you for a second?" The man spoke up again. This comment did not elicit any verbal response from Steve. "I see that nice piece of arse you have standing next to you."

Steve could feel the blood rising in his veins.

"That 'nice piece of arse,' as you call her, happens to be my girlfriend!"

Ox smiled and started laughing through his teeth.

"Well, is she, now?" he asked, reaching over and placing his hand on Kate's trembling back. "Just as long as she isn't your missus, I suppose it would be all right."

"What?" Steve asked, inches away from Ox's face.

Kate finally gained the courage to stand up straight next to Steve. She knew that there was no way that Steve was going to let him touch her again.

"That means we can come to some kind of arrangement, can't we?" The man then looked over at Kate, not seeming to realize that she was the girl he'd accosted outside earlier.

"What do you say to that, my lovely? Your old man might be willing to share." He smiled his greasy smile again and put his hand on her face.

Kate turned away, completely disgusted.

"You bastard! Don't you dare touch her again!" Steve exclaimed.

Ox ignored Steve and pulled Kate in toward him. He kissed her on the mouth, while she struggled to push him away.

Kate broke the kiss, and Ox frowned.

"Oh, come on now, don't be that way. You know you want a little piece of meat from me." He reached out his hand to touch Kate again, but Steve caught his wrist and started to bend it backward.

Ox cried out in pain.

"Ow!" he groaned. "Let go of me wrist."

Steve gripped Ox even tighter, causing him to cry out in pain again.

"You're asking for it now, matey!" Ox said, enraged.

Steve let go of his wrist, and the man charged forward, nearly knocking him to the floor. Steve, however, managed to stand his ground.

"You fucking bastard! Stay away from my woman, or I'll kick your arse to the curb!"

"Oh-ho," Ox retorted. "If it's a fight you want, then it's a fight you'll get!" The man pushed Steve again, and this time, he fell to the ground.

Steve got up and charged Ox, just like he had when they fought over Sherry.

"You sorry piece of shit!" Steve exclaimed. "Was Sherry not enough for you? Now you have to come in here and try to take my Kate? Well, you are *not* going to take her away from me!"

Steve hesitated while Ox formed a confused look on his face. It was abundantly clear that he really did not know what Steve was talking about.

If Steve picked up on this, he did not seem to show it. All that he seemed to portray was the rage building up inside him.

Meanwhile, everyone watched the fight unwind. While there were some cheers from the more rowdy people in the crowd, Kate looked on nervously, wishing that someone would come to assist Steve.

Steve charged hard into Ox, knocking them both into the ground. Through all the grunting, fists and limbs flew all around the place. Meanwhile, a small crowd had gathered to watch the entire spectacle.

While Steve was a strong man, Ox was a lot bigger. He found it took all the strength in his body to keep up with him.

Kate, in a state of panic, tried kicking Ox in the ribs, but this angered him even more. He grabbed her leg, which caused her to trip and fall. She landed with a thud, and someone helped her up.

Steve saw this, and a surge of anger ran through his body.

Russell and the rest of his band mates rushed to his side. They held the man while Steve delivered the final blow, which rendered him unconscious.

Everyone in the crowd appeared to be speechless, as they had just left the man lying there on the floor.

Of course, with these rough types hanging around at the pub; it seemed that things like this were an everyday occurrence.

As the man started to come to, he was dragged out of the pub and taken out to the side curb. If he tried to come back inside later, one of the bartenders would throw him out again and threaten to call the police if he did not leave immediately.

Kate, still a little disoriented because of what had just occurred, finally snapped herself back into reality.

"Steve!" Kate exclaimed. She immediately rushed to his side. Even though he did not want to let on very much, he was injured. Kate went to inspect him further and noticed that he was bleeding from the head.

"Someone get me a napkin and some ice!" she yelled.

Within seconds, Gloria returned with ice wrapped in several napkins.

Kate began dabbing at the blot of blood on his lower lip.

A man returned with a small baggie of ice, which Kate placed on Steve's head after she had finished wiping away the blood.

"My poor baby," she said, feeling as if his injuries were completely her fault. "How badly does it hurt?"

"My head's all right," Steve said, trying to sit up.

Kate put her arms around Steve's waist, but he winced in pain as she touched his right side. Kate immediately removed her hands.

"It's my ribs that hurt," Steve said, "but at least I made out better than that son of a bitch," he said gesturing to the entrance of the pub.

"What's wrong, mate?" Russell asked, coming to Steve's aid. "Do you need us to take you to hospital?"

"No!" Steve exclaimed. "I think I'll be all right."

He started to pick himself up off the floor. As soon as he was back on his feet, he walked around the room a little, as if to prove a point.

"Yes, Russell" Kate agreed. "We probably should take him to the hospital, just to make sure that nothing is broken."

"Okay, Kate, come off it, now. I don't need to go to any hospital; I'll be all right. See, I'm walking around just fine."

Steve walked around some more. And while he did not limp, one could tell that Steve was still in pain. He touched his right side a few times before he tried heading out the door.

"See, perfectly fine. There is nothing wrong with me, love. I just need to get outside and get some fresh air."

Kate frowned. She did not like the fact that Steve was trying to hide his injuries from her and everyone else in the room.

Just as soon as Steve reached the front door of the pub, Russell seemed to come from out of nowhere and blocked his way.

"No way, mate," he said. "We are taking you to a hospital just to make sure that's nothing's broken."

"No, Russell, I just told Kate that I am fine, so you don't need to worry anymore."

"Like hell," Kate said, rushing to his side. "We need to get you checked out immediately."

"Kate—" Steve said before being interrupted by Russell.

"Listen to your woman, Steve," he said. "We are going to take you to the hospital."

Russell hesitated, urgently looking into the eyes of his best friend. "And if you don't get in the car, right now, so that we can drive you over there, I'm going to thrash you. And, believe me, it will seem like Ox took it easy on you!"

Steve rolled his eyes and groaned.

"Okay," he said, relenting. "You and Kate help me in. Russell, you drive." Steve handed his keys to Russell.

Russell went out into the parking lot and pulled the car around.

Kate walked Steve out the door, holding his left side.

"My left side doesn't hurt, babe," Steve said. "You can let go of me now."

He looked over at Kate and noticed that tears formed in her eyes.

"That's just it, Steve," she said, tears streaming down her cheeks. "I don't want to let go!" She began to cry. "It's because of me that you got hurt; it's because of me that Russell has to drive you to the hospital."

Kate stopped speaking and began quietly sobbing into Steve's chest.

Steve felt a little remorseful for the way he'd been acting. He put his arm around Kate and kissed her on the forehead.

"Darling, I'm sorry," he said putting his arm around her again. "It's just that I hate hospitals. I don't like going into them, and I don't want to leave the pub."

Kate looked into Steve's eyes.

"But you are doing it for me," she said.

"Yes," Steve replied, "and I am doing it for Russell, who said he'd kick my arse if I didn't go."

Kate gently wrapped her arms around Steve and laughed. He looked down at her and smiled.

"Don't worry; it will be all right."

"I know it will, Steve, I just know," she said right before Russell came around.

The two of them helped Steve into the car; they let him lie on his back and stretch across the backseat, which was not an easy task because of Steve's height. He had to arch his shoulders and sit up a little to allow his head to fit.

Russell drove them safely off to the hospital.

***

The next day, things seemed to quiet down a little. Luckily, Steve did not have any broken bones, just the pain in his right side. Also, the small wound on his head did not need any stitches.

Both Russell and Kate were very relieved to hear this news, but they did not want to reprimand him for his action at the pub, especially since they thought his fighting to protect Kate's was a very noble gesture.

Kate was also worried that Steve would not be able to make tomorrow's tea, but he assured her that he would be there with bells on.

The band decided to play their scheduled show for tonight. If the drunken lunatic wanted to show up again, he would have to do so at his own risk because Steve would be willing to fight him again if it came down to it.

The show went very well, but Russell was anxious to get it over with. He decided to tell Gloria and Kate that he wanted to designate a special night for the band members, so they would have to find their own thing to do after the show.

The girls were a little nonplussed by Russell's claim, but they went along with their wishes, anyway. They had met up with Judy at the show, and they decided to spend the evening with her. After Gloria called home to notify her mother of their decision, she and Kate were ready to enjoy their evening.

Judy's father was anxious to meet Kate, but it would have to wait until tomorrow; it was too late for that tonight. Instead, they went to her apartment and listened to records.

Since Kate had never seen Judy's flat, or Steve's for that matter, she didn't quite know what to make of it. The apartment was small with four rooms, one living room, one tiny kitchen, one bedroom, and one even smaller bathroom. It's not that Kate was the condescending type, but she had not seen a building this small before. Even her dorm room at NYU seemed a little bigger than this.

The overall condition of the flat was nice, though, as Judy seemed to keep everything in order. After a while of looking around, Kate thought the place was actually cute. She began to see why Judy would like a place to herself, especially since she got to make her own rules. Since Kate had never lived alone, that was a freedom she did not have the privilege of knowing.

The three of them began talking, and Judy offered them some drinks.

While Gloria easily accepted a margarita, Kate was a little reticent to touch alcohol. Though she had imbibed so a few times since she was in London, drinking reminded her of her days with Fred, and those were memories she did not want to have.

With Gloria and Judy egging her on, however, Kate felt that she needed a little something to drink.

Judy handed her a glass of ale. When she insisted that Kate and Gloria spend the night with her, Gloria said that she would need to phone her parents to let her know about her plans.

Mrs. Cunningham thanked Gloria for informing her, and she told the girls to have a nice evening.

The three girls spent the night listening to *Led Zeppelin I*, which was the first "real" rock 'n' roll that Kate had heard outside of The Peppermint Eyes' music. After hearing the song "I Can't Quit You Baby," Kate was convinced that she liked Led Zeppelin.

***

The next morning, Gloria was the first to rise.

Judy had offered them some nightclothes, which they accepted but promptly removed once they discovered how hot it was underneath the blankets.

Gloria put on one of Judy's long T-shirts, walked into the living room, and looked at the small clock that sat on top of the television set.

"11:35," she said. "We sure did sleep in late."

She looked around for either Kate or Gloria. She did not see them stirring, so she assumed that they were both still asleep. Gloria tiptoed back into the bedroom. She had to wake Kate so they could get dressed and head home.

"Kate," she whispered to her sleeping cousin.

"Mmmm," Kate mumbled, as she turned over on her side.

Gloria watched her remain still for a moment before trying to wake her again.

"Kate!" Gloria hissed, shaking her by the shoulder.

Kate opened her eyes, which were still heavy with sleep. She glared angrily at her cousin.

"It's time for us to go. It's nearly noon, and we need to get home before lunch."

Kate rolled her eyes then groaned.

"What, do we have a curfew now?"

"No," Gloria said. "We just need to get out of here before Judy throws us out. We don't want to seem like we are im—" Gloria's sentence was cut short with the sound of a flushing toilet and running water.

Seconds later, Judy emerged from the bathroom.

"Good morning, girls," Judy said. "Have a good sleep, did we?"

"Yes, I slept like a rock!" Gloria exclaimed.

"And you, Kate?"

"I slept fine," Kate replied. "I just still feel like I didn't get as much as I am used to."

"Yeah," Gloria replied, winking at Judy. "It seems like you got a lot *more* of something else than you're used to."

Kate jokingly stuck her tongue out at Gloria. Why did she have to drink so much?

"Well," Gloria said. "Thanks for a lovely evening, Judy, now we know how you really feel about Geoffrey Stevenson."

"Shut up!" Judy said, lightly slapping Gloria on the shoulder. "You know that he is far too young for me!"

"He is not," Gloria replied. "In fact, I overheard him talking to Steve one night about how he wished that the two of you would get together."

Judy raised her eyebrows. Now she felt like Gloria was toying with her.

"When did he say this? I don't believe a word of it!"

"Guys," Kate said, putting on her nightshirt. She had remained silent during this entire awkward conversation. "I hate to interrupt, but Gloria thinks that we should be going."

"Oh, right," Gloria said, coming back into reality. "Yeah, Judy, we don't want to impose anymore. We don't want to take up your time on your day off."

"Nonsense!" Judy said. "I told you that me dad wanted to meet you and Kate. I could phone him right now and tell him that he should expect three more for lunch." Judy went over to her phone and started dialing her father's number. It started to ring.

"Of course," she said, putting the earpiece to her chest. "You girls should really get dressed first. If my father saw the two of you like you are now, he would probably have a heart attack."

Gloria and Kate laughed. During their conversation, they had completely forgotten that they were still nude underneath the nightshirts. The two of them went back to the bedroom to put on their clothes.

Judy's father had lived so close by that it was almost unnecessary to drive over there. Still, Judy liked to show off her car. It was a used model, but it was still nice enough to make people in the neighborhood admire it.

***

All three women arrived at Mr. Spellman's house and knocked on the door. There was the sound of footsteps; the door opened, and they were greeted by the face of a kindly, old man.

"Hello m' dear," Archibald said, kissing his daughter on the cheek. "It's nice of you to stop by and visit your old father."

Judy laughed. This statement was clearly a joke because Judy had stopped by at least five times every fortnight.

"And these are your friends," Archibald said, transfixed by both Gloria and Kate.

"Yes, Dad," Judy said. "I am very pleased to introduce to you Gloria Cunningham."

"Hello, sir," Gloria said, giving Archibald a big smile.

"Hello, young lady," he replied, taking Gloria's hand and placing it to his lips. "It's a pleasure to finally meet you. Judy has told me so much."

"And this is Kate Richards. She is the American woman who so graciously gave me the ten dollars."

"Ah," Archibald said, "so this is the other lovely young woman who wandered into your store." He took Kate's hand and kissed it. "What a pleasure to finally meet *you* as well. I want to thank you for the ten dollars. As Judy may have mentioned, Kate, I am collector of money worldwide, and your contribution had made a fine addition to my collection."

Kate smiled. She was glad that her contribution made Mr. Spellman so happy.

Lunch had gone well, and the four of them talked about many things. When Archibald learned about Kate's love of literature, he promptly showed her his library, where most of his books were housed.

Kate was impressed with his vast collection. She could never remember a time when she had seen so many books in one person's room. Although, she did feel proud that she had read a great deal of them.

After more pleasant conversation, however, Gloria and Kate made the announcement that they had to leave. The Cunninghams would probably want them to return shortly.

"Let me give you a ride back to my place," Judy offered, no doubt eager to show off her car once again.

"We can walk; we'll be okay," Gloria said. Since she had her purse and car keys, and there was nothing left in Judy's flat that belonged to either of them, Gloria had felt that there was no need.

"Besides, this will give you more time to spend with your dad."

"Okay," Gloria said. She certainly did not mind spending more time with her father. Judy got up to hug Gloria and Kate.

"Well, I will see you girls later, eh?" Judy said. "We will have to get together again sometime soon."

After both girls had bid farewell to Mr. Spellman and extended their thanks to both he and Judy, they departed.

It only took them a few minutes to walk back to Gloria's car. Gloria and Kate had driven home, completely unaware of the excitement which was about to unfold.

Chapter 17

"Sir, there is a serious matter I would like to discuss with you," Russell said in an almost pleading tone.

"And what is that, my boy?" Stuart asked, feeling like he knew what Russell had on his mind.

"Well, I've known Gloria only for a short time, but in all the time I've been with her, I feel that she is the one for me."

"I see," Stuart replied, still showing no emotion.

Gloria had brought Russell around several times in the last few weeks, and each visit brought more promise. While it took her father a little time to warm up to him, both Gloria and Russell noted how his behavior toward the whole relationship improved. And though Stuart and Russell were clearly not best friends, one could easily see that Stuart was growing a little fond of the young man.

"Well, sir, to be quite frank, I have come here today to ask your permission for Gloria's hand in marriage."

Stuart raised his eyebrows and leaned back in his chair. Russell had really done himself up for the occasion. He'd dressed up in the same blue suit he had worn to their house the first time he was invited to tea. He was also clean-shaven, and he'd had his hair trimmed. Stuart smiled a little. He was clearly impressed with all the effort Russell had put into his presentation.

"And you thought that by coming here that I would willfully give you consent to marry my daughter?"

"Yes, sir," Russell replied, hoping and praying that Stuart would do just that.

"Well, what if you don't have my permission?" Stuart asked, sitting up in his chair.

Russell froze. He knew that Stuart was putting him on the spot somehow, but he knew exactly what he wanted to say to him. Russell was determined to have Gloria one way or another, and nothing was going to stop him.

"It wouldn't matter," Russell replied in a firm tone.

"What was that?" Stuart asked, eyebrows raised.

"It wouldn't matter," Russell said, repeating himself. "It wouldn't matter because I am determined to marry Gloria, and I am not going to let anyone, or anything, stand in my way." Russell paused, looking Stuart square in the eyes.

"And if you do not approve, then Gloria and I will still go ahead with our plans, somehow. And you cannot stop us, no matter how hard you may try. My love for your daughter is deeper than any ocean; it can reach beyond any plane of existence. Surely, if two people are in love as much as we, then that will lead us through any obstacle."

Russell couldn't believe what he'd just said. It's not that he'd doubted his own bravery, but he was not really the poetic type. Usually, that was Steve's department.

After having heard all this, Stuart said nothing.

Seconds had passed, which discouraged Russell, as he was at a complete loss for words. In his mind, he was just about to give up hope, when he saw a smile form on Stuart's lips.

"Well said, my boy," Stuart proclaimed.

"Sir?" Russell asked, a little confused.

"You said that your love for Gloria would clear any obstacles in your way."

Russell nodded his head, still wearing the same confused expression on his face.

"Well, that was the answer I wanted to hear," Stuart further explained. "I admire you coming first to ask my permission to propose to Gloria, but that was really not important. What is important is that you proclaimed your love for my daughter, and you were determined to let nothing get in your way, not even me.

"It takes a great man to be kind and polite and follow all the rules presented in this life, but takes a greater man to be dedicated to something so passionately that he would let nothing stand in his way. I know that you will make a great life for my daughter, and I feel that she is lucky to have you. And if you love Gloria just as much as her mother and I, and I know you do, then she will want for nothing."

Russell stared at Stuart, open-mouthed and incredulous. He couldn't believe what he was hearing. The great Stuart Cunningham was giving Russell *permission* to marry *his* daughter!

And just when I thought he had a huge bug up his arse, Russell thought, happy to renounce that claim. He had gotten up out of his chair and went over to Stuart.

The two men shook hands, and Stuart clapped him on the back.

"Now, all I ask of you is one thing," Stuart said.

"Anything!" Russell replied.

"Wait until tomorrow to pop the question to Gloria. I think it would do well to gather the family together for tea, don't you? As soon as the girls get home, I will talk to Kate about this as well; I know that my niece is good at keeping secrets. We had originally had it in mind to invite your friend over for tea tonight, but we will put off the whole thing until tomorrow so we can all celebrate together, don't you think?"

"Yes, sir," Russell replied. "I think that would be a wonderful idea."

Stuart smiled. Though he did not care much for Russell before, Stuart found him to be an easy-going and polite fellow. Russell had certainly grown on him, especially since he saw Gloria's reaction every time someone had mentioned his name. It was amazing how much things had changed in a mere matter of weeks.

"Good lad," Stuart said. "Anyway, I will keep it a secret from Gloria, so all you have to do is show up looking your best."

"Absolutely!" Russell replied.

He still couldn't believe that he has his future father-in-law's consent! The first thing he would do once he got home was tell his mates all about it. Then, they would probably head over to the pub across the street and celebrate. Of course, they would have to take it easy on the alcohol, as difficult as that could be sometimes, but Russell and Steve could not show up all hung over to tea.

***

After tea, however, was an entirely different story. It had not even been five minutes since Russell left when Gloria and Kate returned home. Though they wanted to hurry upstairs and change their clothes, Olivia was waiting inside the kitchen to talk to them.

After the girls talked about their night at Gloria's, leaving out all the details about listening to Led Zeppelin while getting drunk, Olivia told the girls to go ahead and change for tea.

Gloria headed upstairs to her room. When Kate tried to leave, however, Olivia caught her by her arm. She told her all about Russell's plans to propose to Gloria tomorrow.

Kate was tempted to squeal in delight, but she held back because she didn't want Gloria to hear.

When all the initial excitement of the talk was over, Olivia told Kate to go upstairs to phone Steve and let him know that tea had been postponed until tomorrow. Kate was happy to oblige. She went up to her room and immediately closed and locked the door. Kate dialed Steve's number, and he answered on the first ring.

"Hello," Steve said.

"It's me," Kate replied, virtually whispering into the phone.

"Hey, babe," Steve said. "Why are you whispering?"

"Because I need to tell you something, but I don't want Gloria to hear me."

"I already know," Steve said excitedly. "Russell's going to propose to Gloria; isn't that great?"

"Yes!" Kate said dreamily. "It's wonderful." Kate paused, thinking about how happy Gloria was going to be come tomorrow evening. "Well, I figured you already knew, but I wanted to call and give you a heads up. It wouldn't do to have you show up for tea tonight if it's just going to be the five of us."

Steve laughed. While he was eager to meet the family, he felt he needed one more night to wrap his mind around the concept.

"Okay, darling. Russell is coming into the room now. I swear, I don't think I've ever seen him this happy. The boys and we are going over to the pub soon."

Kate laughed.

"Well, don't drink too much!" Kate joked, but with a hint of concern in her voice.

"Okay," Steve replied, "but don't you go hanging about in your knickers getting drunk while listening to Led Zeppelin records."

Kate stared at the phone, open-mouthed. "How did you…" she asked, not completing her sentence.

"Judy is here with us; she ran into Rus and the boys earlier outside."

"Oh, that explains it," Kate said with a giggle.

"Yeah," Steve replied. "Good thing there were no men in the flat with you. I would have to smash open their heads because they saw my woman dressed like that."

Though Kate knew that he was only joking, there was a hint of truth in his statement. She loved how Steve had become so protective of her. It made her feel secure.

"Well, on that note," Kate said. "I think I will go. I've got to get changed then go downstairs to help Auntie Olivia and Gloria prepare a boring tea."

"Don't have too much fun," Steve said jokingly. "You need to leave some over for tomorrow evening."

"Will do," Kate said. "See you tomorrow night."

"Until then, love," Steve replied before hanging up the phone.

***

Gloria was absolutely beaming. Today, they were going to have Russell over for tea again. Steve would also be joining them as well. The only bad thing was that Uncle James and Aunt Lois would also be there, and they were bringing the twins.

Gloria had not seen her cousins since they were there nearly two months ago. She had not forgotten about the things they'd said about Kate, and she would not let them forget if they even thought of turning the conversation into something ugly like that again.

"Mum, please let me help you," Gloria protested. "You've been going back and forth, doing all this work in the kitchen and dining room. Please stop, or I'm going to get dizzy."

Olivia laughed. She was clearly not worried about herself. "It's you who are acting nervous, love," Olivia said. "You've been hanging about and looking over at the front door to see if anyone's come yet."

"I am just so excited, Mum. Steve is a gentleman, just like my Russell. I think that you and Dad are going to like him." Gloria hesitated a moment, thinking about how her father had warmed up to Russell in what seemed to be such a short time.

"I mean, the thing that makes me most glad is the fact that Dad is starting to take a liking to Russell."

"All it took was a little time," Olivia said, feeling just as pleased as her daughter. For the duration of their entire conversation, the two women walked back and forth between the kitchen and the dining room, placing various decorations and articles of food onto the table.

Gloria still couldn't get over her busybody mother doing most of the work.

"But why does Kate get to help you and I don't?" Gloria asked, on the verge of pouting like a child.

"Kate only prepared the salad and made the scones," Olivia replied. "And that was only because she *absolutely* insisted that she do something for me."

Kate was currently upstairs, changing her clothes.

"Well, all right then," Gloria said. "But I wanted a chance to make Russell something nice. I know that I'm no great chef, but I want to prepare a nice meal for my man."

Olivia smiled and headed back into the kitchen.

Gloria wasn't absolutely sure, but she could have sworn she'd heard her mother utter the words, *soon enough* under her breath. Besides, Gloria was too nervous to do much of anything, anyway.

The combination of Russell and Steve, with her father's relatives, was almost enough to send her into overdrive.

Gloria paced back and for the between the kitchen and the dining room. The anticipation was enough to make her want to climb the walls. If only Russell and Steve would show up before her dad's relatives.

There was the sound of a car pulling into the driveway, which made Gloria excitedly race to the door. Once she was in the foyer, she checked her reflection in the mirror. She pulled back a few loose strands of hair and tucked them behind her ears. This was it!

Gloria opened the door and was greeted by the smiling face of her Uncle James. Though she was clearly disappointed that it was not Russell and Steve who showed up first, she put on her best face.

"Hello, my dear," James said, kissing his niece on the cheek.

"Hello, Uncle James," she said, artificial smile stretched across her face. "How nice to see you again."

"Yes, my dear, it has been a while," he said making his way inside the house.

"Hello, Auntie," Gloria said, greeting Lois who had followed her husband into the foyer.

"Hello," Lois said in a voice which sounded entirely too saccharine. "My darling, you look absolutely lovely!"

"Thank you," Gloria replied. She had worn yet another nice dress that she retrieved from the back of her closet. And though the garment was extremely uncomfortable, she did not want anyone to hear her complain. After all, poor Russell would have to don his suit again, which he was not looking forward to, no doubt.

Syd and Sebastian came in after their mother. So much for them staying away this time.

"Hello, Syd, Sebastian," Gloria regarded her cousins. Though their actions were polite, she could tell that they would rather be anywhere than there. Gloria, however, wanted to one up her cousins and show them that she could be just as dignified and mature as they.

"Hello, Gloria," each of them had said before placing kisses on her cheek.

"Please, follow me into the dining room," she said once everyone had gathered into the foyer.

Stuart, Olivia, and Kate were all waiting by the dining room entrance, ready to receive their relatives' presence. They all exchanged their mutual greetings, and everyone began to talk, making sure not to mention the proposal.

James Cunningham and his family had already heard the news. Stuart could tell that his brother did not fully approve, despite the fact that he had never met Russell before. However, he was determined to let nothing stand in the way of his daughter's happiness.

Gloria was wondering about the other Cunninghams' suspicions when she heard the doorbell ring again. She formed an excited look on her face. This time, she would not be disappointed.

Kate excused herself from the company and walked to the door with Gloria.

"They're finally here!" Gloria said, bouncing up and down on her heels.

Kate smiled. *My sentiments exactly!* she thought.

Gloria opened the door a second time. She and Kate were greeted by the smiling faces of Steve and Russell, each dressed up in his finest suit, and each carrying a bouquet of a dozen roses.

"Hello, ladies," Russell said. He gave Kate a peck on the cheek. He went over to Gloria and kissed her on the mouth.

"You look absolutely beautiful," Russell said as he got an eyeful of Gloria in her dress.

"Oh, come off it," she said, lightly slapping him on the shoulder. She leaned over and whispered in his ear. "You know how much I hate this dress."

"I know," Russell whispered back. "It's just that seeing you here, in this light, really does something to me." Russell looked deeply into Gloria's eyes. He couldn't believe that his moment was nearly here.

"Of course, you always look beautiful to me." Russell kissed Gloria again and handed her the bouquet.

"Thank you," she replied, on the verge of tears, "so do you." This made both of them snicker, quietly, like two people sharing a private joke.

Russell and Gloria stepped back so Steve could come into the house.

"Steve—" Kate said, almost speechless at seeing him in a suit. Unlike Russell's, his suit was a dark navy blue. It looked like something that the boys back home in Oklahoma used to wear; it looked like something which would actually impress her father.

"I know what you're thinking," Steve said as he laughed. "Don't feel badly, though, because I am going to charm the hell out of everyone here."

Steve leaned over and kissed Kate on the lips. Just as Russell had done for Gloria, he handed her the bouquet of flowers.

Gloria, still bouncing on her heels, wanted to get the dinner progressing. She hoped that her cousins would be on their best behavior today, but she did not expect any miracles, though she had *hoped* for one.

"Shall we?" Gloria asked after a few more seconds of conversation.

"Lead the way, girls," Russell said, extending his hand.

Gloria and Kate strode ahead of the boys, carrying their flowers, like a couple of prom queens. All eyes were on Kate and Gloria once they went into the dining room. Gloria smiled and called attention to the gentlemen who stood by their side.

"Everyone," Gloria said. "This is Russell and Steve."

Both men smiled and addressed the entire family. Introductions were made all around.

Surprisingly, no one on James's side of the family seemed condescending toward the two musicians; Syd and Sebastian were actually very polite, which was enough to arouse some suspicion.

Gloria, however, did not want to be cynical because she liked to believe that her cousins were on their best behavior because they wanted to be.

Olivia wanted to do something special since everyone was gathered together. She and Stuart stood up, making and announcement and leading everyone in prayer.

The entire party bowed their heads and thanked God for this gathering, the food, and each other's company. As soon as everyone said, "amen," they started into the food.

Everyone, with the exception of Gloria, was waiting for the moment when Russell would propose to her.

Kate and Steve seemed to be the most anxious because knew that there would be plenty of celebrations after everything became official.

Russell knew that everyone was waiting with bated breath, but he wanted everything to be perfect. He did not want anything to be done at the wrong moment.

After everyone was well into their meals, Russell noticed that the conversation had waned a little.

Gloria sat beside him, radiant as ever, and completely unaware of what he was about to do.

Russell, having determined that it was finally the right time, turned sideways in his chair so he was facing Gloria. He looked her in the eyes.

"Gloria Rachel Cunningham," he said, getting out of the chair and lowering himself down on one knee. "Will you make me the happiest man alive and become my wife?"

Gloria just sat there, open-mouthed and incredulous. She couldn't believe that this was happening to her, and in front of most of her family! Of course, she did not have to think anything over, for the answer was always going to be "yes." Anyone would be crazy to think otherwise! All the noise around the table seemed to stop, and everyone anxiously awaited Gloria's response.

"Yes!" Gloria exclaimed.

She had been waiting for this day ever since she had fallen in love with Russell. "Yes" was the only word that Gloria managed to say because she was still caught up in the moment, part of her still not believing what had just happened.

She and Russell kissed. The entire party cheered and applauded after Gloria accepted Russell's proposal.

Hugs, kisses, and handshakes were exchanged all around the table.

Everyone seemed genuinely happy with the proposal, which made Gloria feel very secure. She was worried about her father and how those on his side of the family were going to react, but it did not matter in the long run because Gloria would have accepted Russell's proposal, no matter what.

Stuart disappeared into the kitchen and came back out with a bottle of red wine and two wine glasses. He gave them to Russell, who handed one to Gloria. Stuart then went back into the kitchen with Olivia, and they had brought out eight more glasses.

Once everyone was back in their seat, Stuart went around the table and filled each person's glass half full. He then resumed his place at the head of the table and took held his wine glass into the air.

"If I may have everyone's attention," he said, clanging his knife against his glass. Once again, there was silence throughout the room. "I would like now to make a toast."

Stuart looked over at his daughter and gave her a smile. He noticed that she was on the verge of tears, but these were tears of happiness.

"The day when Gloria was born, Olivia and I were the happiest people in the world. We felt very blessed to have such a healthy, happy, and beautiful child."

Tears started streaming down Gloria's cheek, but she managed not to cry out loud.

Russell noticed this and put his arm around her so that she could lean into him.

"Anyway," Stuart resumed, "when my brother, James Cunningham, first heard about the birth about my daughter, he presented us with this bottle of fine red wine, dated 1947. Olivia and I decided to save it, for James had given it to us to mark a special occasion. It was always my intent to save this for the day when I found out that our daughter was going to get married.

"I know today is only the announcement and not the date of Gloria's actual wedding, but I want nothing more than to share the wine with everyone here so that we all may remember this momentous occasion." Stuart lifted his glass, and everyone else did the same.

"To Gloria and Russell; may your love last beyond eternity." Everyone raised their glasses high into the air.

"To Gloria and Russell!" they toasted before taking their first sips of wine.

Once everyone was still and full from their meals and excited by tonight's events, Olivia went back into the kitchen and retrieved a large, two-layer carrot cake that she had made.

Even though everyone was still full from their dinners, they could not resist having a slice of this home-cooked delight.

All in all, the events of the evening were a success, and no one had any reason to complain. Stuart smiled and knew that he made the right choice by giving Russell permission to marry Gloria. He was relieved that he got to know him because it would have been disastrous if he tried to dissolve the relationship because of any disapproval on his part. This way, he knew that his daughter was happy, and despite the fact that Russell was a musician, he knew that he would find a way to make a living so that he could provide for her.

He then thought about his conservative brother-in-law in America, and he knew exactly what he'd say. Stuart did not care, however, because he was the one who was in control of his family, not Isaac.

After tea, everyone departed and went their separate ways. Though Russell and Steve felt like they were in the mood for a celebration, Gloria and Kate said that they wanted to stay home, if only for the fact that they wanted a chance to talk and recover from the events of the evening.

The four of them agreed that they would go out again Saturday night, which would give everyone enough time to spread the news around. There was still more that needed to be done, however, and Steve now knew what he needed to do. It was time that he introduced Kate to his family.

Chapter 18

Since Steve's family were not people who planned ahead very much, he felt that it would be no problem if he brought Kate over the very next day. Mr. and Mrs. Maddington were delighted because they had been waiting such a long time to meet her.

Meanwhile, Olivia and Stuart, who were still delighted over Gloria and Russell's engagement, urged Kate to go over and meet Steve's family. As soon as she received permission from her aunt and uncle, Kate went up and told Steve that she would be attending.

"Stop pacing around the room; you're making *me* nervous!" Gloria said. She was trying to get her cousin to calm down.

Kate was just as nervous as nervous now as Gloria was last week. Kate was terribly worried about what kind of first impression she would make.

"I can't help it!" Kate exclaimed. "I don't know what Steve's family is going to think of me, if they are actually going to like me or not."

"Don't worry," Gloria replied. "Russell's family absolutely adored me, so Steve's family is bound to like you! Trust me."

"I don't know; I haven't met any boyfriend's family in a long time. As you know, Fred did not even take me around to meet his parents." Kate paused, feeling uneasy at just having mentioned Fred. "I had a few boyfriends during high school, but they were nothing serious.

Joseph, my date to the senior prom, had brought me home to meet his family. They were very nice people, but I did not feel very comfortable around them. It's as if they were scrutinizing my every move. They probably thought I was not good future wife material for their son."

Gloria went over to Kate and put her arm around her shoulder.

"But you've gotta remember, m'dear, you are not in conservative, old Oklahoma anymore. If Steve's parents are anything like Russell's, then they are going to *love* you." Gloria removed her arm then patted Kate's shoulder.

Kate took paced nervously over to her closet.

"You don't have to make me reiterate the same thing over and over again, do you?"

"But what am I going to wear?" Kate asked, seemingly frustrated.

"Katie, you know that Steve's folks are very casual people; he even told you so himself."

"Yes, but—" Kate started to say.

"But nothing," Gloria replied. "You are going to go into your closet and find something comfortable to wear. Just put on a pair of blue jeans and a nice shirt." Gloria gave her cousin a gentle push into the closet.

"And if there's nothing in there that you like, just let me know, and I will loan you something of mine."

Kate sighed and started to look through her clothes. She finally settled on a nice purple shirt that she had bought at Judy's. She pulled it out and showed Gloria, looking for her approval.

"Good, that's a start," Gloria said. "Now, go look in your dresser "drawers and find a nice pair of trousers."

Kate did as she was told, while Gloria crossed her arms and waited. Kate threw the clothes down on her bed and looked over at her cousin.

"What?" Gloria asked, thinking she had done something wrong.

"Do you mind leaving the room while I change my clothes?"

"Oh," Gloria replied, looking slightly embarrassed. "Okay, I will be in my room, but as soon as you get into those clothes, you have to come in and show me!"

"All right," Kate replied, resisting the urge to laugh.

Perhaps she really *was* making Gloria nervous. Gloria exited the room, gently closing the door behind her.

Moments later, Kate appeared in the doorway of Gloria's room.

"So how do I look?" Kate asked.

Gloria looked at her cousin. While the outfit was very casual, it was also very tasteful, in that it was not too tight or revealing.

"Perfect," Gloria replied. "It's very nice, very casual, and there's still something left to the imagination."

Kate looked at her cousin quizzically.

"That means they really can't see your enormous tits."

"Gloria!" Kate exclaimed.

"Well, it's the truth. And besides, Steve would be proud of how beautiful, yet modest, you look." "You really think so?"

"I know so. Now, go on downstairs because he will be here any minute."

"Okay," Kate said. She actually seemed to be getting less nervous by the minute. Leave it Gloria to always know how to make her laugh.

Kate made her way downstairs and saw that Aunt Olivia was in the kitchen preparing tea. She offered to assist her, but her aunt declined, stating that she should just sit there and wait for Steve. This was her big night.

Moments later, the doorbell rang.

Kate fidgeted for a second then answered the door. Steve stood there wearing a sexy smile. Kate could tell that he was really excited that he was finally going to introduce her to his family.

"Hello, my love," he said, leaning over to give Kate a kiss. The two of them embraced.

"Oh, Steve," Kate replied, still hugging Steve and not wanting to let go. "It feels so good being in your arms." While Kate was doing her best to hide her emotions, Steve could still tell that Kate had reservations.

"Don't tell me that you're nervous," Steve said.

"Well, just a little." Steve made a little grumbling noise, feigning exasperation.

"Oh, Kate, you're such a silly girl," Steve said, letting go of her. "I've already told you that you don't have to worry about me folks. They are going to love you; just give them a chance."

Kate did not say anything, but she gave Steve another hug. She wanted to feel the warmth of his arms one more time before they left.

After Steve and Kate bid farewell to Olivia and Stuart, they headed out to his car.

While the two of them drove to Steve's parents' house, which was about a half hour away, Kate quizzed him on such things, like if she wore the wrong clothes and how she should act.

Steve listened to her, but he had a hard time keeping a straight face. He knew that she was being far too worried. It took at least half of the car ride there to assure her that everything was going to be all right.

Once they arrived at the Maddingtons', the two of them got out of the car. They headed to the front door, hand in hand.

"Now, remember," Steve said. "If you even so much as *think* a nervous thought, I am going to give you a big old kiss right in front of my family."

Kate laughed. She knew that Steve was only teasing her to make her feel at ease.

"I'm serious," Steve continued, placing his hand on her rump. "And I won't stop at kissing; if I have to take you up to my old room and make love to you so everyone can hear, then I will do it."

Kate laughed again. "Now you're the one who's being silly."

Steve smiled and placed a small kiss on her lips.

"Yes, but you know you love it."

Kate blushed then smiled.

Steve rang the doorbell and waited for someone to answer. He took Kate by the hand, trying to ease her nerves one last time. Seconds later, the front door opened. The two of them came face to face with Steve's mother.

"Hello, love!" she exclaimed, gathering in Steve for a quick hug and kiss.

"Hello, Mum," he said, parting the embrace. "Thank you so much for allowing us to come over tonight."

"It's not a problem, my dear. You know how much we've been wanting to meet Kate."

"And here she is," Steve replied, putting his hand on Kate's back.

She took a shy step forward to greet Mrs. Maddington. Steve's mother took a good look at Kate. She put her hands on her face and squealed out of delight.

Kate was actually used to people in England making over her so much, so she tried not to think much of it.

"Oh, and you must be Kate," Mrs. Maddington said with great enthusiasm in her voice.

"Yes, ma'am. It's lovely to meet you."

"And it's such a pleasure to meet you, too, my dear."

She leaned over to give Kate a hug. Once the embrace was over, Mrs. Maddington kissed Kate once on each cheek. That part she was not used to, as it seemed like something Europeans did very often.

"As you know, I'm Mrs. Maddintgon, Steve's mum, but you can call me Nancy." Nancy let out a big smile, hoping that Kate was completely at ease.

"Thank you, Nancy. I want to thank you for inviting me into your home."

Nancy smiled again and looked over at Kate. She was a big woman with short brown hair and pale skin. It also seemed that she greatly admired Kate, which both flattered her and puzzled her at the same time.

"Oh," Nancy crooned. "You just have the most adorable accent I've ever heard. What do you call that?"

"Southern," Kate offered, not really sure. She had been hearing people talk with those accents all her life, but she had just started getting used to the way people talked in England. She adored Steve's accent, though, because it somehow added to his male swagger and charm.

"Well," Nancy said. "Won't you please both come inside? My husband and Steve's brother are just dying to meet you!"

Steve took Kate's hand again and followed her into the house. As soon as they walked in, they were greeted by two more smiling faces.

Mr. Maddington and Nick, Kate thought. She thought that Mr. Maddington looked like a nice man, though a little older. His grey hair was balding, and his face did have a few wrinkles, but he also had kind, blue eyes. Kate had a good feeling that she was going to get along with this man.

Nick, just like Steve, looked nothing like his parents. He looked like a slightly younger version of Steve, which needless to say, meant that he was also very handsome.

"Hello, hello," Mr. Maddington said, coming in to embrace his son. "Good to see you again, mate!" Mr. Maddington released Steve then looked over at Kate.

"Well," he said, making his way over to Kate. "This must be the young lady you've been telling us all about." He then said to Kate, "Hello, my dear. It's wonderful to meet you!"

"Hello, sir," Kate said. "It's such a pleasure to meet you, too. Thank you for agreeing to have me over for tea."

"It's our pleasure," Mr. Maddington replied with a smile. "And, please, call me David."

"Thank you, David," Kate said. "I am very happy to be welcomed into your home."

As soon as David took the opportunity to greet Kate just as Nancy had, with kisses on each cheek, she felt completely at ease. She knew that she had worried all for nothing.

Nick went over to introduce himself to Kate. "Hello," he said. "I'm Nicholas, Steve's brother."

Nick took her hand and kissed it. She could tell, like Steve, that he, too, was a charmer. "Steve has told us a lot about you, but he never said you were this beautiful."

"Thank you," Kate replied, taking a compliment which would have made her feel uneasy merely a few months ago.

"Now, watch it, Brother," Steve said. "This here is my woman." Steve put his arm around Kate's shoulder. "You'd better not try to make any moves on her."

Steve and Nick both laughed, like they were sharing some kind of private joke.

Kate smiled along with them. Though Kate knew that Steve was only teasing his brother, she wouldn't be surprised if Steve really *did* have to warn him.

After a few more minutes of pleasant conversation, Nancy directed everyone to the dining room.

"Well, it's best time we eat. We don't want to burden poor Kate with all this chit chat and questions about America. I also don't want the roast get cold."

Roast? Kate thought, as she headed over to the table with Steve.

Sure enough, Nancy had gone all out and prepared pot roast with mashed potatoes and greens. There were also two dishes with scones and rolls, along with some assorted jellies and jams.

Kate was hungry, but she didn't know if she could handle such a meal. The last time she had seen a spread that large was at Christmas with her parents.

"My goodness," Kate remarked as she sat down next to Steve. "This meal certainly looks delicious."

Nancy smiled. "I hope you've brought your appetite."

"Yes," Kate replied. "I am very hungry. I haven't seen a meal like this since Thanksgiving."

"What's Thanksgiving?" Nick asked.

Steve just looked over at his brother, not believing that he'd never heard of the holiday. Of course, no one in his family has ever been to the United States, so part of him understood Nick's "silly" question.

"Thanksgiving is a holiday similar to Christmas," Kate said. "It's a celebration commemorating the time when the Native Americans welcomed the early English settlers to their country. It was the first time they broke bread together.

"The first Thanksgiving was held in 1621 at Plymouth Rock, Massachusetts." Kate paused. "Ironically, Massachusetts is one of the six states that make up New England..." Kate trailed off. She stopped speaking because she was afraid that she was boring the poor family with her "history lesson."

"Really," Nick said. "I didn't know all that."

"That's because you're such a great big git," Steve teased.

"Oh, right," Nick replied. "Come off it, Steve, you didn't know that, either."

Nick was right; Steve had actually *not* known that much about Thanksgiving himself.

"Now, boys, stop it, the both of you!" Nancy said. "Don't talk so much; let the poor girl get something to eat. She's going to need to satiate that appetite of hers if she wants to keep up with us."

Nancy looked over at Kate and winked.

"Right," Steve replied, "like we're that hard to keep up with."

David, Nancy, and Nick all looked at Steve like they could not believe what he was saying.

Then, everyone burst out into laughter, Kate included. She took a piece of pot roast and started carving into the meat.

Nancy smiled as she took her first bite.

Kate was having such a good time around Steve's family. She had complimented Nancy on her food, which seemed to make her feel pleased. Kate also made it a point to eat a lot, because she wanted to show Nancy how much she enjoyed her cooking.

Kate also remembered that she needed to leave some room for dessert. She felt very at ease with Steve's family, probably even more so than with her own parents sometimes.

Kate was happy to know that they had been so accepting of her upon their first meeting. She was also relieved to know that her conversation was not boring them. They all seemed to be fascinated with her life stories and historical facts about America. It was like they were all living vicariously through her.

During some points throughout the evening, it seemed like Steve would just sit there and listen to her talk. He also had the same smitten look in his eyes as he did that first night at the pub.

Kate smiled, contented knowing that she was in good company.

As soon as everyone had their fill of the main course, Nancy had brought out the dessert, which was a beautiful velvet cake with white frosting.

Kate looked at the cake and was glad that she had saved some room for dessert.

"Teatime must be something special for you, especially since you do not have it in America," David said, "so I hear."

"Yes," Kate replied, "but since I've been living here, I have enjoyed it most every night."

"Pretty girl like you must have been over to dinner at a lot of folks' houses," Nick said.

"Not really," Kate said, holding her head down to the table. "I'd only been over to one boy's house during high school, and it seemed like his parents did not like me very much."

"They must have been mad!" David replied. "You are an absolute delight."

Nancy and Nick both nodded their heads, agreeing with the statement.

Steve put his arm around Kate again; she knew that Steve would not beg to differ.

Just as soon as those words were said, Nancy changed the subject.

Kate was relieved they did not talk more about her past relationships, especially since she was just meeting Steve's family for the first time.

She shuddered after thinking about Fred Beaumont. Just the mere mention of his name, by her lips or anyone else's, would have been enough to upset her for the rest of the evening.

But Kate told her mind to forget all about Fred because there was no way that she was going to let anything interfere with her happiness.

Now that she had met Steve's family, everything seemed to fall into place. Kate was extremely pleased with how the evening was progressing, and she could tell that everyone else was having just a good time as she.

But, as the feast and pleasant conversation turned into more than just a few hours' worth, Kate knew the Maddingtons would have to call it an evening soon.

Sure enough, Steve announced that he needed to get Kate back home, which was just a polite way of saying that he was getting tired. Also, he didn't want to overwhelm his poor girlfriend with too much of his family on one night.

That will come at another time, he thought as he drove Kate back home for the evening.

Chapter 19

Steve and Kate decided to meet up with the rest of the gang at the pub. Though they were not scheduled to perform any shows tonight, they decided to stay there anyway so they could continue to celebrate with Russell and Gloria.

Kate was relieved that Steve's family liked her, but that was the very thing which had also made her sad. Her three-month visa was nearly expired, and she would have to return to America shortly. In fact, she only had three weeks left in this wonderful country, but it depressed her to even think about it. Gloria, sensing her cousin's distress, went over to her and put her arm around her shoulder. "What's wrong, Cousin?"

"Nothing," Kate said, looking ahead and sighing.

Gloria knew that there was no truth to that statement.

"Bullshit," she said. "Like I have said to you a million times, I know when something's bothering you."

Kate turned her head away and started so that Gloria would not see her cry, but her attempt was unsuccessful. Soon, Kate was a mass of tears, putting her head down on the table.

Steve heard this and came rushing over to Kate's side. He wore a confused look on his face.

"What's wrong?" he asked Gloria, who had put her arm around Kate.

"I don't know," Gloria replied. "She won't tell me. Here we were having a good time, and all of a sudden, she started bursting out into tears. Maybe you should try to talk to her, Steve."

Steve went over to Kate, whose head was down on the table again. He put his hand on her back and leaned down closer to her.

"What's wrong, babe?" he asked.

Kate looked up; her face splotched from crying. She sniffled and wrapped her arms around Steve. "I love England!" she exclaimed.

"Okay," Steve replied. "I know you do, but I can also tell that something is wrong. Do you need to tell me anything?"

Kate started sobbing even harder. She unburied her face from Steve's side and sat up straight.

"I love England, and I don't want to leave!" she said, looking at both Steve and Gloria. She knew what she had to say, but she didn't want to say it. Her time here was almost over.

"Who says that you have to go anywhere?" Steve asked, not understanding where all this had come from.

Surely, her mother and father had not called Kate and told her that she needed to come home. At least, Steve had not heard anything about that.

"My passport!" Kate exclaimed, looking like she was ready to cry again. "My three-month visa is almost up, and I have to go back to the US soon!"

Steve and Gloria looked at each other. They were both aware of the issue, but had completely forgotten about it in relation to Kate.

Steve tried to put his arm around her again, but she lightly shrugged him off. Steve was somewhat surprised; never before had he seen her this upset. He didn't know quite how to respond, but he felt that he had to find a way to comfort her.

"Don't worry, babe," he said. "We can get around this."

Kate still did not stop crying. He was ready to tell her that he would renounce his British citizenship and go with her to America, but he hoped things would not come to that.

"Don't worry?" Kate asked, sounding a little offended. "How can you say that? This is my life!"

"But—" Steve tried to interject, but Kate cut him off.

"Steve, please," was all she said until she looked into the eyes of her cousin.

Gloria looked genuinely sad for Kate, and it made Kate feel even worse in turn.

"Oh, Gloria," she resumed. "I'm so sorry. This is your night to celebrate. You and Russell should be having a good time, and here I am ruining it for you."

Kate got up out of her chair and started walking to the entrance of the pub.

"Where are you going?" Steve demanded.

"I need to get some air," Kate replied, still walking. "I can't stay in here another moment longer."

Kate had reached the door, opened it, and went outside.

Steve tried to follow her, but Gloria held him back.

"Just give her a moment," Gloria said. "She just needs to be alone for a while. If she doesn't come back in soon, I will go out there and fetch her."

Steve was about to tell Gloria that she was right, but it was at that exact moment that he looked out the window and saw Kate trying to cross the street.

"Dammit, Gloria!" he exclaimed before racing to the door.

Before anyone could say anything to Steve, he was out the door and closing in on Kate.

"Where the hell do you think you're going?" he asked, only a few steps behind her.

"Steve, I'm sorry," she said, now moving faster and not bothering to turn back to look at him. "I just can't. I—" was all she said before making it across to the other side of the street.

Within seconds, Steve had caught up with her and grabbed her by the arm.

Kate tried to struggle, but her efforts were futile.

Now that Steve had her in his grip, there was no way that he was going to let go!

"Steve, please, let go of me!"

"Like hell!" he exclaimed, angry at the fact that Kate tried to run away from him.

"But don't you see?" Kate said, her eyes still full of tears. "Seeing you again would actually make things worse. Steve, I just can't bear it anymore. I can't!"

Steve huffed. Though he could feel his temper rise, he did not want to harm Kate or upset her anymore. Besides, he knew that this wasn't her talking; it was the result of some deep-rooted fear that resided within her. He decided to take a slightly different approach.

"So you want to just give up on us? Do you really want to end it here and now? After I have introduced you to my family, and you introduced me to some of yours?"

"Steve..." was all she managed to say.

He could see the sadness in her eyes, but he could also see something else, pure fear. What had made Kate try to run away like this?

"I just want to say this to you, and I *need* to say it now. I love you, Kate, more than anything in this entire world. Sometimes, I love you so much that it hurts!"

Steve hesitated, looking into Kate's eyes for a second. He could see that there was a fair amount of hurt and confusion, but he attributed it to the fact that she was unsure of herself. Steve knew that he had to find a way to reassure her that everything was going to be all right.

"And having said that," Steve continued, "there is no fucking way that I am going to let you walk out of my life!"

He held Kate tighter and gathered her into his chest, where she began to cry again. Steve began stroking her hair and whispering into her ear.

"I mean it, Kate. I will do everything in my power to keep you here, including marrying you. Whatever it takes, my love."

In an instant, Kate looked up at Steve, not believing what she was hearing.

"You would really do that for me?" she asked, drying her tears with her fingers.

"Yes," Steve whispered into her ear. "My love, I would do anything, anything as long as it would get you to stay with me."

Kate looked up at Steve and saw the sincerity in his eyes. And, for the first time in what seemed like an eternity, as opposed to mere minutes, Kate began to smile. She grabbed just as tightly as he did to her moments ago. Kate had no intention of ever letting him go now.

***

It was Saturday night, and The Peppermint Eyes were getting ready to perform another show at the Banner Alehouse. They were brought back by popular demand. Steve was particularly happy about the news that the band was going to receive a whopping £500 for their performance, which meant 100 quid for each man.

That was not the only thing that Steve had in mind for tonight, however, because he thought of something really special, something which would change his life for the better.

Steve was in the back room, getting ready for the show. Everyone else had already made their way out to the stage, where he would join them shortly. He reached into the pocket of his jeans and pulled out a little box. Inside was a 14K gold diamond ring, on which Steve had spent a fair amount of his savings.

But Kate is worth it, he thought to himself as he made his way out onto the stage.

Steve had clued in Gloria, Russell, Judy, and the rest of his band mates, but he swore each one of them to secrecy. He did not want them to ruin the surprise. Steve, however, knew that his friends and Judy had no problems keeping secrets.

It was Gloria he was worried about. She promised to be good, however, because she did not want to spoil this evening for either Kate or Steve. Why not? It was a special night, indeed. It was not every day that one's cousin and best friend received a marriage proposal from the man that she loved.

Once Steve joined his band mates on the stage, who had already hooked up their equipment, they looked like they were ready to play. Steve was both nervous and excited at the same time, as he knew this was his big moment. Since no one in the audience knew what was going to happen, they, too, were in for a big surprise.

Kate and Gloria took their usual seats upfront.

Judy had joined them a few moments later.

When Kate and Gloria noticed that she was smiling, Gloria had asked her why she was so happy.

Judy sighed and giggled like a schoolgirl. She said that Geoffrey had kissed her earlier backstage. He also told her how much he liked her. Judy did not have to say anything, however, because she was floating on cloud nine. She clearly had the look of love in her eyes.

"All right," Steve said into the microphone. "Welcome to Banner Alehouse; we have a great show lined up for you tonight!"

The crowd cheered. Steve waited for the noise to die down a little. As soon as it did, he started speaking into the microphone again.

"But first, I want to introduce someone very special in my life," he said, looking over at Kate. "This is someone who means the entire world to me; my beautiful girlfriend, Kate Richards."

Everyone looked over at Kate, who sat blushing in hear seat. She was very surprised but flattered that Steve mentioned her in front of an entire audience.

"So," Steve resumed, looking Kate right in the eyes, "without further ado, I would like to ask Kate to please come up and join me on stage."

Kate blushed again but out of embarrassment rather than anything else. She slowly and quietly got up out of her seat and made her way to the stage. All eyes were set upon her as most of the room had gone quiet. It was that eerie kind of silence which no one would expect in a place like this.

As soon as Kate made her way to the stage, she climbed up the two stairs and went to stand right by Steve. Instead of hugging or kissing her, he immediately got down on one knee. Kate's pulse quickened, and the blood started flowing faster through her veins. She knew what was going on, but she wasn't sure if it was real or just in her head.

"Kate Richards," Steve said, producing a diamond ring from his pocket. "Will you marry me?"

All eyes were upon Kate, and the audience grew dead silent, waiting for her response.

"Yes!" Kate replied, without any hesitation.

The couple was met with thunderous applause and loud cheers after Kate had accepted Steve's proposal.

While Steve knew that The Peppermint Eyes had a large following, he had never heard applause that loud before. And, in front of everyone, he kissed Kate.

Neither one of them wanted this moment to end, though the show had gone really well that night. Now it was official, Kate and Steve were going to be married in one week.

Chapter 20

Once Gloria and Kate returned home, the first thing Kate did was locate her aunt and uncle. She proudly showed off her engagement ring, which elicited emotional responses from both of them.

Aunt Olivia was so happy that she wrapped her arms around her niece and offered Kate her most sincere congratulations.

Stuart was also very pleased, and he approved of the marriage, just as he did for Gloria and Russell.

There was, however, still something that seemed to be bother Kate. She still had not yet told her parents about Steve! She knew that she had to go into the other room and try to call them, but she would give it a few hours until it was midafternoon in Oklahoma, after their breakfast was eaten and their morning chores were through.

Kate would have to be brave and tell her parents all about Steve and the fact that she was going to be a married woman in one week.

Kate was so excited about this news that she actually gathered up the nerve to call her mother. She was not sure if her father was outside tending to the farm or if he was in the house. Either way, she was sure that her mother would tell him the news. She crossed her fingers and dialed her parents' number.

Kate and Susan talked for a while and expressed formal pleasantries before Kate dropped the news.

For a moment, there was dead silence.

Then, Kate swore that she could hear sighing on the other end. She was optimistic about this phone call up until this point, especially since her mother did not seem pleased.

Susan sighed. She hated the fact that she had to tell Kate about the truth why they sent her to England, but she felt it had to be done, especially since Kate had talked her about marrying some man that she hardly knew. The more Kate talked about the wedding; the more surprised Susan became. The last thing that Susan or Isaac thought Kate would do was fall in some love with some hooligan musician.

"Sweetheart, I have something to tell you," Susan said after sighing. She has dreaded this moment ever since she and Isaac had put Kate on the plane to England.

"What is it, Mom?"

"I don't quite know how to say this, so I'm just going to say it. The reason why we decided to send you to England is that some horrible boy came down from New York looking for you."

Kate's heart skipped a few beats. She couldn't possibly be talking about Fred Beaumont, could she? Though this news came as a complete surprise to Kate, she promised herself that she would not panic until she found out if it was her psycho ex who showed up at the farm.

"You're not talking about Fred Beaumont, are you?"

"Yes, that was his name. He was a very rude and crude young man. He upset your father so much that he shot at him with his gun!"

Kate's throat tightened. She couldn't believe what she was hearing. Why had her mother and father waited this long to tell her about Fred coming to their house? And, worst of all, why did they not tell her about the truth behind her taking this trip?

"Mom!" Kate exclaimed. "Why are you telling me this? No, I take that back, why are you telling me this *now*?" Kate could hear Susan sigh on the other end of the phone.

"Because, darling, we don't want you to make a huge mistake by marrying Steve. For one thing, you hardly know the man, and you tell me that you are going to get married in one week!" Susan paused.

"From what you've told us, he seems like a nice, young man, but he doesn't seem to show any promise. Besides, your uncle told us that he had found a nice fellow who is going to be a banker. He's going to school at Oxford. Your father and I think he would be a much more suitable husband."

Kate could feel her blood boil. How dare she; how dare either of them try to do this to her now?

"Well, if either of you think that piece of news is going to stop me from marrying Steve, then you are dead wrong!" Kate exclaimed. "Besides, only the ceremony will be in one week, just so that I can stay here legally. I plan on having a proper wedding sometime later."

Kate wanted to add that she could have her "wedding" closer to Gloria and Russell's actual wedding, but she did not feel the need to mention her cousin at this point. What good would it do right now?

There was heavy silence on the other end of the phone. Neither woman knew just what to say to the other.

Kate thought that her frantic and distraught mother would try to get Isaac on the phone. Kate would actually welcome it because there was a lot she wanted to say to him right now.

"Sweetheart, I—" Susan continued.

"No," Kate angrily spat into the phone. "Save your breath, Mother, because I don't want to hear anymore! I am marrying Steve, whether you and Dad like it or not! The arrangements are soon to be made, and we are not backing out now!"

"But just listen to me for a minute, Kate. If you don't want to think about your father or me, think about your Aunt Olivia and Uncle James. Surely they will be disappointed if you go through with this."

"I have news for you, Mother, Aunt Olivia and Uncle James are fine with it! Are you forgetting that your niece is now also engaged to one of Steve's band mates?"

Kate felt her heart pulsing and her veins contracting with anger. Despite all that was going on right now, she still loved her parents, but she did not think that they were at all being fair.

"Uncle James and Aunt Olivia *accept* Russell for who he is. They accept Russell because Gloria loves him! Why can't you and Father just be happy for us?"

"Sweetheart," Susan said, in a desperate tone of voice.

"Mom, please put Dad on the phone."

"Your father's indisposed at the moment."

"That's bullshit, Mom! Don't lie to me."

"Katie!" Susan exclaimed, surprised at her daughter's colorful language.

"Mom!" she replied. "If Dad doesn't want to talk to me, fine. At least have the guts to tell me the truth!"

"Kate..." Susan said, trailing off. Kate still felt angry, but her anger dissolved into frustration and sadness. She felt like she was going to start crying any minute.

"You know what, Mom, just forget it. I don't want to talk to Dad right now, anyway on the account of both of you being so unreasonable!"

Kate was greeted with complete silence. It seemed that Susan backed herself into a corner with nothing else to say. She could swear that she heard the faint sound of sobbing on the other end of the phone. Kate began to feel a little sorry about how she'd been acting, but the thought of her father was enough to make her realize the importance of standing her ground.

"The ceremony is in one week," Kate resumed. "And the wedding will happen whether or not you and Dad decide to show up or even support me. Goodbye, Mother."

Kate's mother did not say anything on the other end of the phone. There was nothing but dead silence. After giving her mother a few more seconds to speak, Kate got frustrated and finally hung up the phone.

Within seconds of hanging up, tears welled up in Kate's eyes. She was a bit relieved that no one else was in the house at the moment, but, at the same time, she felt very alone.

She wished that Steve was there to hold her. She wished that Gloria and Olivia were there to give her words of comfort. Even having her Uncle Stuart around would make her feel better because *he* had given Kate and Steve *his* blessing. This was more than her own father had done, and nothing made Kate feel sadder.

Then, she realized how rudely she'd treated her mother on the phone. Kate felt bad, especially since it was not her mother with whom she was most angry. It was her father, her selfish, controlling father, whom she was very mad at.

Kate just wanted to take the first flight back to the United States and give him what for, but she was not the type of person who would do that. Her parents had done a fine job of raising her, and, despite everything, she still loved him.

But just because I love my father does not mean that I am going to give up Steve! Kate thought. No, she was determined to walk down that aisle next week because she was going to be Mrs. Steve Maddington. And, if her father would not come to England to give her away, Kate would walk herself down the aisle. The only thing which really comforted Kate was the fact that, starting next week, her true happiness would begin.

***

Since Kate and Steve did not have time to plan any kind of proper wedding ceremony, their only main concern was that it would make Kate a legal citizen of England so that she would not have to leave the country. Although Kate had always dreamed of a big wedding since she was a child, she knew that that was not going to happen, but she loved Steve so much that she would give all that up just to be with him. Besides, once their relationship was legitimized, her father would have to accept Steve as his son-in-law, at least she hoped so.

There was a nice Anglican church on the other side of town, near the bank where Kate went on her third day in the country. Luckily, the church was not that difficult to book, so they were relieved that they could find a place where the ceremony would take place.

***

Kate stood there, looking beautiful in the white wedding dress, which Judy had loaned her; it was Judy's mother's, who was now deceased. As much as she was excited about today, Kate wished that things could have been different. She felt a little bit awkward wearing the wedding dress of a woman she had never met.

Her childhood dreams of walking down the aisle while wearing her mother's dress and holding her father's hand had been thrown out the window. Kate was determined not to let that get in her way, however, because she loved Steve more than anything. A smile formed across her face; she knew that everything was going to be all right, despite recent events.

Kate was not nervous as she walked down the aisle to meet Steve. Rather, she was glad that she getting through the day without shedding any tears. Kate also did not want to forget the promise that her aunt and uncle made to her. A proper gathering would be made at a later date, especially because both Steve and Kate wanted to make sure all their loved ones were going to attend the ceremony.

All those in attendance at the small church were Olivia, Stuart, Gloria, Russell, Nancy, David, Nicholas, John, Joan, Geoffrey, Judy, and Henry. Though Kate and Steve knew that their other friends and family would have liked to attend today's ceremony, they knew they would be understanding, knowing that everyone would have to wait until they could throw a decent party.

After the ceremony, everyone went out for a nice dinner at Livingston's, a fancy restaurant on the upper side of Putney. And while all the excitement of the day did make Kate a little hungry, she was still basking in the glow of her happiness. And, even though she did not get that big wedding she'd wanted as a child, Kate knew that Steve would do everything in his power to make sure that she was happy.

Of course, Kate was determined to keep the same promise, as well. Still, something did not feel quite right, and she knew that it was due to the fact that her parents were not there to share in her bliss.

In fact, neither of them had tried to call the Cunninghams' since Kate had that horrible argument with her mother last week. It was probably just as well, though, because Kate knew that her father was probably beyond furious.

Everyone else had known this as well, but they would dare not to speak a word of this to Kate. This was her and Steve's day, and nothing was going to ruin it for them.

Kate looked over at her Uncle Stuart, who sounded like he was trying to clear his throat. When she realized that he was trying to get her attention, she stopped what she was doing and listened to him.

"My dear," he said handing a small envelope to Kate. "I know this isn't much, but I want you and Steve to have this."

Kate didn't quite know what was in the envelope, but she felt like crying.

"Thank you, Uncle Stu," she replied, beginning to tear it open.

When she opened it up, her eyes became as wide as saucers. Inside the envelope was £2,000. She couldn't believe that her sweet uncle and aunt would give her this much money, especially since she was not their child.

But, ever since being invited to their home, she felt like she was. Gloria was like a sister, and Aunt Olivia was like a second mother. Kate also couldn't help but think of her Uncle Stuart as a second father.

He was more like a father than the one who had raised her back in Oklahoma. They had not even bothered to give her and Steve so much as a congratulations on their upcoming nuptials. In fact, it felt like they had disowned her due to this circumstance.

Still, Kate couldn't help but feel happy, especially because she wanted to be that way for Steve. Seeing her kind uncle smiling at her just now made her heart want to melt.

"Uncle Stu!" Kate said, getting up to hug him. "Thank you and Auntie so much for your generous gift, but this is really too much." She then formed tears in her eyes as she looked over at her new husband.

"Take the envelope, Steve, and look inside it."

Steve reached over and took the piece of paper in his hand.

"2,000 quid!" he said, sounding incredulous. "Mr. Cunningham! Kate's right; this really *is* too much."

"Nonsense, my boy," he said to his new nephew, showing him the same amount of warmth that he showed for Kate. "And another thing, please call me Stuart or Uncle Stu." Steve smiled.

"Right, Uncle Stu, thank you so much!"

He reached over the table and patted him on the shoulder.

"And thank you too, Auntie." Steve got out of his chair and hugged Olivia. "This means so much to us. I mean, we haven't even found a place to live yet."

After hearing this, Kate felt something unsettling in her stomach. With all the rushed preparation and excitement regarding the wedding, they did not have a chance to look around for an apartment. Surely, they would not have to live in The Peppermint Eyes' flat.

"Oh, Steve!" Kate said with a sudden realization of horror in her voice. "We don't even have a place to live. Where are we going to go tomorrow morning?"

Steve pondered this too, but he did not seem near as panicked as Kate. Surely, they could find a flat to rent nearby. Steve knew there were plenty where Judy lived in downtown Putney.

"Not necessarily," Stuart said. "If you dig deeper into the envelope, you will find lease papers, ready to be signed. I took the liberty of finding you a flat very close to our place."

Steve dug deeper into the envelope and retrieved the papers. A look of both happiness and shock formed on his face.

He then looked over at Kate, who was on the verge of tears. He put his arm around his new wife.

"Isn't this wonderful, babe?" he whispered into her ear. "Now we've got some place to start our life together."

Kate let a few tears leak then formed a smile. She was glad that they were not going to have to impose and live with her aunt and uncle. Kate did not have to say anything because Steve seemed to know what she was thinking. He leaned in a little closer and brushed a loose strand away from her ear.

"Besides," he continued, "this will give us a lot more privacy."

Kate smiled then turned a crimson shade of red. Now, they would not have to worry about anyone hearing their lovemaking sounds.

It was official, the couple was that they were going to have a place of their own, somewhere where they could start their married life together. Steve and Kate enjoyed the rest of their wonderful day, knowing that everything was eventually going to work itself out.

Chapter 21

It was one month later. Gloria paced back and for the across the room. Today was the big day. She and Russell were finally going to be married!

Kate and Steve had been happily married for a month, and they Never in her life has she recalled ever being this nervous.

"Will you calm down?" Kate said, on the verge of getting nervous herself. "You look absolutely gorgeous!"

"Kate, it's not that," Gloria replied. "I mean, I know that Mum and Dad have accepted Russell, but I'm so nervous. What if he doesn't meet up to their expectations once we are married? What if The Peppermint Eyes don't make it? Dad would be very disappointed if he thought that Russell was not going to be able to take care of me!"

After having finished that statement, Gloria felt herself become even more nervous. She started pacing back and forth again until Kate grabbed her by the shoulders.

"Stop it!" Kate ordered. "You are going to work yourself into a frenzy, and we won't have such a thing on your wedding day."

Kate turned her head and looked over at the other side of the room, where Jody was looking at herself in the mirror.

"We don't want that, Judy, do we?"

"Absolutely not," Judy said from the other end of the room. "This is your day, and nothing should be upsetting you at all!"

"That's what I keep telling her!" Kate said, looking at Gloria, still pacing the room. "You know, if you aren't going to stop pacing around, then we will have to order you to sit down."

Gloria looked at Kate, like she couldn't believe what she was hearing. Her eyes wanted her to remain focused and serious, but it wasn't long until her face started to tell the truth. The corners of her mouth started to twitch, and seconds later, she burst out into laughter.

"Now, is that hysterical laughter," Judy asked, "or is it because you've finally gotten over your nerves?"

"Both," Gloria said, not really sure how she should respond to the question.

"Okay, that's a start," Kate said. "Now, we just have to keep you under control because your mom should be coming back soon with Joan. "Now, it is my duty as your matron of honor to keep you happy, and if that doesn't happen, people are going to be very disappointed. Russell will be angry with me if he has to deal with a nervous wife."

Gloria smiled again, indicating that she was finally starting to calm down. She's even stopped pacing the room. Kate was about to open her mouth and tell her how proud she was of her cousin when the door opened. The three girls looked over to see Joan enter with her bouquet in her hands.

"Hey guys, have we made any progress?" she asked as she approached Gloria.

"Yes, finally, thank God!" Judy said, going over to the other side of the room. She went up behind Gloria and put her arm around her shoulder. This made Gloria smile again, much to the pleasure of everyone in the room.

"Where's Mum?" Gloria asked, looking around the room and noticing that her mother had not come back with Joan.

"Your mum will be here directly," Judy said. "She's outside talking to one of the guests."

Judy looked at Kate, which Kate hardly noticed because she was still getting used to the idea of Gloria having calmed down.

Kate felt content because Gloria was getting back to her old self again. Any nervous feelings that resided within her only moments before they cast themselves out of her body. All it would take was anyone to look at her to tell that she was ready to proceed with the ceremony.

Seconds later, Olivia entered the room. She took her first look at Gloria fully dressed in her wedding gown, and tears started to form in her eyes.

"Oh, Gloria," Olivia said, trying not to choke on her words, "you look absolutely beautiful. Just wait until your father sees how you look in this dress."

Kate and Jody nodded in agreement.

"Mum," Gloria said, looking at the tears streaming down her mother's face. "Please, don't cry. If you keep this up, you are going to make me start crying." She hesitated, looking around the rest of the room.

"Besides, it would not do for the photographer to take pictures of you with red splotches all over your cheeks."

Olivia laughed and pulled out a handkerchief she'd had in her purse.

"You're right, my dear," Olivia said. "That would not do at all."

She went over to her daughter and put her arm around her. Now, it was Kate's turn to look like she was going to be ready to cry. She didn't, though, because she had managed to make it through her wedding last month without shedding a tear. And though not everyone was there to share in her joy, the day that Kate and Steve were married was the happiest day of her life!

"Now, poppet, Daddy will be coming in to get you very soon," Olivia said, wanting to make sure that her daughter's nerves were finally soothed.

Gloria smiled, finally feeling a little more at ease. And even though she had been both nervous and excited about this day for a very long time, she still could not believe that it was here! If it weren't for the fact that they were in such a dignified setting, Gloria would grab Kate by the arms and giggle, while the two of them jumped up in the air together. And, as juvenile as that sounded, it was something that they would have done.

Before Gloria could have another thought, however, her father entered the room. He was accompanied James. As soon as he laid eyes on his daughter, his breath appeared to be taken away.

"Oh," Stuart said, completely at a loss for words. "My dear, you look absolutely lovely!"

Gloria smiled at her father. She could tell that her uncle had thought the same thing, even though he hadn't said anything yet.

"Thank you, Daddy," Gloria replied with tears on her eyes.

After she realized what she was going, Gloria began to fan her face with her hands in an attempt to dry her tears.

"Oh, this won't do," she said. "How am I going to keep the mascara from running into my eyes?"

Judy smiled then looked over at her friend.

"I suppose one of us will have to say something funny to keep you in line."

Gloria chuckled, though no one was quite sure if it was nervous laughter or if Judy's comment had really done the trick. Either way, it seemed to work all the same.

"There, that's the trick," James said, speaking for the first time since he entered the room. "By the way, my darling," he resumed. "You look absolutely delightful. Both Lois and I are very proud."

"Thank you, Uncle James," Gloria replied, knowing that she was through crying. "I am delighted that you could be here."

She went over to James and gave him a hug. And, despite the fact that Gloria never really felt close to her uncle, she felt like a happy child in his arms.

They hugged just like they used to when Gloria was little. She could feel any and all reservations regarding her family begin to melt away. And she no longer feared the idea of Syd and Sebastian ruining her special day.

Everyone turned their attention to the door being opened. Joan entered the room, with Lois trailing behind her.

"Sorry I'm late, everyone," Joan said, apologetically.

"I told her she was going to make us late," Lois added.

And, though her tone was not very pleasant, she did not want to make a big deal of it and ruin Gloria's special day.

"Oh, Gloria!" Joan said after first setting eyes on her friend. "You look gorgeous!"

"Thank you!"

"Yes," Lois agreed, "you look absolutely stunning in that dress."

"I'm glad that you think so, Auntie," Gloria replied, looking down at the frilly ruffles and the long train.

It was the very same dress her mother wore the day she married her father. In all honesty, Gloria was relieved that it actually fit!

Here she was, about to be married to Russell. Gloria could not think of a time in her life when she had been happier, except for the moment when she found herself in love with him.

She made her way over to the mirror to check her hair and makeup. Her hair looked fine, and she was relieved to see that her mascara was not running.

Kate went over to Gloria and put her hand on her shoulder.

"You look like royalty," she said.

Gloria turned to look at her cousin, seemingly incredulous.

"What?"

"I mean it," Kate replied. "I cannot think of a more beautiful bride than you. Russell will be awestruck when she sees you!"

"Oh, stop it!" Gloria exclaimed, even though she relished all the attention she was getting.

"You're not nervous anymore?"

"Nope, I think I will do fine from here on out."

"Good, that's what I like to hear!"

Gloria smiled and wrapped Kate in a firm embrace. The two women remained hugging until Stuart made his announcement.

"It's time," he said, having looked out the door, seeing all the men lined up at the altar. He could see a well-groomed Russell standing there, waiting for his bride.

"Daddy," Gloria said, linking her arm with her father, "I still can't believe that I am getting married."

"Neither can I, love," Stuart replied, "but I have never been happier for you than I am today."

Gloria smiled then smiled and embraced her father, knowing that he had meant every word he'd just said.

"Shall we get going, then, Dad?"

"Not yet. The bridesmaids have to go before you. There's no use in jumping the gun, darling."

Gloria let out a little nervous laughter. She couldn't believe how she had forgotten an important detail such as that, despite the rehearsal last night!

Oh well, she thought. *At least I won't have to worry about anyone tripping up behind me.*

She let out her last bit of nervous laughter before preparing to head out the door and down the aisle. Gloria and her father watched as Cynthia was the first one to walk down the aisle and take her place. Joan followed, as did Judy, and then Kate. Now time seemed like it was going faster.

Now, it was Gloria's turn to walk down the aisle. She could feel all eyes upon her as she walked down the seemingly long aisle, arm-in-arm with her father.

All the breath seemed to leave Russell's body as soon as he took his first look at his bride. He motioned his head to look up at the ceiling as if to thank the Lord for this special moment. Especially since months ago he never would have thought that he would be here!

Wedlock was something he couldn't really fathom until this very moment, but he felt extremely blessed all the same. As soon as Gloria and Russell had another moment to bask in each other glow, they turned their attention to the minister, who has just started to recite the vows.

It all seemed to go by in such a blur that Gloria hardly remembered the details. All she could recall after her father giving her away and the recitation of the vows was Russell giving her the sweetest and best kiss she had ever received in her life! It was such a cherished moment that Gloria thought she would give away *all* the memories in her head to hold onto that one for the rest of her life!

Her life. She said the words in her head and found that she was happy with the way they sounded. Today, she and Russell were going to start their life together, and they knew that happiness would always be within their reach. Gloria gazed lovingly into her new husband's eyes as he grabbed hold of her hand again. Gloria couldn't help but think that this truly was the greatest moment in her life!

***

Moments later, everyone was enjoying themselves at the party which followed. The reception took place at James and Lois' house, which had a large backyard. Gloria couldn't help but think about how grateful she was to her aunt and uncle for holding the party in her backyard. Even Syd and Sebastian were behaving like perfect gentlemen, complimenting both she and Russell. She couldn't help but think that there was hope for them yet.

Kate could not believe her eyes, as this was the largest private residence she had seen during her entire time in England. Granted, it was nothing compared to acreage of her father's dairy farm, but it was an impressive size, nonetheless.

The party had been going on for an hour when Stuart and Olivia went around and got the attention of the large crowd. They needed to make the announcement that dinner was ready to be served.

As soon as everyone received the message, they stopped whatever they were doing and sat down. The entire bridal party, including both sets of parents, had their designated places at the head table.

Stuart stood up and clanged his knife against his glass after everyone had been given ample time to start into their food. Everyone turned their heads in attention, as they anticipated that he had something very important to say.

"If I may have everyone's attention," Stuart said before the crowd quieted down. "First of all, we would like to thank everyone for coming out tonight and sharing this special day with us."

There were cheers and applause all around.

"As I said the same night Gloria and my new son-in-law, Russell got engaged, 'I can't believe this is happening.'"

Chuckles emanated throughout the area.

"But speaking for both Olivia and I, we couldn't be any prouder of Gloria."

Gloria looked over at both her mother, who was nodding her head, and her father as he was giving the toast. Her eyes began to fill with tears again.

"And," Stuart continued, "we would like to welcome Russell into our family. I couldn't have asked for a finer man to call my son."

Stuart looked over at Russell, whose arm was around his new bride's shoulder. He felt himself begin to mist over, but he hid it well by looking in the other direction and wiping the tear out of his eye. It would not be very manly of him to let his new family catch him crying.

Gloria looked over at Russell and was about to say something. He was afraid she had seen what he tried to hide from everyone just now. Luckily, however, before she could say a word, the applause started up again.

"So," Stuart resumed, after giving himself and everyone else a moment to compose themselves, "without further ado, I would like to present Gloria and Russell with this. Would the new couple please rise from their seats?"

The newlyweds were a little embarrassed about being called to attention like that, but they did not want to disappoint anyone, so they did as they were told.

And, without another word, Stuart handed an envelope to Gloria. She took one look at it and thought that her parents had bought them a flat similar to the one they'd purchased for Steve and Kate.

It wasn't until seconds later when after Gloria dug further into the envelope, did she feel her heart stop. Russell hovered over his new wife in anticipation. Inside the envelope was a simple-looking key and the deed to a house on the other part of town. Gloria felt like she was going to explode with happiness; she couldn't believe the generous gift that her father has just given her!

"Dad!" Gloria exclaimed, reaching over and hugging her father. "A house! However could you afford one?"

Russell was completely dumbfounded. He couldn't quite find the right words to say. Now it was no mystery because he felt this was truly a sign that he was welcomed into the family with open arms.

"Stuart!" Russell said, going over to shake his new father-in-law's hand. "How can we ever thank you?"

Stuart looked at Russell then smiled. He retracted his hand and opened his arms. He and Russell embraced briefly before Stuart continued with his explanation.

"The house is not new, my dear. It belonged to a nice old couple on the other side of town. But it is of very good quality, and I know that both you and Russell will be pleased with it."

He hesitated for a brief second to look over at his wife, who was dabbing the tears away from her eyes.

"The funny thing is, as soon as Russell came to me asking my permission so he could marry you, I knew the house was available. I saw it on the market a few days earlier when I was driving into town."

Gloria and Russell looked at each other, their faces alit with smiles.

"To me, it seemed like a message from God. Then, when Russell came to me with his good intentions, I knew that this was the house I was going to give to you."

After Stuart finished his statement, there was a great silence at the table, as if they were hinging on every word that he said. It was a truly special and tender moment.

Then, turning to Russell, he said, "You're quite welcome, my boy. All that I ask of you is that that you keep my Gloria happy. And what I hope for both of you is that you love and cherish each other as long as you live!"

"Here, here!" John shouted from the groom's side of the table. He raised his glass in the air, "I propose a toast!"

"A fine idea, my lad!" Stuart replied. "A toast we shall have."

He retrieved his wine glass and led everyone else to raise theirs in the air.

"To Gloria and Russell. May their happiness be theirs to last longer than a lifetime!"

"To Gloria and Russell!" everyone repeated before bringing their glasses back down for a sip of whatever they were having.

It would have been safe to say that there was not a dry eye anywhere near the perimeter of the backyard, as this was truly a cause for celebration.

Gloria and Russell shared a kiss, as did Kate and Steve. And even though their wedding was only one month ago, Steve and Kate felt like they were reliving each moment of their special day.

Kate smiled and couldn't help but feel satisfied that she and Gloria were married to the two best men in the world. Kate no longer worried that her cousin would be unhappy with her family or her life, for everything was unfolding before their very eyes.

Chapter 22

Kate and Steve have been married for a little over four months, and they grew to love each other more each day. While the couple enjoyed their flat and their new life together, Kate decided it was time that she would try to make amends with her parents.

When she told Steve about the idea, he was all for it. He knew that nothing would be accomplished if he did not go back with her. Kate *knew* that her parents had to like Steve if they got the chance to meet him and get to know him. That was what they were going to try and to right now, to make things right. They had to go back to Kate's hometown and try to talk to her parents.

Since Kate had married Steve and was now a legal resident of England, the two of them had simply gotten passports and travelled back to the United States.

Geoffrey volunteered to go to Steve and Kate's flat and keep an eye on their place while they were gone. Nick was more than happy to take his brother's place in The Peppermint Eyes. The visa said that they had three months to visit, but they did not think it would take that long to reach Isaac and Susan.

Though it might take longer than they originally thought was needed to accomplish this goal, Steve knew that he was there to assist his wife. He knew he had to remain strong to help her during her weakest moments.

Steve was her rock. And, while Kate was very optimistic about the whole thing since the beginning, she was glad that she could rely on her darling husband for emotional support.

Steve was very excited since this was his first time in America, but Oklahoma would not have been his first choice of places to visit.

Somewhere like New York, or even California, would have been on the top of his list. He never mentioned this to Kate, however, because he did not want to hurt her feelings.

She was still very sentimental about Oklahoma, even though they were staying in Locust Grove, a few towns away from where she had lived most of her life. Despite everything that had been going on, Steve did not want to disillusion Kate.

Since Steve was not a legal resident of the United States, and Kate had just gained citizenship in England, it would be a little difficult to adjust to everything. Ironically, they decided that they wanted to live in Oklahoma, merely thirty-two miles away from the Richards' dairy farm.

While both Kate and Steve knew that they had not received her father's blessing, they hoped that the two of them trying to live a self-sufficient life, albeit back in England, would help him change his mind. But, if they had to move back to Oklahoma to get her father's full acceptance, then they both decided that was what they were going to do. Kate would be the first person to tell her parents about how Steve is very intelligent and hard-working. Plus, he is a fast learner. Maybe Isaac would eventually realize that his son-in-law could be cut out for farm work.

***

"You're my wife, and I love you!" Steve exclaimed, giving Kate a kiss. He then set the bag of groceries down on the curb. The two of them had been out shopping so that they could have a few days' worth of food. Since they had just come back to the United States, money was tight. Steve did have a little money from The Peppermint Eyes' recent gigs, but it did not go as far as he needed it to. The two of them knew that they would have to tighten their belts while staying in Oklahoma.

"Please, don't be sad," Steve said, trying his hardest to comfort Kate. We'll find a way around this. We can make this work."

She looked up at him and frowned. And, without having to say a word, Steve could tell what she was thinking. Part of him wanted to land a fist in Isaac's face for what he was putting his daughter through.

Kate did not actually have the nerve to show up at her parents' door like Fred Beaumont had months ago. She just couldn't bring herself to do it, especially since she was so afraid of the rejection.

Steve insisted that Kate take them to their house so he could give Isaac a piece of his mind, but that idea only made her feel worse. So the two of them settled on a town on the opposite end of the state. That way, they could venture to her parents' farm when she finally gathered up the nerve to go there.

They'd only been back in Oklahoma for two weeks, and Kate had already begun to feel herself give up. Instead of looking for an apartment, Kate and Steve were living with a nice, elderly couple who was renting out a room. They were lonely because their two grown sons had finished college and were out of the house.

Kate and Steve lived in a room upstairs, and the sweet couple had only asked them to pay twenty dollars rent for a whole month. The young couple was not sure how long they were going to stay there, but at the rate that things were going, Kate was very close to throwing in the towel.

"It's not you, Steve, it's my stupid father! I don't know why he isn't willing to accept the fact that we are in love with each other! I mean, we've even legitimized our relationship and gotten married, for God's sake! What more does the man want?"

Kate started sobbing again, this time, uncontrollably.

Steve went over to Kate and wrapped his arms around her. He stoked her hair and tried his best to soothe the shaking bundle that was enveloped in his arms.

"He can be such a bastard sometimes!" Kate sobbed.

"Shh," Steve whispered into her ear. "Please, no more crying, love. I am here now, and I will always take care of you. Everything will be all right; you'll see."

As reassuring as Steve sounded, it seemed as if nothing he could say or do could console his sad and frightened wife. Steve was no pacifist, and sometimes he had a little trouble keeping his temper in check, but he knew how to relate to Kate. He had a way of soothing her and calming her down like no one else could.

Just thinking about Isaac Richards, a man whom he was not proud to call his father-in-law, made his blood boil! Steve just wanted to take a swing at him. He wanted to grab him by his shoulders and shake him until his brain rattled! Isaac had to see how he manipulated his daughter was wrong, even though she did get into that trouble with Fred.

Fred. There was another person who Steve wanted to pummel, and badly. He had never met the man, and that was a good thing.

It's a damn good thing that Fred has not shown his face around here anywhere, Steve thought.

He was tempted to let Kate hear his words, but he thought that would upset her even more. Sometimes certain things are better left unsaid.

"Please, love," he whispered into her ear. "Do it for me. Do it for your old husband."

Kate stopped crying, and Steve slowly began to release her. When she faced him, he saw that there were still tears in her eyes and that they had also stained her cheeks.

He wiped away the tears with his fingers. "All better?" he asked.

"I'm working on it," she replied.

Her tone seemed to indicate that she was feeling better, but it did not seem to promise that everything was going to resolve itself soon. Steve knew this, and he was determined to stand by his wife as they started to think about ways to confront her father.

***

Mr. and Mrs. Thomas and Lily Emerson were both in their early 70s, and they were kind and God-fearing folks. And while they were aware of all the corruption which polluted the world, they were not the types of people who wanted to believe that it existed much around them.

They took to heart Jesus' most important commandment, *Love thy neighbor.* And, when a nice young couple had come to them from off the streets asking about the room for rent, they knew they could not deny them. Besides, they were in need of some company.

Of course, the older couple had noticed Steve's accent, and they inquired about it. They were simply amazed when he said he'd come from England. They also asked how long he had been in the United States. Steve told Mr. and Mrs. Emerson all about growing up in England, his aspirations, falling in love with Kate, and finally getting to marry her. Of course, he left out all the dirty details, including the fact that he and Russell were getting high when they met their future wives.

Mr. and Mrs. Thomas seemed pleased with Steve's explanation, and one could tell merely by looking at Mrs. Emerson that she was picturing the whole romantic scene of Steve calling out to Kate in the street.

The one thing that Kate and Steve did not actually volunteer was the fact that they were trying to get back into contact with her parents. As far as Kate was concerned, since they did not ask what they were doing in Oklahoma, she felt she did not have to tell them.

There was no point in having a third party know all about the sad details of their lives, albeit a sweet and kind third party. Kate and Steve were just relieved to have a place to live with people who did not criticize of judge them.

Judging from what they had been told, Kate and Steve figured that the older couple had lived interesting and fulfilling lives. Mr. Emerson was a veteran of WWI, for which he was immediately drafted right after high school. And though he'd served his time with a smile on his face, he did not have any epic ware stories which to relay to Kate and Steve.

He had, however, told them about how he'd met his wife and the job that he held as working in a car factory to support his wife and sons. He was also proud to tell Kate and Steve that they had lived in the same house ever since they were married. Steve smiled, and Kate couldn't help but think about how romantic the whole idea was.

As the days came and went, Mr. and Mrs. Emerson bonded more with Kate and Steve.

In a way, Kate felt like they were surrogate parents because of how comfortable she felt talking and being with them.

Even though the Emersons had no pictures of the young couple in any of their photo albums, and even though all the memories they shared were very recent, the elder couple made it abundantly clear that they cared about Kate and Steve as though they were their own children

Steve also liked the older couple very much because they began to feel like his own set of American parents. He was very relieved at the fact that they did not seem to judge him because of his occupation. And while Mr. and Mrs. Emerson did not seem like they were the types who really understood rock 'n' roll, the fact that he was living out his dream did not seem to bother them.

Kate and Steve hoped that they would have a house of their own someday, be it in England or the United States. A home would be something that could share and quite possibly stay for the rest of their lives. They did not care where they lived, just as long as they were happily united with their family.

Chapter 23

Kate and Steve were walking down the street of the little town. During the two months which had passed since Kate broke down and cried in the street, they had made no progress in reasoning with Isaac, and Susan even refused to talk to them most of the time.

Kate and Steve tried to write a few letters, and they even made a few long-distance calls to them a few times, but he stopped answering the phone. Susan would always pick up, and she would tell Kate or Steve, depending on who dialed the number, that Isaac was "indisposed."

Unlike the other times, long ago, when Susan used that word, these times it meant that Kate's father did not want to talk to either one of them. Since things were not going very well, between Kate's father not wanting to talk to them and with Steve's dwindling luck at trying to find a part-time job, the newlywed couple seriously contemplated going back to England.

While things were not going their way, Kate and Steve did receive a bit of good news. Gloria had written them and told them that she was pregnant! When they had read about this news, both of them were equally excited.

"Thinking about Gloria always seems to help," Kate had told Steve one night after she felt herself feeling down. Kate enjoyed receiving her first letter from them after their honeymoon in Spain. Gloria wrote and told her all about their trip and how Stuart had arranged for the movers to take care of everything while they were gone.

When they got back, their house was completely furnished. All they had left to do was gather their small and personal belongings, which they did shortly after they were comfortably settled back in from their trip.

Kate wanted desperately to call Gloria; she missed the sound of her cousin's voice. She knew that Gloria wanted to talk all about her, Russell, and the baby which was growing inside her.

The Emersons, however, did not have a phone on which they could call long distance and overseas. One of the things they would not be deprived of if only they could be with Kate's parents right now.

Steve did miss talking to his best mate and Gloria, and he was on pins and needles regarding the band. Though Nick had graciously agreed to take over for him in his absence, Steve wanted to hear any and all news about The Peppermint Eyes' progress. While both of them had their reasons for wanting to call England, they could not let whatever feelings they had get in the way of them achieving their main objective. Still, the young couple was determined that their patience would help them persevere.

"I'm tired of this, Steve," Kate said after returning herself to the real world. In her mind, she could not help but fantasize about being back in England, where people truly loved her. As of late, she felt like she had no family here, but there was this small part of her that was hanging on.

"My father has gotten to the point that he will no longer talk to me," Kate resumed, "and my poor mother is caught in the middle of it all." Kate sighed. "What are we going to do?"

Steve kissed his wife on the forehead.

"I venture a guess to know what you are thinking, and I think we would be better off leaving," Steve said.

The two of them stopped walking for a second.

"Do you really mean that, or are you just saying what you think I want to hear?"

Kate was not angry, but she did not want her husband to feel that he had to lie on her behalf. Kate was still willing to make things work in Oklahoma if Steve truly wanted to stay here.

"No, Kate, I am not just saying that. I really have had enough of all this, as have you. I miss my home, and I miss playing in my band. Though Nick is starting to write music for us, and he has taken over for me for the last few months, I know that he's only doing it for me. The Peppermint Eyes are not his life."

Steve paused, looking over to see Kate's reaction. She was neither smiling nor frowning. She turned her head and looked down at the road ahead of them. Today was a quiet day in town, as no one else was about.

"What are you thinking?"

Kate still had not said anything, and Steve knew that he asked a silly question. He wanted to talk to her more about this, but he could tell that Kate was deep in thought. Before he upset her anymore, he decided to just be quiet for the time being. There was no sense in talking much more about it anyway, especially because Kate could be just as stubborn as her father sometimes. It was one of the family traits which did not pass her by.

Up until this point, the streets were so quiet that the couple thought they were the only ones walking around outside that day. They did not take long to notice a man walking down the other end of the road, his hands in his pockets.

"Look, there's someone else out here," Steve said, casually.

Kate looked directly ahead of her and noticed that the man, who seemed to be wandering aimlessly. His head was down to the ground.

"I wonder who that is," Kate said, though she did not really care.

Seconds later, the person came closer. Kate knew that something about him was familiar, but she could not quite put her finger on it. Then, when they got even closer to the man, Kate's eyes widened in fear.

It can't be! she thought.

The man on the other end of the street looked a lot like Fred Beaumont. Kate mentally panicked and frantically tried to hide behind Steve.

"What are you doing?" he asked, curious as to why she was now walking behind him.

"It's *him*," Kate whispered, as the faced the opposite direction.

Steve wasn't quite sure who Kate had referred to as him, but the trembling in her voice made it clear that she was afraid of this man for some reason.

"Who is he?" Steve asked, now worried because Kate seemed terrified.

"Fred Beaumont," she replied, still not looking at the man on the other side of the street.

Steve squinted.

"Are you sure?" he asked.

Though Steve did not know what Fred looked like, he already disliked this man because he was frightening his wife. Steve looked at the man again. He hoped for the other guy's sake that he was *not* Fred Beaumont because if he was, he was going to give him a sound thrashing! It was a good thing that Kate could not read his mind because his thoughts had turned real ugly real fast.

Kate clutched Steve as the two of them walked further down the street. Now, they were mere seconds away from crossing the man on the street. Kate was no longer facing the other direction; she tried her best to look ahead because she was afraid that not doing so would attract too much attention.

"Hey, there," the strange man said as he passed Kate and Steve. "Nice day we're having, isn't it?"

"Yes, lovely," Steve replied as they walked farther in the other direction.

Kate finally allowed herself to get a good look at the man. She realized that she was wrong because this was definitely *not* Fred. Come to think of it, this guy even had a southern accent, which was something Fred certainly didn't have. She breathed a sigh of relief.

"I'm sorry, my love" she apologized. "I could have sworn that man was Fred. He looked just like him, even had on the same kind of clothes. I guess I am just being paranoid, being that Mom mentioned that Fred had come looking for me."

Kate shuddered as a chill ran across her spine. Just mentioning Fred by name was enough to make her feel terrified, especially since her mother had told her about the visit he made to their house.

Steve was beginning to get a little concerned. This wasn't the first thing he'd noticed different about Kate since they came back to the United States. Something about her seemed different, and it was not just the sadness that came from being rejected by her parents. It was a certain something else, which seemed more like regret.

Steve knew enough not to ask Kate what was bothering her, but he sensed that she felt more out of place in her home state than she had ever been before. He could strangle his father-in-law for all that he had put them through, but even Isaac couldn't take all the blame.

Kate was homesick for her new home. She missed Gloria, Aunt Olivia, Uncle Stuart, and all the others. Steve knew that he wanted to go home, too, but it was mostly for the sake of his wife and the band. He said now what he had been thinking for a long while.

"Kate, I know that I may be premature in saying this, but I think that we should go back home. Since you are my wife, you are a legal resident of England, and I think that everything which has happened here has only upset you all the more."

Kate stopped in her tracks. "But what about Mr. and Mrs. Emerson?" she asked, showing concern for her surrogate parents. "This will certainly break their hearts."

Steve held his head down.

"I know," he replied. "I don't know how or even what we are going to tell them." He hesitated for a second to life up his head and look into Kate's eyes.

"But we can't stay here. You know it, and I know it."

While she knew that Steve was right, she still questioned if going back to England now would further strain the relationship between her and her parents.

She couldn't handle that thought, but going back to England may be the only thing that could save their happiness. And just like she thought when she decided to give a relationship with Steve a try, Kate decided that she would let Steve take over all the decisions which led to their happiness.

Chapter 24

While Steve was downstairs, happily talking with Mr. and Mrs. Emerson, Kate sat in their room, not looking out the window, but lying down on their bed. She knew that she had to leave Oklahoma soon, for the sake of her sanity, but a part of her was a little sad, not the same kind of sad she felt when they'd departed England, but a different kind of sad. Kate's mind transported her back to a few months ago when she had just graduated from NYU.

***

As soon as Kate got back home from college, she found that part of her really missed New York. Even though she had some bad memories of that place, part of her felt like she belonged. It felt weird thinking about it, but she missed the freedom; she missed knowing that she was able to go out and discover new places.

Now that she'd had her degree in journalism, Kate still had not had any job offers. She was sure that her mother and father were both going to tell her what a mistake college was and that she never should have went in the first place.

"Your place is here with us," she could hear her father's words echo in her head. He would then go on to tell her that she needed to forget all about college. And, while Kate was grateful for the loving environment in which she was raised as a child, she missed being able to do her own thing in New York. She actually missed sitting in her lectures and writing papers for her classes. In fact, she saved most of them, which resided on the top shelf of her closet. She was in the same situation then as she was now, not quite depressed but torn.

She knew that her friends would be coming to pick her up soon, but that was not first and foremost in her mind. While she was proud of the piece of paper she received at her graduation, the local paper was not hiring at the moment, and her parents did not really see the need for her to apply in the first place.

Story of my life, she thought as she knew her folks were going to do most anything to ensure that she would stay on this farm for the rest of her life.

Kate sighed and got up from her bed. She was tired of simply sitting there and pining. She did not feel like going back downstairs because that would mean talking to her parents. Right now, she was definitely not in the mood, so her mind had to think of something else for her to do, and fast!

She started to walk over in the direction of her window, but then she remembered the papers she wrote for her classes. Even though she wasn't feeling her best at the moment, she felt that looking through all her papers and assignments might cheer her up.

There were three boxes on the shelves, each of them containing something special. One box contained all her "college clothes," things that her parents would not much like her wearing, especially in mixed company. Many of these were the blue jeans which she had proudly donned around the campus.

Now that she was back home, she didn't know when she would get to wear them much, as they were not the same as her work overalls, which she had on right now. But, at that point, she was beyond caring. She decided to take the box down and fish out her favorite pair. She was going to wear them tonight. Kate did not care if her parents objected to this, especially since she was only going to be with her girlfriends this evening.

To hell with it, she thought as she slipped comfortably into the faded, blue pants legs. *I deserve to enjoy myself; I just finished school!*

Kate took a quick look at her white T-shirt and determined that it was not dirty enough to throw in the hamper with the rest of the laundry. She was going to wear it tonight for no other reason than she felt comfortable.

Hopefully, her parents were not really going to look at her before she left. Kate also hoped that they would not ask her where she was going and who with. It's not because they didn't trust her, but she knew if their minds were going to be wondering if she would come into contact with any handsome, available men. Just the thought of it alone was enough to make Kate feel nauseated. Meeting and finding a man was the last thing on her mind!

She carefully placed the box back on the top shelf after she'd put on her favorite pair of jeans. The one she dug into next had a little tear on the top right corner; this is how she knew it was the one which contained all her school assignments, including the articles she had written for the school paper. Kate began to tug at it from the top shelf. It was heavier than she remembered.

Once she yanked it down, she carried it over to her bed and gently set it down on the floor. Kate sat down on her bed and looked out the window facing the front of the house. The window on the left side was where she could see the barn, which obscured most of her view of the field and the cows. That did not seem to bother her too much, though, because she saw those damned cows every day when she and her parents milked them.

As for the fields, she could walk them anytime she wanted. The window by the front of the house had a perfect view of the dirt driveway. This was a good thing because she could see her friends as they came to pick her up. She would not have to stand out in the foyer and wait. After taking a quick glance to notice that none of the dust had stirred, Kate turned her attention to the box on the floor.

She pulled out her first student article at random, which also happened to be her first class assignment that she wrote in 1967. The headline was appropriately titled: **STUDENTS ADJUST TO CAMPUS LIFE**, which seemed to encompass the entire freshman class. Kate certainly could relate to this because she was a stranger to these lands. And the fact that she was a dairy farmer's daughter from Oklahoma did not exactly help her blend in.

The next one she pulled out of the box was written in the fall of 1969, which was a brief piece about peoples' reaction to

Woodstock. Aside from the hippies on campus and the people from her and Fred's circle of friends, not many people were in favor of the festival, which came as no surprise to Kate. After she finished reading her second article, she quickly glanced out the window again to see if she should get ready to run downstairs.

Kate was right, reading her old school articles and assignments did bring a smile to her face. She was glad that she retrieved the box from her closet.

Now, she wanted to mix things up a little. Instead of merely picking the one that lay on top of the pile, she stuck her hand down into the stack and shook it around like she was going to pick out a winning raffle ticket. Her hands felt something which resembled an envelope. Naturally curious as to what the item was, her fingers carefully gripped it as she took it out of the box. She turned over the envelope and inspected the writing on the front side. It was a letter from Gloria.

What's this doing in there? Kate thought while looking at the postmark. It was sent on August 28, 1970, not even a year old yet. Kate was about to pull down the other box so she could put it in with Gloria's other letters, but she decided to read it instead.

She loved getting letters from her English cousin because they were special to her. And though Kate had never met this fun and interesting person, she hoped she would get the opportunity to someday. She took the letter out from the envelope and began to read:

Dear Kate,

Hello. How are things going in the good ol' United States? Me, well, I have nothing new to report. Mum's doing the same things around the house, and Dad is Dad.

Oh! I take that back, I did make a trip to my favourite clothing boutique a few days ago. If you're into cute and trendy clothes, then this place would certainly be your bag.

Kate smiled then made a face. Sure, she had seen people on campus wearing some of those "cute and trendy" clothes, but they were not for her. She only wanted to wear what made her most comfortable. Kate continued to read on:

Just because me folks have money doesn't mean that I have to dress up all the time. Still, my clothing choices should not come as a complete shock to people because some of them don't seem to be bothered by it. Well, at least Mum doesn't seem to mind me spending some money on these items, but Dad, that's another story!

Oh, you would have to come here to see what I mean. And I really do hope you get to do that someday, as I really want to meet you. Mum says she has met you a few times but wouldn't be able to pick you out of a crowd.

Well, I suppose I need to sign off for the time being because there is nothing else to say for the moment. Please give your parents a fond shout of 'hello' for me!

Love,

Gloria

Kate closed the letter and let out another sigh. How it would be nice for her to get to go to England, though she never thought her parents would allow it! Granted, her Aunt Olivia got lucky and married a rich man, whom her grandfather and grandmother approved. Still, that kind of thing was very rare and did not happen every day. No chance it would ever happen for someone like her.

She folded the letter up again and neatly placed it back in the envelope. Then, she went over to her vanity and placed it down neatly beside her jewelry box and a bottle of perfume that she had received as a gift from her mother. Kate wanted to look in the mirror and brush her hair because she knew that there really was not much time until her friends would arrive.

And, while Kate did not completely dislike what she saw staring back at her from the mirror, part of her still felt empty because she had yet to find her niche in life. She couldn't help but think that it would have to be evidently clear to her at some point.

No sooner had she taken her eyes off the lonely blonde in the mirror did she hear a car coming down the drive. Kate went over to smile as she saw her friend's red card pull up to the house. Quickly and quietly, she retreated downstairs where she was ready to embark upon a long-awaited evening of fun.

Chapter 25

The year had turned over to 1972.

Steve and Kate had been back in England for the last few months. They knew that they had to leave because they were not making any progress with Kate's parents.

Steve knew that Kate was really hurting inside, and he could tell that she wanted to go back to the place which had made her most happy. Returning to England was not so much an option as much as a necessary means for happiness. Besides, they both had their legitimate excuses to go back home.

Of course, Mr. and Mrs. Emerson were sad to know that the nice, young couple was going to leave them, but they were quickly satiated with promises to keep in touch and come and visit next time they were in the area.

Kate almost cried when she saw Mrs. Emerson smile at her for the last time, because a part of her felt that the older woman knew about her woes and the trouble she was having with her parents. Some things simply did not have to be said. Still, Kate knew that she and Steve would need to get yet another fresh start on their life together.

As soon as Kate and Steve had arrived back in England, it felt like déjà vu. Gloria and Russell were the ones who picked them up from the airport. Kate could already tell that her cousin was glowing, even though she had not yet started to show. As soon as Gloria had spotted Kate, she ran right over to her.

"Kate!" Gloria squealed, wrapping her arms around her cousin.

Kate reciprocated the hug, seeming to have a harder time than Gloria letting go. Kate stood back a little and inspected her cousin;

she could already tell that Gloria was glowing, even though she had not yet started to show. Kate was not sure how far along Gloria was, but she estimated her to be about four months pregnant.

"Good to see you again, mate!" Russell said to Steve.

The two of them gathered in a quick embrace. Steve noticed that Russell looked the same, except that he'd let his hair and moustache grow a little longer. He wore the expression of a proud papa-to-be on his face.

"I've got so many things I need to ask you," Steve said. "How are you and Gloria faring? Have you talked to me mum and dad? Any new news concerning Nick and The Peppermint Eyes?"

Russell laughed, as he felt that his friend's first priority was the band.

"I know that you missed The Peppermint Eyes. Actually, Nick has been doing a great job, though our audiences know that he's not you."

Steve smiled.

"Of course, he is also relieved that you will be back taking over the next gig. While he loved taking over for you on guitar, he does not want to feel like he has to fill your shoes anymore.

"Right," Steve said, resisting the urge chuckle, "as if it was any trouble or inconvenience for him."

Steve then looked over at Kate, who was happily talking to Gloria, no doubt about the pregnancy. He was glad to be back home.

And though Kate was completely engaged in her conversation with Gloria, she could not help but think about how happy she was to be back in England.

Kate and Steve had not succeeded in making her parents see reason, their trip back to the United States was not a complete bust. After all, the young couple got to meet and befriend a nicer old couple, whom they promised they would visit if they ever came back to that part of Oklahoma. And regardless of how things turned out with Kate's parents in the future, they made a promise to themselves that they would come back another time to explore other parts of the country. Besides New

York, Kate had not been anywhere other than her native state. Both of them had picked out many other states they would like to visit someday.

Chapter 26

Both Steve and Kate were optimistic. Though they did not even verbally express it, they knew that something good was going to happen this year. Ever since she thought back on it, Kate decided that she would try to give writing a try, not necessarily for a career, but for a therapeutic means of release.

Maybe she could learn to write rock lyrics for The Peppermint Eyes if Steve ever decided to stop writing songs, but she was getting way ahead of herself. But, as far as the good feeling went, Kate sincerely hoped that it meant that her mother and father would finally acknowledge her marriage to Steve.

Of course, with every breath came a new prayer that such a thing would happen. It had even gotten to the point where the rest of the extended family, and most of their friends became involved. While some of them cursed out Isaac, others just hoped that prayer and reasoning would do the job.

Whatever happened, however, was up to God. He would be the one who would help them remain optimistic during the most turbulent of times, and He would be the one who would bring the families back together. It was all just a matter of time.

***

Gloria had her baby, a boy, who is loved very dearly. She and Russell decided to name him George Colin Bryson Stokes, after Gloria's maternal grandfather George Colin Bryson. Kate found herself completely smitten with George, and she was happy that she now had a second cousin. She hoped that George would come to know her and Steve as his "aunt" and "uncle" as soon as he got to be old enough to know the meaning of the words.

Though this was a very happy occasion for everyone in the family, Kate could not help but feel a little jealous. Her parents, or her father, rather, had not been happy about her marriage to Steve. She did not want to have to expend any more thought about the entire situation because she felt that things were not going to change, at least, not anytime soon.

Another thing that Kate did not want to do was express any great amount of concern, especially since Gloria would be able to pick up on it immediately. In the short time, comparatively speaking, that she had known her cousin, Kate never doubted her perceptive abilities.

Gloria was not very fond of her Uncle Isaac of late, to say the least. The last thing that Kate wanted to hear was her own cousin saying bad things about her father. It was just too upsetting, even though Kate often thought these same things herself.

It had been weeks since Kate had tried to contact either of her parents. She'd only called once to say that she arrived there safely, and her mother answered the phone. The conversation was short, but Kate knew that Susan truly missed her daughter and probably wished that she and Steve were still back in Oklahoma. Kate fully realized that her mother had never gotten the opportunity to meet Steve, although they had talked on the phone a few times.

Susan was a good woman, but she was completely old-fashioned. She played the role of the submissive wife, while Isaac was the definitive authority of practically everything that went on in their house. She never dreamed of flying to England alone to attend her daughter's wedding or meet her son-in-law.

While this did upset Kate a little, she also had to understand. Not everyone she knew was lucky enough to be a modern woman, especially some of the people she knew back in Oklahoma.

"Kate," chimed in the slightly impatient voice of Gloria. "Russell is talking to you."

"Huh?" Kate said, snapping back into reality. "I'm sorry, Russell, my mind must have been elsewhere. Would you mind repeating that?"

"I said, isn't George the most handsome baby you've ever seen?" Russell repeated. "And, I'm not just saying that because he got his good looks from his dad."

"Of course not," Kate replied with a laugh. "I've never known parents to claim that their children are the best!"

"Oh, right," Russell said jokingly to Kate, "but this is our first kid; you've gotta let us have the right to brag."

"Okay," Kate said, relenting. "I could at least grant you that."

Kate couldn't help but smile, seeing Gloria and Russell as happy as they were. She was truly happy that her cousin finally had a house and family of her own.

As far as her own marriage was concerned, she couldn't be happier with the way Steve was treating her. Though they had yet to leave their flat and move into their own home, and Kate has not talked to her parents in weeks, things were going well. For the first time in her life, Kate was starting to fully realize that this was where she was supposed to be.

***

Two more months had passed, and life was peaceful, as everything seemed to stand still. George was already starting to grow into a large baby, and he would soon want to start to crawl and try to do things on his own.

Kate could tell that Gloria and Russell were sad that he seemed to be growing up so fast.

Relations between Kate and her parents were still strained, though she had tried to write and call several times. Her mother would answer the phone on occasion, but she would quickly hang up if she knew that her father nearby or ready to come into the house.

***

It wasn't until that Tuesday night that Isaac called to talk to his brother-in-law, who he had blamed for Kate's "downward spiral." He was thoroughly disappointed that Stuart had lost of most of his conservative ways, which should have become inherently clear when he decided to let Gloria marry Russell.

If Isaac had known about Steve earlier, then he would have cut the whole thing off at the pass! Stuart disapproved of the fact that Isaac had called to stir up even more trouble.

The two of them exchanged harsh words for the next several minutes, though Stuart tried to control the tone and volume of his voice. Gloria and Russell had brought George over for tea. Kate and Steve were also there, which was why it was all the more difficult for Stuart to carry on this conversation. He was trying to rationalize with his brother-in-law, who was on the verge of blowing his top.

"Isaac, Kate is a grown, married woman," Stuart said calmly into the phone. "You cannot dictate her actions anymore."

"But that's why I sent her to you in the first place!" Isaac argued. "You were to give her the proper guidance."

"Really?" Stuart said. "Is that really the reason why you sent Kate all the way to England, or was it because of the boy whom she dated in college?"

"Fred Beaumont is history," Isaac fumed. "I done run him off my property with my shotgun! He will never have the nerve to come back here again."

Of course, per Isaac's request, Stuart did initially have nice gentleman in mind for Kate. Once he saw her in the flesh and looked at her innocent face, however, he decided that he would not force Kate to meet the young man. His gut instinct had told him that he was all wrong for her.

"So violence is the answer to everything?" Stuart asked, feeling ashamed that Isaac would resort to such drastic measures.

"And what would you have done?" Isaac screamed into the phone. "What would you have done if a horrible boy like him showed up your doorstep? Tell me something, Stuart, why did you let Gloria marry that hippie musician, answer me that!"

"Because," Stuart retorted, "when your children grow up, everything changes. My Gloria is a grown woman now, and it almost took me far too long to realize that! When she was a child, I did the same thing that you are doing to Kate now. I was too overprotective, too conservative." He paused, looking over at Olivia, who was smiling. Stuart knew that she was rooting for him in her mind.

"And, yes, I will be honest. When I first met Russell, I did not think him worthy of my daughter. I thought he was a no-good man with whom Gloria should not waste her any of her time." He paused again to take a breath.

"When Russell first came over here for tea, I wasn't very pleased, thinking that I hardly even got a change to know the man, what with all his musician friends and late-night gigs. But I actually sat him down, I talked to him, and I came to know that he is a true gentleman. Not only do I know this because I've seen how he treats my daughter, but I can also tell it by the way she looks at him. By the way he fills her with happiness every time he walks into the room.

"Now I am glad that I got to the chance to talk to Russell get to know more about him. And it is because of my daughter's marriage and happiness that I am now the grandfather of a very beautiful little boy. Besides, my opinion wouldn't have mattered because Russell even told me, himself, that nothing would stand in the way of him marrying Gloria.

"Listen, I remember what I was like when you first met me. I remember that I was a lot like my older brother James and that is the only reason why you and your father thought I was worthy enough to marry Olivia."

"Now, hold on there, Stuart," Isaac interrupted. "Hold on right there. That is absolutely not true."

"Oh, don't bullshit me, Isaac. Of course, it is! Like it or not, your daughter is married to Steve Maddington, who everyone around here thinks is a very fine man! Your little Kate is now Mrs. Steve Maddington, and there is not a damn thing you can do about it!" Stuart hesitated.

"In fact, she and Steve are sitting right here in the living room. We were enjoying with tea with them, Gloria, Russell, and George until you so rudely decided to interrupt our evening."

"Now, Stuart, can't you see what I'm going through, all the stress that this has put on both Susan and me?"

Stuart sighed, but Olivia kept nodding her head, indicating that he should not back down.

"Now, you just shut up and listen for a minute, you self-righteous bastard!" Stuart exclaimed, exploding into the other end of the phone. "The only reason there was every any stress to begin with was because *you* had created it! You've brought it all upon yourself, so don't go blaming Susan. And don't you dare go blaming, Kate, Gloria, Steve, Olivia, or myself anymore!

"And you especially need to apologize to your daughter the most. Do you have any idea how hurt she was that her own two parents did not show up to her wedding, that her father was not there to walk her down the aisle?

"Do you know how much pressure you put on Susan for forbidding her to come see her only child get married to the man whom she loves? You are damn lucky to have a daughter like Kate, and if you had even bothered to take the time to get to know Steve better, you would know that he is an excellent son-in-law who would give up his music to try and impress you!

"When you sent Kate to live with us, Olivia and I made a promise to 'keep her on the straight and narrow,' as you stated. But, sometimes, the straight and narrow is not always inclusive of being too conservative. It's about leading a good life." Stuart sighed again.

"And I will keep talking to you about this until I am blue in the face, foolish as that is on my part, because I know one day you will listen to reason!"

After Stuart was finished speaking, there was a long pause on the other end of the phone. It was likely that both men were thinking about what had just been said.

There was still another moment before Isaac broke the silence.

"May I speak to my daughter, please?" Isaac asked in a remorseful tone.

Stuart felt his hard exterior begin to soften, and he decided to be merciful to his brother-in-law.

"He wants to talk to you," Stuart said, holding the phone out to Kate.

She rose from the living room couch, where she and Steve had been seated during the entire conversation. Kate took the phone from her uncle and spoke the first word she'd said to her father in a long time.

"Hello…"

Epilogue

"Son, come on over here," Isaac said. "I'll show you the proper way to milk a cow." Isaac pointed to the stool right next to the animal's side.

Steve sat himself down and awaited further instruction. Kate was hovering over him. Though Steve and her father had not become best friends overnight, they were finally taking time to make the effort, and that meant the world to Kate.

The couple had gone back to Oklahoma to visit her parents. Things had really calmed down since Kate had discussed things with her father over the phone.

Isaac actually broke down and cried, which Kate had never known him to do in all her life. He spent a lot of time apologizing to his daughter, promising that things were going to be better between them now.

Both Kate and Susan had to admit that Isaac was doing his best to make up for all the things he'd said and done, including not showing up at her wedding. He'd even gone so far as to shake Steve's hand and ask his forgiveness upon meeting him, and Kate could tell that the gesture was sincere. Isaac also addressed him as "Son."

Steve was ready to forgive his father-in-law and give him a chance to start fresh.

Kate and Steve agreed that their home did not lie in one country alone, so they decided to obtain dual citizenship; they thought that it would be best that they divide their time between the United States and England. Though it was a lengthy process, it was worth it in the end. This way, they could divide their time equally between Oklahoma and London.

Steve resumed his place as lead singer and guitarist in The Peppermint Eyes, who had sent one of their demos to a producer at Polyphone Records. The producer seemed like he was genuinely interested in their music, so the band set up an appointment for their first professional sound recording.

Steve was very excited with the band's deposit, which was £2,000. He had taken some of that money and put in into savings. He and Kate planned to use it as a down payment for their first house. Kate had taken over writing most of the lyrics for the band, and they were all grateful to her because they thought she was the reason why their music got them a record deal!

Isaac and Susan resigned themselves to the fact that they were getting older and growing closer to retirement. They knew they were going to have to sell Richards' Dairy Farm, but they would not have the problem of changing the farm's name for its new owners.

Isaac had a cousin, Christopher, whose last name was also Richards because he was born to Isaac's uncle.

Christopher had recently passed away. His wife, Edna's, death had preceded his by seven years. Christopher's son, Kevin, however, was very skilled in the trade.

Kevin was thirty years old and has worked as a dairy farmer's assistant ever since he was fourteen. The farm at which he worked was a much smaller dairy farm, Stevensons', also located in the state of Oklahoma, in Minco.

Kevin was also married and the new father of a little baby girl, Jessica. Isaac met Kevin once, nearly fifteen years ago, and he thought he was just the man to keep the farm up and running.

Once Kevin got his share of the estate, the other half going to his younger sister, he was going to sell house and the three acres of land his father had owned. He was also going to put all his money into the Richards' Dairy Farm. This would enable Kevin to expand the farm and hire extra workers to keep it running productively and efficiently.

Since Isaac was obviously excited about his second cousin taking over the farm, he'd made plans for Kevin and his family to move in right after Christopher's house and land sold. Since Kevin was anticipating the large sum of $300,000 from his half of the estate, he planned to build an extension on the Richards' farmhouse where they could live so Isaac and Susan would not have to give up their home.

Isaac and Susan finally realized that their daughter was destined for something different. Though she had been a great farmhand, she was also an excellent daughter. Kate was meant to spread her wings and fly. She proved this when she went away to NYU and came back with a bachelor's degree in journalism, and she proved it when they had sent her off to England.

It was there where Kate found good company with her extended family and the love of a wonderful man. And for the first time in more years than she could count, Kate was truly happy. Both Susan and Isaac noticed a great difference in their daughter. She was the happiest she had ever been, and they knew the reason was because they let her have the freedom to let her live her own life.

Isaac sighed, fully contented in knowing that he finally made amends with his entire family. From here on in, he knew that everything was going to be all right.

About the Author

Jen Selinsky was born in Pittsburgh, PA. In 2003, she earned her bachelor's degree in English from Clarion University of Pennsylvania. In 2004, she earned her master's degree in library science from the same school. Jen is a semi-retired librarian. She has published more than 200 books, many of which contain poetry. Her work can be found on the following sites: Amazon, Lulu, Barnes & Noble, Kobo, iTunes, Smashwords, Pen It! Publications, and Books-A-Million, as well as many others. She has also been featured in publications such as: *The Courier Journal*, *The News and Tribune*, *Pen It! Magazine*, *Explorer* Magazine, *Liphar* Magazine, and *Indiana Libraries*. She works as the Senior Editor for Pen It! Publications and also edits for *Pen It!* Magazine, Hydra Publications, and Write Your Best Book. One of her children's books, *You Are You!* won the IMADJINN Award for Best Children's Book 2019. Jen lives in Sellersburg, IN with her husband.

Milton Keynes UK
Ingram Content Group UK Ltd.
UKHW032144170324
439604UK00012B/1776